Queen of Babble
GETS HITCHED

AVON

An Imprint of HarperCollins*Publishers*

MEG CABOT

Queen of Babble
GETS HITCHED

FIRST AVON PAPERBACK EDITION PUBLISHED 2009.

The Library of Congress has catalogued the hardcover edition as follows:
Cabot, Meg.
    Queen of babble gets hitched / Meg Cabot. — 1st ed.
        p. cm.
    ISBN 978-0-06-085202-3
    1. Young women—Fiction.   2. Weddings—Fiction.   3. Americans—France—
Fiction.   I. Title.
    PS3553.A278Q445   2008
813'.54—dc22   2007044817

ISBN 978-0-06-085203-0

09 10 11 12 OV/RRD 10 9 8 7 6 5 4 3 2 1

For Benjamin

Acknowledgments

Many thanks to:
Beth Ader
Jennifer Brown

Carrie Feron
Michelle Jaffe
Laura Langlie

Tessa Woodward

and especially Benjamin Egnatz

Queen of Babble
GETS HITCHED

A HISTORY
of
WEDDINGS

In ancient times, weddings were a little more casual than they are today. Rival tribes, in order to increase their population, would frequently stage raids against one another, with the sole purpose of acquiring brides. That's right—they'd steal one another's ladyfolk. The raiding party was kind of what you'd consider your modern-day groom and his groomsmen.

Only, you know, they wouldn't be wearing tuxes. More like loincloths.

Sometimes the young ladies in question got wind of the raiding party beforehand and didn't necessarily put up much of a fight.

But this didn't mean there wasn't ill feeling on the part of their families and friends.

Always have more gifts on your registry than you do wedding guests. This way you can avoid receiving the same gift twice . . . and those guests who can't actually make it to the festivities will still be able to find something lovely to get for you!

LIZZIE NICHOLS DESIGNS™

Chapter 1

Whatever souls are made of, his and mine are the same.
—Emily Brontë (1818–1848), British novelist and poet

"Chaz," I say, poking the man in the tuxedo who lay sprawled across my bed. "You have to get out of here."

Chaz brushes my hand away as if it's annoying him. "Mom," he says. "Stop it. I told you, I already took out the trash."

"Chaz." I poke him some more. "I mean it. Wake up. You have to go."

Chaz wakes up with a start. "Wha— Where am I?" He looks blearily around the room until his unfocused gaze finally comes to rest on me. "Oh. Lizzie. What time is it?"

"Time for you to go," I say, grabbing hold of his arm and pulling on it. "Come on. Get *up*."

But I might as well be pulling on an elephant. He won't budge.

"What's going on?" Chaz wants to know. I have to admit, it's not easy, being so mean to him. He looks downright adorable in his tuxedo shirt, all stubbly faced and confused, with his dark hair sticking up in tufts all over his head. He squints at me. "Is it morning already? Hey—why do you still have your clothes on?"

"Because nothing happened between us," I say, relieved that it's true. I mean, stuff *happened*. But my Spanx are still on, so not *that* much stuff. Thank God. "Come on, get up. You have to go."

"What do you mean, nothing happened between us?" Chaz looks offended. "How can you say that? That's my beard burn you're wearing."

I lift a hand guiltily to my face. "What? Oh my God. You're kidding, right?"

"No, I'm not kidding. You're completely chafed." A look of self-satisfaction spreads across his face as he stretches his arms. "Now come over here and let's continue where we left off before you so rudely fell asleep, which I'm going to try not to hold against you, although I will admit it's going to be difficult, and will probably necessitate punishment in the form of a spanking if I can figure out how to get those things off you. What did you call them again? Oh, yeah. Spanx." Chaz brightens. "Hey, how appropriate."

But I've already dived for the bathroom and am examining my face in the mirror over the sink.

He's totally right. The entire lower half of my face is bright pink from where Chaz's stubble rubbed it as we made out like a couple of teenagers in the back of the taxi on our way home from the wedding last night.

"Oh God!" I cry, staggering back into the bedroom. "Do you think he noticed?"

"Do I think who noticed what?" Chaz has seized me by the wrist, pulled me over, and is fumbling with the tiny buttons to my gown.

"Luke!" I cry. "Do you think he noticed I've got beard burn all over my face?"

"How would Luke notice that?" Chaz asks. "He's in France. How do you get this thing off, anyway?"

"He's not in France!" I cry, swatting at Chaz's hands. "He was just downstairs. That was him, at the door!"

"The door?" Chaz pauses in his attempt to disrobe me, looking more adorably confused than ever. Not that I have any business noticing how adorable Chaz is. "Luke's at the door?"

"No, not anymore," I say, swatting his hands away once more. "But he's coming back in half an hour. And that's why you have to leave now. He doesn't know you're here. And I want to keep it that way." I wrestle his tuxedo jacket from beneath the knee he's resting on it and hold it out for him. "So if you wouldn't mind putting this on and kindly vacating the premises—"

"Wait a minute." Chaz raises a dark eyebrow. "Wait just a minute here. Are you honestly trying to tell me that you and Mr. Romance are getting back together?"

"Of course we're getting back together," I say, throwing an urgent glance at the clock. Twenty-five minutes! Luke will be back in twenty-five minutes! He only went in search of a Starbucks to grab us coffees and a couple of Danish . . . or whatever it is Starbucks has available on New Year's Day. Which, for all I care, could be rancid pig fat in plastic containers. *What does it matter?* "Why else do you think I've been standing here asking you to please get up? I don't want him to know you spent the night—or that you gave me beard burn."

"Lizzie." Chaz is shaking his head. But he's putting his tuxedo jacket on. Thank God. "He's not a little boy. You can't protect him forever. He's going to have to find out about us sometime."

Icy tentacles grip my heart. "Us? What us? Chaz . . . there is no us."

"What do you mean, there is no us?" He looks up from the inside coat pocket he'd been investigating, evidently in search of his wallet. "Did we, or did we not, just spend the night together?"

"Yes," I say, with another exasperated glance at the clock. Twenty-four minutes! And I have to wash my hair. I'm sure there's confetti in it from the wedding. Not to mention, I probably have raccoon rings of mascara around my eyes. "But I already told you. Nothing happened."

"Nothing?" Chaz looks wounded. "I distinctly remember holding you tenderly in my arms and kissing you beneath a sky full of falling stars. You call that *nothing*?"

"Those were balloons," I remind him. "Not stars."

"Whatever. I thought we said we were going to work on the physical part of our relationship."

"No. *You* said that. I said we'd both just come out of painful breakups and needed time to heal."

Chaz reaches up and runs a hand through his hair, causing it to stand even more comically on end. Plus, confetti falls out of it and onto my bedspread. "Then what was all that kissing in the cab about?"

He has a valid point. I'm not sure what all that kissing in the cab was about.

Or why I enjoyed it so much, either.

But I do know one thing. And that's that I'm not going to stand here and talk about it. Not right now.

"We had too much to drink," I explain, with another frantic glance at the clock. Twenty-two minutes! And I have to blow-dry too! "We were at a wedding. We got carried away."

"Carried away?" Chaz's blue eyes look unnaturally bright in the winter sunlight filtering through my new lace curtains. "That's what you call my hand down your bra? *Carried away?*"

I rush forward to place a hand over his mouth.

"We must never speak of this again," I say, my heart booming—yes, booming—in my chest.

"Don't even tell me," Chaz says from behind my hand, "that

you're giving him another chance. Yes, he made the big romantic gesture, flying back from France on New Year's Day, or whatever. But, Lizzie . . . the guy is a complete commitment-phobe. He's never followed through with anything in his life."

"That isn't true," I cry, wrenching my hand away from Chaz's mouth and flipping it around for him to see. "Look!"

Chaz stares at the third finger on my left hand.

"Oh God," he says after a minute. "I think I'm going to be sick."

"That's a nice thing to say," I point out hotly, "to the girl your best friend's just proposed to."

Although the truth is, I feel a little sick myself. But that's from all the champagne last night. It has to be.

"Lizzie." Chaz flops back across my bed and stares up at the cracks in my ceiling. "Do I have to remind you that less than twenty-four hours ago you two were broken up? That you moved out of the apartment the two of you were sharing precisely because he said he couldn't see you in his future? That you spent most of last night with your tongue down *my* throat because the two of you were supposed to be through?"

"Well," I say, looking down at the emerald-cut three-carat diamond sitting in its platinum band. It seems to catch the light just so. Luke told me the certificate authenticating the gem is blood-free is on its way. "He changed his mind."

"Because your moving out like that scared him shitless," Chaz cries, sitting up again. "Is that what you want? A guy who comes running back to you and proposes just because he's so scared of being alone, he'd rather be with a girl he knows isn't right for him than be by himself?"

I glare at him. "Oh," I say. "And I suppose you think we'd make such a better couple."

"Yeah," Chaz says. "Now that you mention it, I do. But the truth is, a monkey with a paper bag over its head would make a better boyfriend for you than Luke. Because you two are totally wrong for each other."

"You—" I suck in my breath. I can't even believe I'm having this conversation. "What . . . How can— I thought Luke was supposed to be your best friend!"

"He *is* my best friend," Chaz says. "I've known him since he was fourteen years old. I probably know him better than he knows himself. That's what makes me unequivocally qualified to say that he's got no business asking anybody to marry him right now, let alone you."

"What do you mean, *let alone me*?" I can feel tears brimming along the edges of my eyelashes. "What's so wrong with me?"

"Nothing's wrong with you, Lizzie," Chaz says in a gentler voice. "It's just that you know what you want, and Luke doesn't. You're a star. And Luke's not the kind of guy who's going to hitch his wagon to a star. He still thinks *he's* the star. And you can't have two stars in one relationship. Somebody has to be willing to be the wagon . . . at least some of the time."

"That's not true," I say, wiping my eyes with the back of one of my wrists. "Luke's a star. He's going to be a doctor. He's going to save children's lives one day."

Chaz raises his gaze to the ceiling.

"The day Luke de Villiers ever actually becomes a doctor," he says solemnly, "is the day I switch to light beer. For good."

I glare at him. "Get out," I say, pointing at the door. "I mean it. Just get out."

Chaz stands up—then instantly looks as if he regrets it. Nevertheless, when he regains his balance, he says, with as much dignity as he can seem to muster, "You know what? Gladly." He stalks out of the bedroom and into the living room, finding his coat on the floor where he'd dropped it the night before. He scoops it up—holding his head a bit woozily—then heads for the door.

"You're making a big mistake, Lizzie," he turns to say when he gets there . . . looking a little surprised when he finds me right behind him.

"No," I shoot back, pressing my index finger against his sternum. "*You* are. Your best friend is getting married. You should be happy for him. And for me. Just because things didn't work out for you and Shari—"

"Shari?" Chaz shakes his head in bewilderment. "This has nothing to do with Shari. It has to do with you and me."

"You and me?" I let out a stunned bark of laughter. "There *is* no you and me."

"That's what you think," Chaz says, tugging on his coat. "And I'll be damned if I'm going to wait around until you figure out that isn't true."

"Fine," I say. "I'm not asking you to, am I?"

"No." Chaz is smiling . . . but not like he's happy. "But you would if you had the slightest idea what was good for you."

And with that, he yanks open the door and storms through it, slamming it closed behind him with enough force to cause the windowpanes to rattle.

And then he's gone.

A HISTORY
of
WEDDINGS

nce the kidnapped "bride" and her groom had safely escaped the wrath of her relatives, frantically searching for her around the outskirts of the village from which she'd been snatched, they'd lay low for a while, to avoid retaliation from her family (or any possible husbands already in existence).

This was also the period during which the "groom" exerted his dominance over his new captive, stamping out any desire she might have to escape or murder him in his sleep (a not uncommon practice in early "marriages" of this sort where the bride wasn't as happy with the situation as a groom might hope her to be).

This "laying low" period could be considered the ancient predecessor to the honeymoon. Only it probably took place in a cave, not at a Sandals resort. And there definitely wasn't room service.

Tip to Avoid a Wedding Day Disaster

Never try a new beauty product—or, God forbid, get a facial—on the day of or the days leading up to your wedding. The last thing you need is a breakout or rash! Stick to your normal routine, and you'll glow like the angel you are.

LIZZIE NICHOLS DESIGNS™

Chapter 2

Two souls with but a single thought,
Two hearts that beat as one.

Franz Joseph von Münch-Bellinghausen (1806–1871), Austrian dramatist

I blink. I have to admit: this was not the reaction I'd expected from the first person I'd told about my engagement to Luke. I'd expected Chaz to have some concerns, sure. I mean, it's true that Luke and I have been having some problems up until recently. As recently as half an hour ago, as a matter of fact.

But all those problems are over now. Because Luke asked me to marry him. That was the only major obstacle standing in the way of our being together—that he couldn't see me in his future.

But all that's changed now. He's asked me to marry him! I'm going to be a bride! Lizzie Nichols, a bride, at last!

And okay. It's a little weird that every time I think about that, I feel like I want to throw up.

But that's just all the excitement from having gotten engaged before I've had any breakfast. I've always suspected I'm a little hypoglycemic. Just like Nicole Richie.

And anyway, it's all Chaz's fault. Why, instead of being happy for me, had he had to throw that absurd little hissy fit, almost as if . . . well, almost as if he'd been jealous?

Except that that's not possible. Because Chaz doesn't like me that way. We're just friends. I mean, sure, we'd messed around a little last night.

And, I'll admit, it had been . . . well, nice.

Really nice, actually.

But we'd both been a little tipsy. Drunk, even. It hadn't meant anything. It was like I'd said: still smarting over our respective breakups, we'd sought solace in each other's arms.

But that doesn't mean there was anything more going on.

Does it?

Well, I'm not going to waste any more time worrying about it. Luke is going to be here any minute. I have to get myself cleaned up before he arrives. It's bad enough he proposed—and I accepted— while I still had morning breath. I am not going to start my first day as a newly engaged person wearing the same underwear I've had on since yesterday.

By the time the downstairs buzzer goes off, I'm as sweet smelling and coiffed as I've ever been in my life—thanks to the world's fastest shower, a quick change into a stunning 1950s Lorrie Deb pink chiffon party dress (perfect for the newly engaged, soon-to-be-certified professional wedding gown restorer), and a couple layers of undereye concealer—and ready to let in the man to whom I've just pledged my troth.

I feel lighter than air as I make my way down the twin flights of steps to the building's front door (I have to get that buzzer fixed first thing when places open up again tomorrow morning).

"Whoa," Luke says after I fling open the heavy metal door. "You look—"

"Like a bride-to-be?" I ask, holding out the three layers—one chiffon, one net, and one nylon—of my full skirt and giving him a playful curtsy.

"I was going to say hot," Luke says. He triumphantly holds up a Starbucks bag . . . and a six-pack of Diet Coke for me. "Look what I scored. I only had to walk eleven blocks to find a place that was open on New Year's Day."

"Oh, Luke! You remembered!"

Except, of course, it was Chaz who told Luke how much I love Diet Coke in the first place. That's the only reason Luke bought it for me that day in the village back in France last summer. Because Chaz told him that Diet Coke was the way to my heart.

But that doesn't mean I'm in love with Chaz, does it?

Of course not! How could I think anything so silly?

My eyes fill with tears. Really, Luke's the most thoughtful fiancé in the whole world. Also the handsomest, standing there in his Hugo Boss overcoat, with his long dark eyelashes curling so perfectly . . . and without the help of a Shu Uemura eyelash curler, even. He'd looked so cute when he'd been kneeling there in that exact spot in the slush a half hour ago, so hopeful and nervous. How could I have said anything but yes when he'd proposed?

Not that saying anything but yes had even occurred to me. Well, except for a few seconds, maybe. To punish him for that whole "I don't know if I see you in my future" thing.

"I just want to let you know that when I look into my future, I see nothing but you." That's what Chaz had whispered in my ear at some point during the wedding last night.

Then he'd whispered, *"And you're not even wearing Spanx."*

I shake my head. Why do I keep thinking about *Chaz*? He wears University of Michigan baseball caps nearly all the time.

In *public*.

Luke's face falls. "What?" he asks. "What'd I do? You don't drink Diet Coke anymore. Is that it? I can get something else. What do you want? Diet Dr Pepper?"

"No!" I try to laugh breezily. Oh God. What's wrong with me? "Of course I still drink Diet Coke. I'm sorry. Wow, it's really cold out here. Come in." I move out of the doorway so he can do just that.

"I thought you'd never ask." Luke gives me one of those grins that still cause my insides to go weak. He stops in the doorway just long enough to brush my cheek with his lips, letting them linger for a moment in my hair.

"It's good to be home," he murmurs before moving past me. "Which is wherever you are. I know that now."

Oh! How sweet!

And how could Chaz ever accuse Luke of not knowing what he wants? He knows exactly what he wants. *Me!*

It just took him a little while to realize it. He needed a gentle nudge. In the form of my breaking up with him and moving out of the apartment we were sharing.

"So this is the new place, huh?" Luke is looking around at the somewhat dingy and exceptionally narrow hallway.

"It gets better," I say.

"No," Luke says, his tone apologetic. "I like it. It has character."

It isn't, I tell myself as I follow Luke, Chaz's fault. Not really. He's just never known happiness—true, romantic happiness—as great as what Luke and I share. So of course when he sees it, he looks on it with suspicion. Of course he doubts our chances of success.

But when he sees us together—how happy we are, now that we're really and truly committed to each other—he'll change his mind. He'll come around. He'll see how wrong he was to say all those horrible things.

And someday Chaz will find a girl—the right girl for him—who'll make him as happy as I know I make Luke . . . and he'll make her as happy as Luke makes me.

And then everything will be all right.

Wait and see. Just wait and see.

"Here we are," I say when we reach the door to my new apartment, which I fling open. "Home sweet home."

"It's great," Luke says enthusiastically as he follows me inside.

I smile at him. "You don't have to pretend to like it. I know it's horrible. But it's mine. And as soon as I get the time—and some extra money—I'm going to fix it up."

"No, Lizzie, it really is great." Luke sets down the Starbucks bag and the Diet Coke and puts his arms around me. "It's like you. Completely whimsical and totally charming."

"I hope it's not like me," I say with a laugh. "I hope I'm not covered in big blobby rose wallpaper with slopey floors and cracks in my ceiling."

"You know what I mean," Luke says, nuzzling my neck. "It's unique. Like you. It already smells like you. God, I can't believe how much I missed you. And we were apart for only, what? A week?"

"Is that what you want? A guy who comes running back to you and proposes just because he's so scared of being alone, he'd rather be with a girl he knows isn't right for him than be by himself?"

God! Get out of my head, Chaz Pendergast!

"Something like that," I say. Luke's nuzzling is getting more serious. Or at least closer to the bateau neckline of my dress.

I jump away and reach for one of the Diet Cokes.

"So who should we call first?" I ask brightly.

"Call?" Luke's eyes, which tend to have a dreamy look about them even when he's wide awake, are heavy-lidded with a combination of jet lag and, well . . . sex. Sexual desire, anyway. "I wasn't thinking about calling anyone, to tell you the truth. I was actually thinking about trying out that bed I see over there. And I was hoping you'd get out of that dress and join me . . ."

"*Luke,*" I say after I've chugged down a mouthful of restorative caffeine and potassium benzoate. "We have to call people and tell them the good news. I mean, we're *engaged.*"

"Oh." Luke looks longingly back at the bed. "I guess. I mean . . . Yeah. You're probably right."

"Here." I dig into the Starbucks bag and pull out the coffee he'd ordered for himself, along with two muffins. "Drink this. Let's make a list. We should call your parents, of course."

"Of course," Luke says, taking a sip of his coffee.

"And mine. And my sisters. Well, they'll be at my parents for New Year's Day brunch with Gran, so we'll be able to reach them all with one call." I grab a notepad I've left on the tiny yellow kitchen table, while Luke peels off his coat and sinks onto one of the table's matching yellow chairs. "And I have to call Shari, of course. And you should . . . you should probably call Chaz."

Luke has his cell phone out and is punching numbers into it. An overseas number. Too many numbers for him to be calling Chaz.

"What are you doing?" I ask.

"I'm calling my parents," he says. "Like you said to."

I reach out and close his flip phone.

"Hey," he says, looking confused. "What'd you do that for?"

"I think you should call Chaz first," I say. "Don't you?"

"Chaz?" Luke looks at me as if I'd suggested he mainline heroin and then shoot his mother. "Why would I call *Chaz* first?"

"Because he's your best friend," I say, sliding onto the chair opposite his. "And aren't you going to ask him to be your best man?"

"I don't know," Luke says, still looking confused. He must be much more jet-lagged than I thought. "I guess."

"He'd be so hurt if you didn't tell him first," I say. "You know, he was so kind to me this past week, while you and I were . . . apart. He helped me move in here and everything. And last night he even went with me to the Higgins-MacDowell wedding."

Luke looks touched. "He did? That was nice of him. He must be feeling better. You know, after the whole thing with Shari turning out to like girls."

"Uh," I say. "Yeah. It was. Nice of him, I mean. That's why I think you should call him first. And thank him. For being such a good friend. And tell him how much his friendship means to you. I really think he just needs to hear your voice."

"Okay," Luke says, opening his flip phone and dialing. "I think you're right."

A second later, as I'm squeezing my fingers together and praying that Chaz is still in the subway and won't pick up, Luke says, "Chaz? Hey, it's me. I've got some news, man. Are you sitting down?"

I jump from my chair, convinced I'm going to throw up what little Diet Coke I've downed so far, and run to clutch the edge of the sink.

This is it, I think. Chaz is going to tell him. Chaz is going to tell Luke that just twelve hours ago, his hand was down my bra.

And the engagement is going to be off.

Probably I'm not going to get to keep the ring.

"What? Yeah, I'm back. I'm at Lizzie's. I got back this morning."

What is Chaz doing? He knows Luke is back. I *told* him Luke's back. Oh God. Just *do it* already, so we can get this over with.

"Okay. So you're sitting down? In a cab? Where are you going in a cab on New Year's morning? You were? You did? Who was she?"

I grab the edge of the sink. This is it. I'm going to hurl.

"What do you mean, you're not going to tell me?" Luke laughs.

"Fine, you dog, you. All right. Well, here's my news: I asked Lizzie to marry me. And she said yes. And I want you to be my best man at the wedding."

I close my eyes. This is the part where Chaz tells Luke that he can't be his best man because he thinks he's making the worst mistake of his entire life.

And that, oh yeah, by the way, last night his tongue was down my throat.

"Thanks!" Luke is saying into the phone in a cheerful voice. An entirely too cheerful voice for him to be responding to the news that last night his best friend and fiancée were making out in the back of a cab. "Yeah, I do too. What? Lizzie? Sure, you can talk to Lizzie. Hold on."

I turn around from the sink just in time to see Luke cross the kitchen to hand the phone to me.

"He wants to talk to you," he says. Luke is beaming. "I think he wants to extend his congratulations personally."

I take the phone, feeling sicker to my stomach than ever. "Hello?"

"Hi, Lizzie." Chaz's deep voice rasps in my ear. "You were hoping I'd spill the truth to Luke about our illicit affair and he'd call the whole thing off, weren't you? No such luck, I'm afraid. You got yourself into this mess, and you're going to have to get yourself out of it. If you think I'm going to come sweeping in like some kind of prince on a milk-white charger to save your pretty little buns on this one, you're high."

I let out a totally fake laugh. "Thank you!" I cry. "That is so nice of you to say!" Luke continues to beam at me from across the kitchen.

"Yeah," Chaz says. "You know, when you packed up all your stuff and left his ass high and dry, I thought, finally. A woman with some moral fiber. Little did I know that all he'd need to win you back was a big diamond ring and a few crocodile tears. I really expected bigger things from you, Lizzie. Tell me something. Are you going to wait until the invitations have actually gone out before you admit to yourself that Luke is the last guy you ought to be spending the rest of your life with? Or are you going to do the right thing and call it off now?"

"Great, Chaz," I say, with another fake laugh. "It was nice talking to you too."

"This is like watching a lamb being led to slaughter," Chaz mutters. "Is getting married really that important to you? It's just a goddamned piece of paper."

"Thanks, Chaz," I say. I'm not sure how much longer I can keep up the fake laughing. Because I'm ready to start shedding real tears. "Thanks so much."

"Look, I . . . Just put him back on."

I hold the phone out to Luke. "He wants to talk to you," I say.

Luke takes the phone from me. "Hey, man. Yeah? Uh-huh."

I drift away, into the bedroom, unzipping my dress as I go. I can't believe this . . . any of this. I have what I wanted . . . what it seems like I always wanted: The man of my dreams has proposed to me. I'm going to be married.

I should be happy.

Strike that. I *am* happy. I am.

Maybe it just hasn't sunk in yet.

"What's going on?"

I look over to see Luke standing in the doorway, his cell phone closed in his hand.

"What are you doing?" Luke wants to know. His gaze falls on my dress, lying in a pink puddle on the floor. "I thought we were going to call people and tell them we're engaged."

"I changed my mind," I say, flipping the bedclothes back to show him what I have on underneath them. Which is nothing. "I think I like your original idea better. Want to join me?"

Luke tosses his cell phone over his shoulder. "I thought you'd never ask," he says. And dives into bed with me.

• • •

Luke and I are doing some postcoital spooning. It's so nice to be in his arms—a place I seriously thought I'd never be again.

"So I was talking to my uncle when I was in France this past week," Luke is saying.

"Umm-hmm?" I love the way he smells. Luke, I mean. I missed that smell so much. Being a strong, independent woman who stands up for herself and walks out on the man she feels has done her wrong is really empowering and everything.

But it's not easy. Or fun.

It's much nicer to hang out in bed with that man, completely naked.

"You know, my uncle Gerald?" Luke goes on.

"Uh-huh," I say. "The one who lives in Houston. And offered you the job with his firm's new branch in Paris."

"Right," Luke says. "Thibodeaux, Davies, and Stern. It's one of the most exclusive private client investment companies in the world."

"Mmmm," I say. I'm admiring the way Luke's bicep, even when he's totally relaxed, like he is now, is just so . . . big. And round. And satiny smooth. And the perfect place for me to rest my cheek. It's impossible to think about anything else—or any*one* else—when you're resting your cheek on a hot guy's naked bicep. "Except you don't care about that. Because you're working on your postbaccalaureate program so you can finish up the premed classes you didn't take in college because you were getting an MBA, and when you're done, you can start applying to medical schools."

"Yeah," Luke says. "I know. That's what's so great about Gerald's offer."

I have no choice but to reluctantly lift my head from the satiny pillow of Luke's bicep.

"Your uncle Gerald made you an offer?" I try to keep my voice even-sounding. Like I don't care at all what we're discussing. La la la, don't care a bit about STUPID UNCLE GERALD BUTT-ING HIS NOSE INTO MY BOYFRIEND'S—excuse me, MY FIANCÉ'S—BUSINESS. "What kind of offer?"

"That this summer I could work for him, helping to get the Paris branch of Thibodeaux, Davies, and Stern up and running."

"Oh." I lay my head back down. "Instead of taking classes in your post-baccalaureate program?"

But no sooner have I laid my head down than Luke sits up, jig-gling my head to the pillow.

"It's a really fantastic offer," he says excitedly. "Considering it's for only three months. It's about half a year's salary of what I used to be making. It's really generous of him."

"Wow," I say, trying to plump my pillow up so it's as comfy as his arm was. "That *is* generous."

"Not that it won't be a lot of work," Luke says. "I mean, it will be. Seventeen-, eighteen-hour days, most likely. But it's a fantastic opportunity. And, of course, I can use the family apartment."

"Neat," I say. Luke's lucky his family happens to have all these places to live just randomly sitting around empty all over the world. Apartments in New York City and Paris, a house in Hous-ton, a château in the south of France . . .

"And I can make up the classes I'd miss," Luke says, "in the fall. It'll just be another semester tacked on to what I've already got ahead of me."

"Oh," I say.

"And the best part," Luke says, leaning over to drape one of those tanned, muscular arms across my waist, "is that you can come with me."

I blink at him. "What?"

"Yeah," Luke says, giving me a squeeze. "I've thought it all through. You can come with me, to Paris. It'll be much easier to coordinate the wedding at Château Mirac from there than it would be from here . . ."

"Um," I say. I can't believe he's serious. "I can't just take the summer off and go to Paris, Luke."

"Sure you can," Luke says. Apparently, he thinks *I'm* the one who's kidding. "They'll give you time off from the shop. They'll have to. You're getting married!"

"Yeah," I say. "Time off meaning two weeks . . . three, maybe. But not the whole summer."

"Lizzie." Luke looks disappointed in me. "Don't you know anything about the business world? Don't let the Henris tell you how much vacation time you get. *You* tell *them*. If they really want to keep you, they'll let you take off as much time as you want."

"Luke," I say, trying to figure out how I can put this without offending him. "I don't *want* to take the whole summer off. And I definitely don't want to spend it with you in *Paris*."

But no sooner are the words out of my mouth than I realize that I've done it again. Put my foot in my mouth, I mean. God, no matter how hard I try to be tactful, I just never seem to be able to say the right thing around this guy.

"Th-that didn't come out the right way," I stammer.

Fortunately, Luke is chuckling.

"I guess I never have to worry about your not being honest with me," he says.

"I'm sorry," I hurry to say. "What I meant was—"

"You don't want to spend the summer in Paris," he says. "And you don't have to apologize. I understand. You love your job, and you want to be here for it. That's okay. The thing is, Gerald's offer is really too good for me to turn down. Especially with the wedding to pay for. Look, it's all right. We can do the long-distance thing. We're already going to be doing the separate-apartment thing"—he gives me a mischievous smile, because I'd already warned him, before I'd said yes to his proposal, that I wouldn't be moving back in with him until *after* the wedding; it just seems like the wisest thing to do, under the circumstances—"so I guess living in separate countries for a couple of months over the summer shouldn't be that big a deal."

I chew my lower lip. Am I insane? I probably am. I've got this amazing guy who's finally proposed to me, and in the past hour I've turned down an invitation not only to move back in with him but also to spend a summer in Paris with him.

"He's not the kind of guy who's going to hitch his wagon to a star. He still thinks he's *the star. And you can't have two stars in one relationship. Somebody has to be willing to be the wagon . . . at least some of the time."*

Oh! I can't *believe* it! Even a session of hot and heavy makeup sex didn't succeed in exorcising Chaz's voice from my head! What am I going to have to do to get that guy out of there?

"Come on," I say, reaching for my cell phone. "Let's call people and tell them now."

Luke looks amused. "Oh, *now* you want to call your family?"

You'd better believe it. Anything to make the voice of Chaz stop talking inside my head.

"Come on," I say, dialing. "It'll be fun. I'll call my parents first. Because I'm the bride, so you have to do what I say. Hello, Mom?"

"No," a childish voice says. "It's me, Maggie."

"Oh, Maggie," I say to my niece. "Hi, it's your aunt Lizzie. Could you put your grandma on the phone, please?"

"Okay," Maggie says, and I hear the phone thunk to the floor as she goes off in search of my mother. I can hear the voices of my sisters and their husbands in the background as they enjoy my parents' traditional Nichols Family New Year's Day Brunch. Although "enjoy" might be a strong word. Maybe "endure" is more like it. I can hear my sister Rose's husband, Angelo, bleating something about how he no longer eats eggs because of the hormones in them, and my sister firing back that maybe he could use more hormones . . . especially in bed.

"Who's this?" Gran picks up the phone and barks.

"Oh," I say, disappointed. "Gran. Hi. It's me, Lizzie. I was just trying to reach Mom—"

"She's busy," Gran says. Whoever was assigned to make sure she imbibes only nonalcoholic beer has apparently failed in his or her mission. Gran is, as always, three sheets to the wind. "Somebody's gotta feed this crew. God forbid one of your sisters should offer to host one of these things and dirty up *her* house someday."

"Huh," I say, giving Luke a sunny smile to show him everything is going swimmingly. "Well, I've got some news. Maybe you could let everyone know."

"Jesus Christ," Gran says. "You're knocked up. Lizzie, I told you. Always use a rubber. I know the boys don't like them, but it's like I always say: no rubber, no way."

"Uh," I say. "No, Gran, that's not it. Luke and I are engaged."

"Luke?" Gran sounds like she's choking on whatever drink she's just knocked back. "That no-good-nik? What did you go and agree to marry *him* for? I thought you booted that loser to the curb before Christmas."

I cough and give Luke another reassuring smile.

"Are they excited?" he mouths.

I give him a thumbs-up.

"Um, I did, Gran," I say. "But now we're engaged. Can you get Mom, please?"

"No, I am not going to get your mother," Gran says. "Trust me, I'm doing you a favor, Lizzie. She did an aquaerobics class *and* a scrapbooking class at the Y yesterday, plus all the shopping for this brunch, with no help whatsoever from those sisters of yours. This news could kill her."

"Gran." I smile at Luke again. "If you don't put Mom on the phone, I'm going to call her on her cell and tell her you've been hitting the cooking sherry. And don't try to deny it. Because I can tell."

"You ingrate," Gran snarls. "What do you want to go and get engaged for anyway, Lizzie? Husbands don't do anything but cramp your style. Believe me, I was saddled with one for fifty-five years. I would know. Get out now, while you still can."

"Gran," I warn.

"I'm getting her," Gran says. I hear her shuffling off.

I can't help noticing that Luke isn't smiling anymore. I say, "It's okay. Gran's just a little tipsy."

Luke looks at his watch. "It's *noon*."

"It's a holiday," I point out. Jeesh. Some people can be so picky.

Mom's reception of the news that I'm getting married is much warmer than Gran's. She screams and cries and calls for Dad and asks to speak to Luke and welcomes him to the family and wants to know when she's going to get to meet him. Which reminds me that it is a little weird Luke hasn't met my family yet. I've met all of his.

But oh well. They'll meet soon enough, I guess. Mom wants to throw an engagement party . . . and the wedding, which Mom immediately offers the family backyard for, a suggestion I gently brush off, saying, "Well, we'll see." I'm not sure how to break it to her that Luke's already suggested we get married at his seventeenth-century familial estate in the south of France, an offer that's pretty hard to turn down.

Except that my family's never been to Europe before . . . they've never been to *New York* before.

This might actually pose a problem.

But Luke says all the right things to them on the phone, and is as charming and gracious as if my parents were a king and queen and not a professor at the University of Michigan cyclotron and a housewife. Everything, I think, as I watch him proudly, is going to be fine. Just fine.

"This is like watching a lamb being led to slaughter. Is getting married really that important to you? It's just a goddamned piece of paper."

Okay, well, it's going to be fine after a few more phone calls. And more sex.

A *lot* more sex.

A HISTORY
of
WEDDINGS

The declaration of union between two people has long been considered by sociologists to be an important step in the development of human happiness. Societally speaking, a heterosexual male who has paired off with a heterosexual female is generally thought to be calmer and less prone to violence, and a wedded female equally less troublesome. Their offspring benefit from having both a father and a mother, and—in ancient times, at least—the entire tribe benefited from the goodwill generated from a happy union. In other words: weddings were a joyous occasion that brought about less fighting and unpleasantness all around.

I would just like to point out that none of these sociologists came to my sisters' weddings. Obviously.

Is your future mother- or sister-in-law driving you insane as you plan your special day? There's a simple way to get her off your back. Give her something to do! Allowing his family—especially the female members—to take part in the preparations for the big day will not only make them feel special but will also lift some of the burden off your shoulders.

Just make sure you don't ask them to do anything too important. That way when they mess it up (as they inevitably will), it won't matter.

LIZZIE NICHOLS DESIGNS™

Chapter 3

Happy and thrice happy are those who enjoy an uninterrupted union, and whose love, unbroken by any sour complaints, shall not dissolve until the last day of their existence.

Horace (65 B.C.–8 B.C.), Roman lyric poet

"Hello, Chez Henri, please hold."

"Hello, Chez Henri, please hold."

"Hello, Chez Henri, please hold."

"Hello, Chez Henri, how may I help you?"

"Yeah, is this Henri Bridal?" The woman on the other end of the phone has pronounced it *Henry* instead of the correct French pronunciation of my boss's name, which is *En-ree*.

That I can forgive. What I can't forgive is that she's chewing gum. I can feel my toes curling. Of all the annoying personal habits a bride-to-be—or anyone, really—can have, gum-chewing is the one that aggravates me the most.

"Yes, it is," I say, glaring at all the blinking lights on my phone. It's a good thing I had all those months of reception work at the law offices of Pendergast, Loughlin, and Flynn. I can handle an overloaded switchboard like nobody's business.

And the Monday morning after Jill Higgins's New Year's Eve wedding to wealthy socialite John MacDowell—at which Anna Wintour (yes, *the* Anna Wintour, longtime editor of *Vogue*) called my restoration of the ancestral MacDowell bridal gown "cunning"—the phones at Chez Henri are ringing off the hook.

Of all the mornings for Monsieur and Madame Henri to come in late from their home in suburban New Jersey, this would not have been the one I'd chosen. I'm just saying.

"I wanna make an appointment to see that chick," the gum-chewer says.

"I beg your pardon?" I am taken aback. First gum-chewing, then a reference to me—and she can only be referring to me. I am the only employee at Chez Henri who can reasonably be referred to as a "chick," Madame Henri being in her fifties—as a derogatory slang word for "young woman"?

"You know," Gum-Chewer says. "The chick that designed that dress for Blubber."

Blubber. The nickname the press dubbed poor Jill Higgins, because she happens to work in the seal enclosure at the Central Park Zoo. And because she'd deigned to fall in love with one of New York's wealthiest bachelors, and she doesn't happen to be a size two.

"I'm sorry," I say to Gum-Chewer. "The *chick* to whom you are referring happens to dislike people who look down on others due to their weight."

Gum-Chewer appears to have swallowed her gum. "But—"

"And furthermore, that *chick* happens to dislike being called a chick."

"Um, excuse me." Gum-Chewer snaps her gum. "But do you have any idea who I am? I'm—"

"No, and I don't care to know. Good-bye," I say, pressing the END CALL button. "Chez Henri, how may I help you?"

"Elizabeth? Is that you?" The woman on the other end of the line has a heavy French accent and sounds as if she's speaking to me from inside a tunnel. No, it isn't my future mother-in-law, who is from Texas. It's Madame Henri.

"Madame, where are you?" I ask in French, the language I now routinely slip into when speaking to my employers, though I hid the fact that I could speak it—not perfectly, but well enough to understand (and be understood by) them—for months. "It's crazy here. The phones are ringing off the hook."

"Elizabeth, I'm so sorry. I meant to call earlier, but my cell phone doesn't work here. I've been at the hospital."

"The hospital?" The other lines continue to ring. Callers, impatient at being placed on hold, have hung up and are calling back. I turn away from the phone. "Is everything all right? I hope nothing happened to the boys—"

"No, the boys are fine. It's Jean, actually." Madame Henri's voice sounds tiny. She's a petite woman, but the one thing about her that's never seemed small before is just that . . . her voice. She's always had a commanding—even domineering—presence. But not now. "He didn't feel well at breakfast yesterday morning. I thought it was just too much champagne from the night before. But then he said his arm hurt—"

I gasp. "Madame!"

"Yes." Her voice sounds even smaller. "He had a heart attack. He is scheduled for emergency bypass surgery here at the hospital today. Quadruple." Then, with a hint of her old asperity, she adds, "I told him he works too hard! I told him he needed to take more time off! Well, now he's getting it . . . and look how he has to spend it! He could have taken it at our home in Provence. But no! Not him! This is what it has come to."

"Oh, Madame." I shake my head. "Well, I'm sure he's in very good hands—"

"The best," Madame Henri says simply. "But it will be weeks before he can return to work. And I as well, because who do you think will have to play nursemaid to him? His sons? Bah! They are worthless. Worse than garbage."

I'm relieved to hear her bad-mouthing her children. That means the situation is nowhere near as dire as I'd first feared from the way she'd sounded. If she can trash-talk the kids—who, from what I've observed, pretty much *are* worthless—things are okay.

"And just as the shop is doing the best business it has ever done before," Madame Henri goes on. "All thanks to you! And this is how we repay you. When he is well again," she adds matter-of-factly, "I will kill him."

"Don't worry about the shop," I say, keeping my face resolutely turned away from all the blinking lights on the phone. "I'll be fine here."

"Elizabeth," Madame Henri says. "I am not a fool. I can hear the telephone ringing."

"The phone," I admit, "is a bit of a problem at the moment. But not one I can't solve."

"Do what you have to do," Madame Henri says, with a sigh. "Even . . . even hire someone."

I can't help letting out a gasp. The Henris are almost insanely tightfisted. For good reason, of course. Until I started working for them, they barely made a profit. In fact, for the first four months I worked for them, I did it for free, just to prove I'd be worth the eventual investment of my thirty grand a year . . . and the rent-free apartment over the shop.

"Madame," I say, hardly daring to believe what I'd just heard. "Are you sure?"

"I don't see what choice we have," Madame Henri says with a sigh. "You can't do it all alone. Not the phones *and* the gowns. I'll try to stop in when I can, but it won't be often. You're going to have to get some help. It's Jean's own fault," she adds waspishly. "And I'll tell him so if he dares to complain when he hears of it . . . after he's out of the hospital, of course."

"Don't bother him about it, Madame," I say. "And don't you worry about it, either. Leave everything to me. I'll take care of the shop. I'll take care of *everything*."

I have no earthly idea, of course, how I'm going to go about this. I just know that this is a crisis, and, well, I used to be a Girl Scout. Crises are what Girl Scouts are trained for. I'll get through this somehow.

I tell her to let me know if there's anything else I can do, and also to let me know the minute her husband is out of surgery. Then I hang up and stare at all the blinking lights on the phone and listen to the shrill ring of the unanswered line. I have every confidence that I can handle this. I really do.

It's just that I don't have the foggiest notion how I'm even going to begin.

"Hello, Chez Henri, can you hold?"

"Hello, Chez Henri, can you hold?"

"Hello, Chez Henri, can you—"

"Lizzie?" a familiar woman's voice screams hoarsely in my ear, cutting me off. "Don't you frigging put me on hold. It's me, Tiffany."

I pause just as my finger is about to hit the HOLD button.

"Tiffany Sawyer," the hoarse voice continues impatiently. "From Pendergast, Loughlin, and Flynn? The office we both used to work in until you, like, got totally fired, remember? Which, by the way, was last week? God, what is the matter with you? Are you going to turn out to be one of those people who become famous and then, like, forget everybody they knew on the way up? Because if that's the case, you totally suck."

"Tiffany." I glance at the Henris' wall clock. It's barely ten, which would account for the hoarseness in her voice. Tiffany, part-time model, part-time receptionist in Chaz's father's law offices, which is where I met her, rarely makes it up before noon, thanks to her hard-core partying with her married photographer boyfriend, Raoul. "What are you doing up so early?"

"Whatevs," Tiffany says. "It's, like, the day after New Year's. The city was dead last night. But that's not why I'm calling. Do you know—do you have any fucking idea—who made Page Six in the *Post* today?"

"Tiffany." I can't take my eyes off all the blinking hold lights. "I know this might seem hard to believe, but I'm actually *working* right now. My boss had a heart attack, and I'm the only one here, and I don't have time for—"

"You. *You* did. There's a huge story about you, and a photo of you and Jill Higgins at her wedding, and about how you're the up-and-coming wedding gown designer to the stars, and how Anna Wintour—Anna fucking Wintour—said your gown for Jill Higgins was, and I quote, cunning. Do you have any idea what that *means*?"

The other line starts ringing. "I'm starting to get a pretty good idea," I say.

"You are the shit," Tiffany screams into the phone. "You have it fucking made!"

"You know," I say. "It really doesn't feel that way right now. Because right now, I can't get a thing done because I don't have anyone to ANSWER MY PHONES!"

"Jesus Christ, you don't have to yell," Tiffany says. "You need someone to answer your phones? I'll answer your fucking phones."

I blink, not certain I've heard her correctly. "What? No. Wait. I—"

"I'll be right there. Where are you again? I can stay till only one because you know I've got Pendergast at two. God, I wish I could quit that place. But the benefits are so good. As soon as Raoul gets rid of that troll wife of his and I can get on his insurance, I'm giving Roberta my two weeks' notice. God, I can't wait to see her pruny, dried-up face when I do. But I can get someone to come in at one and help you out. I wonder what Monique is doing today. I know she got booted from Chanel for doing blow in the back room. But—"

"Tiffany." I'm gripping the edge of my desk. "Really. It's fine. I don't need your help. Or Monique's." Whoever that is.

"—it's cool," Tiffany goes on, " 'cause she's in Narcotics Anonymous now. So am I. That's how I met her. Coke is for whores."

I realize there's no point in telling Tiffany that the Anonymous part of Narcotics Anonymous means you actually aren't supposed to tell people you—or other people you meet there—go to meetings. It will just go in one ear and out the other, like so much of what I tell Tiffany.

"Look, you said your boss had a heart attack, right?" Tiffany goes on. "We'll just come in and help out until he's back on his feet, or whatever. Don't act like you don't need us. I can hear the frigging phone ringing off the hook in the background."

"Um, thanks. It's just—" How can I explain that if I were stranded on a desert island and Tiffany pulled up in a rescue boat, I wouldn't get in it. Love her like a sister? Yeah. Trust her? Not so much. "I don't have the money to pay you. I mean, we're not exactly making huge profits yet, and—"

"What are we talking about here?" Tiffany wants to know. "Twenty bucks an hour?"

"Twenty?" I gasp. "Who do you think we are, UPS? I was going to call Manpower and offer ten—"

"Ten!" Tiffany lets out a bark of laughter. "I haven't made ten bucks an hour since I used to babysit my neighbor's kid back in

North Dakota. But," she adds, more soberly, "I guess it'll be worth it if I can get my hands on a Lizzie Nichols original. Those things are going to be next to impossible to get by the time Raoul's green card comes in and he can finally ditch the troll, I know it. Just like I know Monique's gonna want one, too. Her boyfriend, Latrell, just popped the question at Christmas. With a four-carat square-cut pink diamond from Harry Winston. Latrell's in the music industry." Her tone becomes reverential. "He knows Kanye."

"Wait," I say. This can't be happening.

"Look, I'll be there in twenty," Tiffany says. "We can discuss it then. You want a muffin or something? I'm starving. I'll pick up muffins on the way. Fuckin' Page Six! Can you believe it? Oh my God, Lizzie, this is gonna be so righteous. You're gonna be so much of a better boss than Roberta. God, I hate her. *Ciao*, baby."

Tiffany slams down the phone. I stare at the receiver, not sure what just happened. Had I just solved the problem—or created a bigger one?

I'm taking messages from everyone on hold—with assurances that Ms. Nichols (I'm posing as her assistant, Stephanie. I've always wanted to be a Stephanie) will be calling them right back—when a floral delivery guy makes his way into the shop, barely able to see past the huge bouquet—two dozen yellow roses in a crystal vase—that he's holding.

"Delivery for Lizzie Nichols," he says.

"That's me," I cry, jumping up from Madame Henri's desk and rushing over to take the flowers from him. They're so heavy I have to stagger back to the desk with them before I can sign for them and tip him.

As soon as he's gone, I tear open the tiny envelope that accompanies them, expecting to find a note from Luke, thanking me for agreeing to be his bride . . . or maybe from his parents, welcoming me to the de Villiers family.

I'm shocked when I read, instead, the following:

Sorry for my bad attitude the other day.
I never was a morning person.
Of course I'm thrilled for you both. If you're happy,
I'm happy.
Congratulations. You'll make a beautiful bride.
> *Chaz*

I'm so stunned, I have to sit down for a few minutes—and ignore the phones—in order to regain my composure. Can he really mean it? Can Chaz *really* be all right with Luke and me getting married?

And if he is, why do I still feel a little bit like throwing up every time I think about it? Not about Chaz being all right with it—I'm pretty sure—but about Luke and me actually going through with it?

Oh, I seem all right enough with the idea of being engaged. I don't seem to mind flashing my ring around. I'd been fine on the phone yesterday—after our prolonged interlude in the bedroom—with our parents.

It's when I actually try to picture the wedding itself—and even more oddly, the dress—that my mind seems to go blank, and the vomit rises up in the back of my throat.

That's not a very good sign.

But prewedding jitters are normal, right? Everyone goes through them. Maybe not the day after they've gotten engaged. But I'm probably just getting mine over with sooner than other people do. I've always been precocious that way. My mom said I used to put together first-day-of-school outfits for all my stuffed animals. And that was before I even started preschool.

The bells over the front door tinkle, and Tiffany, wearing dark sunglasses (even though it's overcast—and winter—outside) and a black catsuit beneath her new fox stole ("Which is totally faux, by the way," she reminds me later. "Do you know what they *do* to the poor foxes to get their fur off? It's disgusting"), walks in and says, "Whoa. Who went overboard with the roses?"

I quickly thrust Chaz's card into the pocket of the Mollie Parnis silk dress I'm wearing.

"Luke," I lie automatically.

"Luke?" Tiffany whips off her sunglasses and squints at the roses. "I thought you guys, like, broke up."

"Not anymore." I hold out my left hand. "We're engaged."

"No shit." Tiffany grabs my hand. She doesn't have to squint at all to see my diamond. "Holy crap, Nichols. That's three carats, at least. Tiffany, right?"

"No," I say. "He got it in Paris—"

"Cartier," Tiffany says, clearly impressed. "Even better. Platinum band, emerald cut. This thing cost as much as a fucking house—well, in North Dakota. He may have acted like a dick," she adds, in reference to the sewing machine Luke gave me for Christmas, which in a roundabout way became the catalyst for our realizing we wanted different things out of life, and led to our breaking up, "but you have to admit. The guy came through in the end. I'm not sure about the roses, though. Interesting color choice. Yellow means platonic friendship, you know."

Platonic friendship? Well, that's good. I mean, because they're not actually from Luke. They're from Chaz.

And that's all I want from Chaz. His friendship, I mean. Platonic is good.

"Well, because Luke and I are friends, first and foremost," I twitter. Oh my God, what am I even talking about?

Tiffany makes a face.

"If Raoul ever bought me yellow roses," she says, "I'd stuff them up his butt. So where do I sit?"

"Tiffany," I say, beginning a speech I've been mentally rehearsing since hanging up the phone with her. "I—"

"Is this good?" Tiffany asks, collapsing her nearly six-foot (and barely one-hundred-and-twenty-pound) body into Madame Henri's chair, behind the desk with the telephone (which is ringing shrilly) on it. "Here. I brought you a chocolate croissant. They were out of muffins. And a Diet Coke. I know how you are."

I catch the white paper bag she tosses to me. It's truly weird how everyone just thinks they can bring me Diet Coke and everything will be okay.

Especially since it's pretty much true.

"Hello, Chez Henri, this is Tiffany, how may I help you?" Tiffany, not skipping a beat, begins picking up calls as if she's worked at Chez Henri her whole life. "Ms. Nichols? I'm not sure. Hold, please." Tiffany places the call on hold. "Do you only do restorations, or do you do original designs? I mean, I know you're doing an original design for me, but for, like, the commoners?"

"Right now," I say, slowly chewing the end of chocolate croissant I've bitten off, "I'm only doing rehab and restoration."

"Got it. Where do I log your appointments?"

I point at the black leather appointment book on Madame Henri's desk.

"But," I say. "Tiffany, we have to talk. I can't—"

Tiffany just looks at the appointment book and snorts. "High-tech," she says, then flips it open, grabs a pencil, and hits the hold button. "Only restorations. All right. I've got an opening next week on the tenth at eleven o'clock. No? Please hold . . ."

I am starting to think hiring Tiffany might not be such a bad idea. She seems to have just . . . well, taken over.

And that's a good thing. A very good thing. For now. Maybe I should worry about how I'm actually going to pay her later.

I'm getting ready to retreat to the back room to look over what I've got to do—if I can at least get my head around that, maybe I can get my head around Tiffany working for me . . . and, oh yeah, the part where I'm engaged—when the bells over the front door tinkle once more, and my confused-looking best friend, Shari, wanders into the shop.

"Oh my God," I say, nearly dropping my can of soda as I rush to hug her. "I'm so glad you came."

"I got your message," she says, giving Tiffany a curious glance. "They said you said it was an emergency. It better have been, to have made me come all the way uptown. What's so important that you have to tell me in person? And what's *she* doing here?"

"Come on," I say, taking Shari by the hand. "I'll tell you upstairs, in my place. Tiffany, can you handle things down here for ten minutes?"

Tiffany gives me the finger while saying, "Ma'am, I'm sure your daughter is a lovely girl, but Ms. Nichols only does restorations. If you have a gown to restore, we're in business. If not, I'm afraid you're going to have to look elsewhere for your daughter's wedding dress. Oh, really? Do you eat with that mouth, ma'am?"

"What," Shari asks again impatiently, "is she doing here? What's going on? Seriously, Lizzie, this better be important. I have clients who could actually be dying as we speak. And I mean literally."

I realize that the speech I've planned for Shari, who's always been my staunchest supporter, isn't anywhere near eloquent enough. So I simply turn and show her my ring.

"Oh," Shari says. "My. God."

A HISTORY
of
WEDDINGS

When brides weren't being taken by force in ancient cultures, they were sold or bartered for gold, land, or even livestock (like a cow—can you *imagine*?).

For many centuries, it was common practice to use the weddings of offspring to bring high-ranking families together, but it wasn't until medieval times that laws were enacted that required any sort of religious rite be part of the actual ceremony (along with the exchange of goods and the signing of contracts). It was also around this time that dowries began to become more common, so that it wasn't just her lovely self the bride brought to the marriage, but some cold hard cash and maybe a few dozen head of cattle too. What's more, often the bride was expected to deliver the cash to her in-laws herself (more on this later).

Tip to Avoid a Wedding Day Disaster

The legal experts at Pendergast, Loughlin, and Flynn agree: the marriages that work best are the ones where both parties are joined at the heart and *the bank account. Couples who share their assets tend to stay together longer. Apply for a joint checking account, at least for shared expenses . . .* unless *one of you has excessive amounts of debt or other legal or financial troubles. If that's the case, the debt-free party should be seeing a lawyer . . . possibly at Pendergast, Loughlin, and Flynn.*

Chapter 4

There is no more lovely, friendly and charming relationship, communion or company than a good marriage.

—Martin Luther (1483–1546), German theologian

Wait." Shari is staring at me over the yellow tabletop in the kitchen. "He asked you to marry him . . . and you said *yes*?"

I'll admit this is not the sort of reaction I was hoping for. In fact, Shari has a lot more in common with her ex-boyfriend Chaz than she'd probably like to know.

"I'm not rushing into anything, Shar," I say to her. "I swear. I've totally thought this through."

"You have." Shari is still staring at me. She hasn't taken her coat off, even though I offered to take it from her. Judging from her body language—arms folded across her chest, head cocked at one angle as she glares at me, legs crossed—I would say she is feeling cranky toward me . . . maybe even downright hostile. "He got home from France yesterday morning. And he proposed yesterday morning?"

"Yeee-es . . ."

"And you said yes as soon as he proposed?"

"Um . . . yes?"

"So you thought this through . . . when?"

"Well . . . since then." I can tell where this is heading, and I attempt to head it off. "I mean, you'll notice, Shari, that he's not living here. I'm not letting him move in. And I'm not moving back in with him. Nuh-uh. I'm not making that mistake again. We're living in our own separate apartments until the wedding."

"Which is?" Shari demands.

I stare at her over the cups of tea I've made for us. "Which is what?"

"Which is *when*, Lizzie?" Shari asks. "When is this alleged wedding taking place?"

"Um," I say, taken aback. "Well. Probably this summer . . ."

"Right." Shari unfolds her arms and uncrosses her legs. "You're insane. I'm leaving. Good-bye."

I pull her back down before she can abandon her chair, however.

"Shari, *come on*," I say. "Don't do this. You're not being fair—"

"*I'm* not being fair?" Shari cries. "Lizzie, come on! Did you, or did you not, just spend a night on my couch last month because that no-good boyfriend of yours pulled your heart out of your chest and crushed it to bits when he told you he couldn't see you in his future—something he might have mentioned, by the way, *before* he asked you to move in? And now for some fucked-up reason—probably because he's gone for a week without getting laid—he's decided, *Oh, hey, I guess I can see Lizzie in my future after all*, throws a diamond ring in your face, and you're all, *Okay, Luke, anything you say, Luke*. Well, I'm sorry, but I'm not going to sit here and watch you throw your life away. You deserve better. You deserve a guy who actually loves you, Lizzie."

I blink at her. The next thing I know, I'm crying.

"How can you say that?" I ask with a sob. "You know Luke's not like that. You know—"

But that's all I manage to get out. Because I'm weeping too hard to say anything more.

After a while, tired of listening to me sniffle, Shari gets up, comes around the table, and puts her arm around me.

"Lizzie," she says in a softer voice than she used before. "I'm sorry. I didn't mean it. I just . . . I worry that the reason you said yes to Luke is because you wanted to marry him so badly, and then when you found out he didn't want to marry you, you moved on. And then when he suddenly came back and wanted to marry you after all, you thought you *had* to say yes because you'd been so adamant that that's what you wanted all along. But you know, Lizzie, it's okay to change your mind."

"I haven't!" I shout through my tears. "Why would I do that?"

"I don't know," Shari says with a shrug. "Because you grew up a little since last month, maybe? I was there, remember? I saw you do it. But look . . . If you really want to marry Luke, then of course I'll support you. If you want to marry Luke, then I want you to marry Luke too."

"No . . ." I'm crying too hard to speak clearly. "No, you hate Luke."

"Now you're just being irrational. I do not hate Luke. I do think he's got a lot to learn about being a man. And, frankly, I think you could do better. But I'll support you no matter who you love, same as you've supported me, so long as you don't stuff me into a lime-green taffeta hoop skirt that matches your sisters'—which you aren't going to do, are you?" Shari asks suspiciously.

"What?" I force a laugh as I wipe away my tears. "Oh God, no. Are you kidding?"

Except that I'd once picked out a bridesmaid dress for Shari.

Dupioni silk . . . Only for some reason I can't picture it in my head anymore. It's kind of funny how, before I'd gotten engaged, all I'd ever done was sit around and planned what my wedding was going to be like.

And now that I'm actually having one, whenever I try to imagine it, my mind just goes blank.

"So, where's it going to be?" Shari wants to know. "Château Mirac?"

"Um," I say. "Maybe. My mom wants me to do it in our backyard."

Shari brightens. "That'd be nice."

I roll my eyes. "*Shari.*"

"Well, why not?"

"It would make so much more sense to do it at the château. That place was practically built for weddings. And it's where we fell in love and all. And there's the added cost-benefit of its being free, since Luke's family owns it."

"Ye-e-ah," Shari says slowly. "Except it's far for your family to travel. And there's your grandmother to consider."

"What about Gran?" I ask defensively.

"Well," Shari says as she sits back down in her chair. "She's getting up there in years. You really think she's going to make it to the south of France and back for a wedding?"

"Sure," I say a little hotly. "Why not?"

"I don't know," Shari says. "I'm just saying. She's old. And . . ."

"And what?"

"And she suffers from chronic alcoholism, Lizzie. Geez, what's the matter with you? You'd think being engaged would make you happy. But you're acting anything but."

I hang my head. "I'm sorry. It's just . . . it's been a bad day. Monsieur Henri had a heart attack and is having a quadruple bypass and is going to be out for a while and I was on Page Six this morning because of the Jill Higgins wedding and the phones are ringing off the hook and—"

"Oh, so *that's* what Tiffany's doing down there," Shari says. "I wondered."

I take a sip of my tea. It's grown cold in front of me. "I should probably be getting back to work. There are a lot of brides who need wedding gowns restored, apparently."

"And there are probably a lot of victims of domestic abuse who need help obtaining public support and orders of protection," Shari says with a sigh.

I look at her from across the table. "How did we end up here?" I ask.

"I don't know," Shari says with a shake of her head. "But I like where I am. Do you like where you are?"

"I think so," I say, looking down at my ring. "It might take some getting used to. I think I might be better at helping other people with their weddings than I am at planning my own. Whenever I think about it, I sort of want to throw up."

"Okay." Shari points at me. "That is not a good sign. Remember what I said. It's okay for you to change your mind."

I give her a queasy smile. "I know. But . . . I really do love him."

"Do you?" Shari asks as she stands to go. "Or do you love the *idea* of him?"

"God," I say with a laugh. "What kind of question is that?"

"For you? I think it's a pertinent question. You have a history of falling in love with guys it turns out you basically didn't know at all."

"Yeah, but, Shari, come on. Luke's not going to turn out to be gay or a gambling addict." I have made some unfortunate mistakes in the guy department. "I mean, I *lived* with Luke, for crying out loud. For six months. I think I know him pretty well by now."

"Yes," she says. "You'd think that, wouldn't you? Still, people can surprise you, can't they? After all, I lived with Chaz for nearly as long as you lived with Luke, and I turned out to be a—"

"Don't say it." I fling up a hand to stop her before she can say the word "lesbian." Not that I mind. It's just that I try so hard not to remember that night at Kathy Pennebaker's when we were both sixteen. I'd been lusting after Tim Daly from the television show *Wings*. Shari and Kathy, it turned out, had been lusting after . . . well, each other. God, I'd been so *blind*. Although I suppose it's just as well they never told me. It would have been all over school in half a second. I'd have *tried* to keep it a secret, of course, if they'd asked me. But somehow I can never seem to keep my mouth shut, despite my best intentions. "I got it. Look. Don't worry. At the rate we're going, it'll be a long engagement, anyway. Luke's got school to finish, and his uncle wants him to come work for him in Paris this summer, and I've got about five thousand dresses to get through before I'll ever be able to lift my head to breathe. I'm not rushing to get married any time soon."

Shari gives me a hug. "That's my girl," she says.

It's as she's squeezing me that I notice it—this weird splotchy thing on the inside of my right elbow. It looks like a mosquito bite, only it's flat, not raised. And besides, it's January in Manhattan. How could I have been bitten by a mosquito?

I don't think anything of it. Then.

It's only later that I realize what it really is: Just the beginning of the ruination of the rest of my life. That's all.

A HISTORY
of
WEDDINGS

In ancient times, brides were traditionally expected to set forth on pre-wedding day pilgrimages from their own village to that of their betrothed. Due to the likelihood of her being set upon by thieves hoping to make off with her dowry (or the bride herself), the bride made this trip accompanied by armed maidens to defend her and her bling against marauders.

Thus was born the bridesmaid—or to be more historically accurate, the WARRIORMAID.

Tip to Avoid a Wedding Day Disaster

Today's bridesmaids perform a much different function than their ancient predecessors, from helping to organize the engagement and bridal showers to shuttling guests— I've even heard of some babysitting and doing the bride's laundry (ew).

Don't forget your bridesmaids on your special day. A special gift—such as a silver necklace or bracelet—will go a long way toward showing them how much you appreciate all their help . . . although the basic human courtesy of not turning into a Bridezilla on them would also be nice.

LIZZIE NICHOLS DESIGNS™

Chapter 5

One should believe in marriage as in the immortality of the soul.

Honoré de Balzac (1799–1850), French novelist and playwright

Gum-Chewer is sitting in the shop when I get back downstairs. Even though my only previous conversation with her was over the phone, I know it's her. I'd recognize that snap, crackle, and pop anywhere.

What shocks me is that I also recognize her instantly from *Access Hollywood* . . . and *Inside Edition* . . . and *Entertainment Tonight* . . . where she can frequently be seen wearing very little on the red carpets at the premieres of movies in which she is not starring, since she has no actual talent—none, at least, that's been detected so far. Ava Geck's only claim to fame, in fact, is that her family owns a chain of discount department stores ("Get It at Geck's"), said to be worth more than a billion dollars. She herself is rumored to have a personal net worth of more than three hundred million dollars, thanks to some savvy fragrance deals and a few less fortunate reality-television appearances.

More impressive—to me, anyway—is that she also happens to be marrying a prince. Not a prince like Luke is a prince back in his father's native France, where the aristocracy was abolished centuries ago, and no one kept track of who really was or was not a royal, and we really have only Luke's father's word for it, but in Greece, where, even if the royal family is no longer recognized as the head of state, they are nevertheless still allowed to hold and be addressed by their royal titles and are invited to state functions.

Somehow, someway, Greek Prince Aleksandros Nikolaos met—and apparently fell in love with and proposed to—Ava Geck.

It's kind of surreal to see her without a television set framing her pointy face. Although the hulking bodyguard standing with his arms crossed beside her—not to mention the enormous rock on the ring finger of her left hand and the trembling Chihuahua on her lap—quickly makes me realize what I'm seeing is all too real.

"Oh, hey," she says, with a quick glance at Tiffany when I walk in. "Is this her?"

Tiffany rolls her eyes. "I already told you, Ava. She won't see you without an appointment."

Tiffany and Ava have apparently already become acquainted. It appears to be an acquaintance of some long standing. And it is obviously not a very happy one.

"Um," I say. "Hi. What's going on?"

"Ms. Nichols." Ava leaps to her precariously high stilettos—which are attached to purple suede thigh-high boots—upsetting the Chihuahua, who tumbles to the carpet with a yelp. This does not seem to concern its mistress in any way. "I'm so, like, sorry I'm here without an appointment. It's just, like, I saw the story on Page Six about you, and the thing is, I live in Los Angeles and I'm in town for New Year's—you know, I was doing a guest spot for *Celebrity Pit Fight* at Times Square for the ball drop?—and I have to get back, but I'm getting married this summer, and I, like, really, really, really want you to do my dress."

"And I already told her," Tiffany says, from between gritted teeth, "you don't do original designs, just—"

"I know this girl keeps saying you only do restorations," Ava says, flicking a scathing glance in Tiffany's direction. "But I'm all, what's the diff? I mean, if I bring in some heinous old dress and ask you to make it over, or if you just, like, make me a new one? Why can't you just make me a new one? Okay? Because that's what I want. I want a dress by someone who's young and cool. Not some dried-up old-lady dress by someone with a freaking four-story shop on Madison Avenue. Ya know?"

Except it was kind of hard to tell what she was saying, between all the chewing sounds.

"Ms. Nichols?" Tiffany stands up. "Can I have a word with you in the back room?"

"God!" Ava cracks her gum. "What is the dealio? I have money. I'll, like, pay you."

"Um," I say to Ava. I notice that the Chihuahua is getting ready to lift a leg against Madame Henri's potted hydrangea. I dive to pick up the dog and place it gently back in a confused-looking Ava Geck's arms. "Let me just consult with my, um, assistant here, to see what the schedule for this week looks like, and I'll be right back."

Ava looks relieved. At least if that's what I'm to believe from the large pink bubble she blows.

"Whatever," she says.

I allow Tiffany to drag me into the back room.

"You cannot design a dress for her," Tiffany hisses as soon as I've drawn the black velvet curtain across. "She's a skanky crack whore."

"Let me guess," I say. "You met her in Narcotics Anonymous."

"No," Tiffany says. "But she's still a skanky crack whore. Seriously, Lizzie. Did you see her on *Celebrity Pit Fight*? She made Lil' Kim cry. *Lil' Kim.* You can't. You just can't."

"She's hugely famous," I say. "She's a bazillioniare. And she's marrying a prince. Do you have any idea what kind of press that will bring in?"

"Yeah," Tiffany says. "Skanky crack whore press. Believe me, that is not the kind of press you want."

"Tiffany," I say, fighting for patience. "You don't understand. At this point in my career, any press is good press. I'm totally doing the dress."

"But she's disgusting," Tiffany insists. "Did you see the way she treated that dog? And what is with those boots?"

"Tiffany, she's obviously deeply troubled. She needs our help, not our scorn. She's clearly had no one in her life to gently guide her on how to act like a decent human being. And she really needs that, now more than ever . . . she's marrying a prince! It's going to be a royal wedding!"

"In *Greece*," Tiffany points out. "Hel-*lo*."

"Tiffany! How can you say that? Greece is the cradle of Western civilization, the birthplace of democracy, political science, Western literature and philosophy, the Olympic games—"

"Um, Lizzie, have you ever even tasted hummus?"

"Tiffany." I glare at her. "I'm doing Ava's dress. You're either with me or you're out."

Tiffany rolls her eyes toward the ceiling. "Is this because of the prince thing? Because, like, you're marrying a prince, and so you feel like you have this moral obligation to help her, because *she's* marrying a prince?"

I ignore that. "Tiffany, we have a moral obligation to help this poor girl, because if we don't, no one will, and she'll just go on doing asinine things like pulling out Lil' Kim's hair extensions on

Celebrity Pit Fight, and she'll never discover her true inner potential."

"And you think *you* can help her find it?" Tiffany sneers.

"Yes, Tiffany," I say gravely. "Yes, I think I can."

Except that the truth is, I don't think I can. I *know* I can.

"Fine. If you want to play Dr. Dolittle to her Eliza Higgins," Tiffany says, "it's your funeral. I'll just do what you're paying me for: answer the phones."

"It's Professor Higgins," I correct her, "and Eliza Doolittle. Professor Higgins is the guy who gives the Cockney flower girl the makeover. Dr. Dolittle is the guy who could talk to animals."

"Fine," Tiffany mutters. "I can tell this was a bad day to cut back on my Adderall."

I throw back the black velvet curtain and find Ava Geck closely examining a dressmaker's dummy wearing a House of Bianchi off-the-shoulder number I've retrofitted with sleeves for a bride who's being married in a conservative synagogue.

"I like this one," Ava says, straightening up when I come in. She's still chomping on her gum. "Can you make me something like this?"

I'm surprised. Pleasantly so. For a girl who's shown her panties so many times on television, it's a surprisingly modest choice.

"I think we can come up with a gown you'll like," I say. "Something a little more Ava-like."

Ava gasps, then claps her hands. The Chihuahua barks excitedly and spins around in circles. Even the bodyguard cracks a smile. A very small one, but a smile just the same.

"Oh, thank you!" Ava cries. "This is gonna be bitchin'!"

"Yeah," I say. "Just a couple of ground rules, though. Rule number one... when you enter Chez Henri, you have to de-gum. When you leave, you may re-gum." I hold out my hand expectantly.

Ava stares at me blankly. "What?"

"Your gum," I say. "There is no gum allowed in Chez Henri. You're welcome to go over to Vera Wang and chew gum, but not here. It's uncivilized to stand around looking like a cow chewing her cud. So either spit it out or leave."

Ava, looking stunned, spits her gum out into my hand. I drop the wad into a nearby trash can, which the Chihuahua quickly runs over to inspect.

"Rule number two," I say, wiping my hand off with a tissue I pluck from the box on Tiffany's desk. "You must show up on time for all fittings. If you're not going to be able to make it for whatever reason, you must call at least an hour before your appointment to let us know. Failure to do this more than once, and your contract with us will be canceled. It's not polite to stand people up. We have lots of clients and could reschedule someone else in your time slot if we know you won't be able to make it in advance. Okay?"

Still looking dazed, Ava nods. The bodyguard, I notice, is still smiling, although now he looks slightly bemused.

"All right, Ava," I say. "Why don't you step into the dressing room over here so I can take your measurements?"

Ava hurries to oblige, tripping a little over her ridiculously high-heeled boots.

It's going to be, it's clear, a long morning.

A HISTORY
of
WEDDINGS

Bridesmaids in ancient Roman times were the first to wear identical gowns—identical not only to one another's but to the bride's as well. This was in an attempt to trick demons from taking the bride's soul prior to her wedding night. Any woman who'd protected three brides from evil spirits was considered too impure to marry herself, having absorbed too much black magic. This is where the expression "three times a bridesmaid, never a bride" comes from.

So they weren't making it up about the *three times a bridesmaid* thing! And you just thought they were talking about your aunt Judy.

Tip to Avoid a Wedding Day Disaster

You love your friends because of their unique personalities. Well, their bodies are unique too. So don't squeeze your bridesmaids into identical gowns. They'll hate it, and if you're really their friend, you should hate that they hate it. Choose a shade that will flatter all of them, and let them each choose a dress in that color that they like, one that they'll really wear again.

So what if they won't all look exactly the same? It's them you love, not their look, right?

LIZZIE NICHOLS DESIGNS™

Chapter 6

Two such as you with such a master speed cannot be parted nor be swept away from one another once you are agreed that life is only life forevermore together wing to wing and oar to oar.

Robert Frost (1874–1963), American poet

*L*uke has promised to come over and make me a nice dinner because of the day I've had—though Madame Henri calls just after five to let me know that her husband has gotten through his surgery with flying colors—but the truth is, all I want to do is take a hot bath, read a fashion magazine, and go to bed.

Only how can I tell this to Luke, who went to the market and picked up two sirloins and marinated them (his postbaccalaureate premed classes don't start up again until after Martin Luther King Day), especially for me?

So when he calls just before six with an apologetic note in his voice and says, "Listen," it's all I can do to keep from clicking my heels together with joy. He's canceling! Alleluia! And hello, this month's *Vogue*.

"There's a Michigan game on tonight," he says. "And Chaz really wants me to watch it with him. You know how he is about the Wolverines. And the truth is . . . he seemed kind of depressed on the phone when he called to tell me about it."

"Chaz is depressed?" This is news to me. He hadn't seemed a bit depressed when he'd had his hand down my bra. Not that I add this last part out loud, of course.

"Well, I mean, it's only natural he'd be a little down, you know," Luke says. "We're getting married, and his girlfriend left him . . . for another woman. I really thought he'd have someone else by now— I've never seen him go without a date for this long."

"Shari only broke up with him at Thanksgiving," I point out dryly. I notice there's a new red splotch on the inside of my elbow where the old one, which has faded away, was. So it wasn't a mosquito bite. What could they be? Maybe an allergy to the detergent I'm using? But I haven't switched detergents lately.

"For Chaz, a month and a half is a real dry spell," Luke says. "Now his best friend is marrying the cutest girl in the world . . . No wonder he's depressed."

"Then you should absolutely stay home and watch basketball with him," I say. I'm already fantasizing about the Chinese food I'm going to order in. Moo shu chicken with hoisin sauce. Maybe I'll even eat it in the bathtub.

"Well, that's the thing," Luke says. "The game's only on satellite. We'll be watching it at O'Riordan's Sports Bar, which is around the corner from your place, on Lexington. So I thought, if you wanted to stop by later . . ."

"Gosh, honey," I say sweetly. "There's nothing I can imagine wanting to do more than sit around with you and your depressed guy friend watching sports."

"We'll be ordering chicken wings," Luke says in an effort to tempt me.

"That is so hard to resist . . ."

"Come on," Luke says in a more serious tone. "Chaz loves you, you know that. He wants to say congratulations in person. And seeing you will cheer him up. You know how much he likes teasing you about your weird outfits. Besides, if you don't show up, I won't see you all day."

Except it isn't my outfit I'm afraid of Chaz teasing me about.

Not that I'm about to mention this, either.

"Luke," I say. "The whole point of our not living together is so that we can use this time of our engagement to explore who we are as individuals, so that when we come together as a married couple we'll have a clearer idea of exactly what we want out of—"

"Lizzie," Luke says. "I know all that. I was there when you made that little speech, remember? Can't a guy just want to see his girlfriend?"

I sigh, visions of my fun evening of high-fashion photos and bubbles going down the drain. Literally. "I'll be there around seven."

The bar is crowded, but thankfully not smoky, since New York City banned all smoking indoors and actually enforces it. I find Luke and Chaz in a booth beneath one of the dozens of televisions hanging suspended from the ceiling and blaring college basketball games. Luke leaps up to kiss me hello. Chaz, I see, is wearing one of his ubiquitous (except when he's in evening wear) University of Michigan baseball hats, pulled down low over his hair. He is unshaven and looking a little rough around the edges . . . rougher, even, than when I'd seen him last, after a night of too much champagne . . .

And too much other stuff as well.

"Come on," Luke says to me, grinning his adorable grin. "Show him."

I've slid into the booth beside Luke, and am taking off my coat and unwinding my scarf.

Chaz is nursing a beer, his eyes on the game above my head.

"Luke," I say, blushing, though I don't know why. "No."

"Come on," Luke says. "You know you want to."

Chaz's gaze flicks down from the television screen and onto me. "Show me what?"

Luke lifts my left hand to show Chaz my engagement ring. Chaz lets out a long, low whistle, even though of course he's already seen it. "*Nice,*" he says.

Luke's grin is now ear-to-ear.

"Let me get you a drink," he says to me. "I'll just run up to the bar, since the waitress takes forever. White wine?"

I nod. "That'd be great . . ." I wonder if I need to remind him to get it with a side of ice. I hate warm white wine, and I can never seem to drink it fast enough. It's tacky, but lately I've started asking for my white wine with a glass of ice on the side. It also lasts longer and has less calories that way.

"Be back in a flash," Luke says before I have a chance to say anything, as I slide to let him out of the booth to go to the bar, then slip back into the seat he's just vacated.

Oh well. He'll remember about the ice.

Chaz has lifted his gaze back to the game over my head. I clear my throat.

"Thank you for the roses," I say quickly, to get it over with, and before Luke gets back. "You didn't have to do that."

"Yeah," Chaz says shortly, still not looking at me. "I did."

"Well." I see that Luke is still frantically trying to get the bartender's attention, so I lay a hand—my right—over Chaz's. "Thank you. It meant a lot to me. You have no idea."

Chaz looks down at my hand. Then he looks back into my eyes. "Yeah," he says. "I think I have a pretty good idea."

I pull my hand away, stung—though I'm not sure why.

"What is *that* supposed to mean?" I ask.

Chaz chuckles and reaches for his beer. "Nothing. God, what are you so defensive for? I thought you and Luke were so blissfully happy."

"We are!" I squeak.

"Well, then"—he tilts his beer at me in a toast—"mazel tov."

"You don't seem very depressed," I can't keep myself from remarking.

Then I immediately want to kill myself.

He seems almost to choke on the mouthful of beer he just swallowed.

"Depressed?" he echoes when he's recovered enough to speak. "Who said I'm depressed?"

I look around for a conveniently loaded pistol. Sadly, there doesn't appear to be one available, so I have no choice but to answer the question.

"Luke," I mutter shamefacedly. "He thinks you're depressed because he's getting married and you're all alone."

"Luke *would* think that," Chaz says with a smirk.

"So . . . you're not depressed?" I ask, feeling a tiny glimmer of hope that maybe suicide won't be necessary, just this once.

Chaz looks me dead in the eye and says, "Why, yes, Lizzie. I'm manically depressed because the girl I've finally realized I've always been in love with, and who I was beginning to think just might love me back, turned around and got herself engaged to my best friend, who, frankly, doesn't deserve her. Does that answer your question?"

It's the weirdest thing, but my heart seems to do a flip-flop in my chest, and for a second, I can't breathe, nor can I drop my gaze from his.

Then I realize he's joking.

And I feel my cheeks begin to burn.

He's joking. Of course he's joking. God, I'm such a fool.

"What does it matter to you?" I demand, ignoring his sarcasm. I'm furious at myself—for thinking he meant it when he said he loved me, but even more, for having felt bad that I'd hurt him. He can't be hurt. I mean, obviously he can. But not by me. Never by me. "You should be relieved you escaped my sights. You don't even believe in marriage. It's just a slip of paper, right? That's what you said, anyway."

"You got that right." Chaz has leaned back to watch the game. "You want a happy romantic relationship? Don't ruin it by getting married."

I blink at him. I can't believe he's serious.

"Since when did you start feeling this way?" I ask. "You never felt like this about marriage when you were with Shari. You two were the picture of connubial bliss. Without the connubial part. But you were always making pies and doing her laundry and stuff . . ."

"Yeah," Chaz says, still not taking his gaze off the television screen . . . although I notice he's set his jaw. "Well, she left me, remember? For a *woman*. Believe me, I won't be making that mistake again. Marriage is for suckers."

"You don't mean that," I say, a little shocked at his bitter tone.

"Don't I?" He smirks at the screen. "I think I know what I'm talking about. My dad's a divorce lawyer, remember?"

"And yet he's been married to your mom," I say, "for like, what, thirty years?"

I can't believe I'm still upset about the *I've always been in love with you* remark, which, considering all the making out we were doing in the back of that cab on New Year's, wasn't really in the best of taste. I'm even more upset about the way my heart had reacted to the information. What had *that* been about?

And how, even for one second, could I ever actually have believed him?

I know I'm a naïve Midwestern girl. But I really try not to act like one. Most of the time.

"I try to keep that on the down low," Chaz says. "The happily married parents thing doesn't really go with my whole persona. You know, newly single philosophy Ph.D. candidate, living alone in an East Village walk-up, hard drinking, hard living, kind of dangerous—"

Now it's my turn to smirk.

"What?" Chaz drags his gaze from the television screen and eyes me. "You don't think I'm dangerous?"

"Not in that hat," I say.

"Oh, I'm dangerous," Chaz assures me. "More dangerous than *Luke*."

"I don't like Luke because he's dangerous," I point out.

"Oh, right," Chaz says. "You like him . . . why? Because he's rich? Handsome? Suave? Debonair? Thoughtful? Kind? Going to save the children someday?"

"All of the above," I say, "except rich. I intend to make my own money, thank you, so I have no need of his. In fact, I just took on Ava Geck as a client today."

"The skanky crack whore?" Chaz looks horrified.

"Why does everyone call her that?" I ask in annoyance. "No one has ever actually *seen* her do crack or have sex in exchange for money, and yet everyone calls her a skanky crack whore."

"I don't have to see her do it," Chaz says. "Have you ever checked out *Celebrity Pit Fight*?"

It's my turn to look horrified. "What is a hard-drinking, hard-living, philosophy Ph.D. candidate doing watching *Celebrity Pit Fight*?"

Chaz grins. "It's a really good show," he says. "I mean, if you're ever in the mood to examine one of the bleaker examples of the depraved depths to which we as a society have sunk. Or at least the

depraved depths to which the entertainment industry is determined to make us think we've sunk."

"Hey." Luke slides back into the booth and hands me my glass
of wine. "Sorry that took so long. This place is a madhouse. There
are five different games on."

I notice with a slight feeling of disappointment that he's forgotten to get a side of ice. Oh well. We've been going out for only six
months, after all. He can't remember *everything*.

"You forgot the ice," Chaz says. "Luke, tell your girlfriend she
isn't going to get ahead in the wedding gown biz if she takes on
skanky crack whores as clients."

I blink, not quite able to believe Chaz remembered.

"What ice?" Luke looks confused. "Wait. *Who*'s a skanky crack
whore?"

"No one," I say at the same time that Chaz says, "Ava Geck."

"Who's Ava Geck?" Luke wants to know.

Chaz guffaws. I take a hasty sip of my wine, knowing what's
coming.

"Do you even *watch* television?" Chaz asks Luke. "Do you ever
even read a periodical besides *The Wall Street Journal*? Tell me,
because I really want to know. When you're in the dentist's office,
do you ever, even by accident, pick up a copy of *Us Weekly*?"

"Stop it," I say to Chaz. I'm getting annoyed with him now.
More annoyed, maybe, than the situation warrants. "Just because
Luke doesn't know who Ava Geck is—"

"*Everyone* knows who Ava Geck is," Chaz bursts out.

"Who's Ava Geck?" Luke asks again.

"She's—" But suddenly I'm so tired I can't even go on. I can't
take it, the voices of the announcers from the televisions and the
screams of the fans and the clapping whenever someone's team
scores a basket—not to mention the drunk homeless guy I can see

bobbing around outside the plate-glass window a few feet away, begging for change from anyone who passes by the place.

But what I really can't take is the voice inside my head that's returned. It's a familiar voice. It ought to be. Because it's the voice of the guy sitting directly across from me . . . the big, rumpled one in the University of Michigan baseball cap.

"Why, yes, Lizzie. I'm manically depressed because the girl I've finally realized I've always been in love with, and who I was beginning to think just might love me back, turned around and got herself engaged to my best friend, who, frankly, doesn't deserve her."

But simultaneously I hear that same voice saying, *"You want a happy romantic relationship? Don't ruin it by getting married. I know what I'm talking about."*

"You know what?" I say suddenly, my own voice tight with unshed emotion. "This has been fun. But I'm really tired. Do you guys mind if I call it a night? I have a big day tomorrow, and I think I'm gonna turn in early."

"Oh, come on," Luke says. "You just got here. Don't go yet. The game just started."

I look at Chaz. His face is impassive beneath the brim of his hat. But he's looking right back at me.

"Yeah, Lizzie," he says. "Don't go yet. The game just started."

It's weird. But something in the way his gaze holds mine—not to mention his tone—tells me he isn't talking about the game on TV.

Not at all.

"Okay, I'll be seeing you guys later," I say, my own voice pitched way too high, as I all but shove Luke out of the way in my haste to leave the booth.

"I'll walk you home," a confused Luke says, but I brush this offer aside with a quick kiss on his cheek and a whispered *No, thanks, I'll be fine, stay and have fun,* then bolt for the door, where I stand gasping in the bitterly cold January air.

"Spare a quarter, miss?" the homeless drunk asks me, holding out a filthy, chipped coffee cup.

I don't even answer him. That's what a jaded New Yorker I've become. I never have a quarter to spare anymore. I need my quarters. I need all the quarters I can get. Do you have any idea how much it costs to do laundry around here?

"Fine," the homeless guy says with a sniff. "Be that way, bitch."

My eyes fill with tears. I'm not a bitch! I'm not! Any more than Ava Geck is a skanky crack whore. Any more than Chaz Pendergast is in love with me. Oh, why did he have to say that, anyway? Why does he have to be so mean? After having gotten those beautiful roses, I'd been completely ready to forgive him for all the nasty things he'd said yesterday morning . . . and then he'd had to go and say *that.*

. . . the girl I've finally realized I've always been in love with . . . who I was beginning to think just might love me back . . .

He'd only been teasing. He's always teased me, the whole time I've known him.

So . . . why does it hurt so much this time?

"You want a happy romantic relationship? Don't ruin it by getting married."

But if you don't get married . . . what's the *point*?

A HISTORY
of
WEDDINGS

The Elizabethan age brought us the flowering of poetry, literature, theater, and romance. So it's no wonder we have Elizabethan England to thank for so many of our modern-day wedding traditions, including the exchange of rings, a more traditional (i.e., non-weapons-bearing) use of bridesmaids, the exchange of wedding vows, even bridal bouquets. Most upper-class marriages were still arranged during this time, often from birth. Only the lower classes had the luxury of being able to marry for love.

But if this hadn't been the case, what else would William Shakespeare have had to write about?

Your sister-in-law-to-be might have the cutest kids in the world—and she just very well may have a point: Maybe they should *have a role in your wedding. But don't let her browbeat you into sacrificing one of your bridesmaid, ring bearer, or flower girl positions for* her *kids. Don't upset one of* your *friends or family members just to placate* his *sister. There are lots of other tasks her kids can perform throughout the ceremony, such as guest book holder, confetti or program passer-outer, or even adorable, if slightly height-challenged, usher. Use your imagination, and you'll both be happy.*

LIZZIE NICHOLS DESIGNS™

Chapter 7

Now join hands, and with your hands your hearts.
William Shakespeare (1564–1616), English dramatist and poet

our friend Chaz sounds like a pig" is Monique's observation when she and Tiffany overhear me relating the details about my evening to Gran (Mom, as usual, wasn't available) while the three of us are having a quick, between-fittings lunch in the shop the next day.

"She's right about that," Gran, on my cell phone, agrees. "Whoever she is."

"He's not really," I say, pausing with my Così tandoori chicken sandwich halfway to my lips. "I mean, under ordinary circumstances. That's what's so weird about this."

"Well, that's it, then," Monique says firmly. She's a beauty every bit as statuesque—and sure of herself—as Tiffany.

Unlike Tiffany, however, Monique has a British accent that makes her sound like a college professor every time she speaks.

A college professor who talks a lot about men being "wankers," I mean.

"What's it?" I ask.

Tiffany and Monique exchange glances. Tiffany nods.

"He's in love with you, of course," Monique says.

"You've never even met him," I cry.

"I have," Tiffany says, stuffing a wad of Jamaican jerk sandwich into her mouth. "And he totally is."

"She's right," Gran says. "I've always thought that boy wanted to put a load of coal into your steam engine."

I nearly spit out the bite of tandoori chicken I'd just taken.

"How can you *say* that?" I cry. "He's Luke's best friend! He's my best friend's ex-boyfriend!"

Tiffany looks at me blankly. "So?"

Monique is giving me the same blank stare. They must teach it at modeling school. "Yeah," she says. "So?"

Gran sounds impatient. "*Dr. Quinn* comes on in ten minutes. How long is this going to take?"

"So . . . so . . . ," I say, for once in my life actually sputtering to find the right words. "So . . . Look. I'm sure men fall head over heels for you two all the time. I mean . . . *look* at you. But in real life—for *real* girls, like me, that is—that just doesn't happen. Men don't go around falling in love with me. And certainly not without encouragement."

"Oh, and your letting him touch your titties in that taxi wasn't encouragement?" Monique asks.

"You let him spend the night too," Tiffany points out.

I put my finger over the mouthpiece of my cell. "Excuse me," I say. "My grandmother is listening in on this."

"Too late," Gran says. "I already heard. This is even *better* than *Dr. Quinn.*"

"We were both drunk," I insist in my own defense for what has to be the millionth time. I'm regretting ever having opened my mouth about any of this, a not unfamiliar sensation. I'm especially regretting not having hung up when Gran answered. "Look, forget I said anything. It was nothing."

Why had I even said anything, especially to these girls? I wouldn't have if I'd been able to discuss any of this with Shari. If I could just call Shari and go, *Shari. This is what my fiancé's best friend said to me. What do you think?* none of this would be happening.

But I can't do that. Because my fiancé's best friend is her ex-boyfriend.

And I can't talk about what happened with Chaz with Shari. Because it would all be too weird.

But Monique and Tiffany, it turns out, are not proving to be adequate Shari substitutes. Not at all.

"That last bit he said," Monique says, "about the game just starting? That didn't sound like nothing to me. Does it to you, Tiff?"

"No way, José," Tiffany says. "I think he's warm for our Miss Lizzie's form."

"Told you," Gran sings.

"Oh my God, you guys." I shake my head. "He is so not. And even if he is . . . it's not going to go anywhere. He's completely damaged from what happened with Shari. He says he—"

It's at this moment—fortunately—that the door to the shop bursts open, and Ava Geck comes tumbling through it, her bodyguard and Chihuahua in tow. Ava has a wild look on her face, as if she's being hunted. She's wearing short-shorts over fishnet stockings, even though it's approximately twelve degrees outside, and her lower jaw is moving rapidly . . . except that she's not speaking.

Tiffany scowls down at the book in front of her. "What are you doing here, Ava?" she demands. "Your next appointment's not for four weeks."

"Sorry," Ava says, still chewing. She collapses onto the chaise longue I insisted Madame Henri place in the far corner for nervous, waiting mothers, and peers out the plate-glass window in the front of the store, her body hidden from view by a display dummy dressed in a princess gown from the 1950s, complete with a voluminous, diamanté-dotted tulle skirt that takes up almost the entire display window. "We were in the neighborhood looking at condos and suddenly . . . paparazzi! Can we hide for a few minutes until they go away? I don't have any eyeliner on."

"Hold on, Gran," I say into my cell. I walk over to Ava and hold out my hand expectantly. "You *may*," I say.

Still crouching behind the tulle skirt, she looks down at my hand with a blank expression on her face. Then comprehension dawns. She spits her gum out into my hand. I walk over to the trash can beneath the desk at which Tiffany is sitting and dump it, then reach for a tissue.

"Little Joey," I say to the bodyguard, to whom we'd been formally introduced during Ava's last visit. "There are blinds if you want to pull them down."

Little Joey—whose hulking three-hundred-pound, nearly seven-foot frame makes it clear that his name is ironic—begins pulling down the black metal blinds I'd bought at the Manhattan Target when I'd been rehabbing Jill Higgins's gown, and she, too, had had problems with stalkerazzi.

"Why are you looking for a condo in Manhattan, Ava?" I ask her.

"It's, like, so much better here than in Los Angeles," Ava says, pulling her shivering Chihuahua onto her lap. "Except for the weather. For one thing, you don't have to drive as far to get to cool places. Which is great if you're wasted. And for another, no one asks you for autographs, or crap like that—*usually*. I mean, people stare. But they don't bug you. Except, like, teenagers at H&M."

It takes us a moment to digest this. Tiffany is the first to recover.

"So are you looking for a one-bedroom or a two-bedroom, or what?" Tiffany asks conversationally.

"She's looking for four bedrooms, three baths, and an eat-in kitchen with at least two thousand square feet of outdoor terrace, and full southern exposure," Little Joey says when Ava just blinks bewilderedly at the question.

When we all turn our heads to stare at Ava, dumbfounded by this information—since to my knowledge, no such piece of real estate exists on the island of Manhattan (for less than five million dollars, anyway)—she just shrugs and says, in her little girl voice, "I've got seasonal affective disorder. Hey, do you have anything else to eat? All I've had today is a PowerBar, and I'm, like, starving."

I hand her the other half of my tandoori chicken sandwich, but she makes a face.

"What's that white slimy stuff?" she asks suspiciously.

This causes Tiffany and Monique to dissolve into a fit of hysterical laughter from which it's clear they won't soon recover.

"Tzatziki sauce," I say. "Ava, how can you be marrying a Greek prince and not know what tzatziki sauce is?"

"I like *him*," Ava says, snatching the sandwich out of reach of her dog—whose name, she'd informed us the day before, is Snow White ("After the Disney princess")—"not his country's *food*."

"Well," I say. "You should try it, at least, before you decide you don't like it."

Ava shrugs and takes a bite. Her mouth occupied, I turn back to Tiffany and Monique, who are wiping their eyes from their shared—if disgustingly raunchy—joke.

"Seriously, you guys," I say to them, addressing my remark into the phone. "Do you think I should try talking to him? Luke thinks he's depressed. What if he's right? Maybe if I talked to him about it, it would help. To bring about closure, you know? Sometimes when things are out in the open, they don't bother people as much."

"Says the girl who can't keep a secret to save her life," says Tiffany with a laugh. Although frankly I don't see what's so funny about that remark. Also, it's not true. I've kept lots of secrets.

I can't happen to think of any right now. But I'm sure there are some.

"What are we talking about?" Ava wants to know. She's already gnawed off a quarter of an inch of the sandwich half I've given her. Snow White is busy with another quarter of an inch. It's not hard to see how the two of them stay so trim.

"Lizzie's fiancé's best friend is in love with her," Monique says lightly. She's split her vegi muffuletta with Little Joey. "And she doesn't know what to do about it."

I roll my eyes. "He's not in love with me," I say. "He—"

"Oh, that's easy," Ava interrupts, licking the fingertips Snow White's just licked. "Why don't you just fuck him?"

"Who's that?" Gran asks over the phone. "I like her."

I have no choice but to set down my Diet Coke and say, "Ava, first of all: Monique is wrong. Chaz isn't in love with me. We're just friends. Second of all, you shouldn't be driving anywhere, short or long distance, if you're wasted. I want you to know that I Googled you after I got home last night, and I know all about your DUI. You need to be more careful. With all your money, why don't you just hire a driver? And last, while I appreciate that, as feminists, we have every right to embrace whatever kind of language we choose, even words considered by previous generations to be 'unladylike' or 'coarse,' it really isn't tasteful or imaginative to use vulgarities in everyday conversation. Sure, if you're really upset about something. But the f-word, Ava, when you're speaking about making love? I think you're better than that. In fact, I *know* you are. Besides, what would Prince Aleksandros say?"

Ava looks at me with the same blank expression she'd worn when I'd held out my hand for her gum. "He says 'fuck' even more than I do," she says.

I sigh. "Let's just drop it," I say to the room—and into the phone—in general. "Pretend I didn't say anything. Especially to Mom. Okay, Gran?"

"Tell you what you should do," Little Joey remarks, after taking a delicate sip of the Diet Peach Snapple he's produced from one of his enormous pockets. "Get this guy alone, in a darkened room. Open up a bottle of Hennessey. Play a little Vandross. That's how you have yourselves some *closure.*"

"Now," Gran says approvingly, "someone is finally talking sense."

I gape at my cell. "That's . . . that's preposterous," I stammer. "I happen to be deeply—*deeply*—in love with my fiancé. I mean . . . come on, Tiffany." I turn to her for help. "You've seen Luke and me together. You had Thanksgiving with us, remember?"

"Right," Tiffany says, thoughtfully tapping on her perfectly aligned—also capped—front teeth. "But I think Little Joey might be onto something, Lizzie. I think you *want* us to say you should go talk to Chaz. I mean, why else would you have mentioned it?"

Monique nods too. "Right. You do seem to want us to tell you that you should go talk to Chaz about it."

"I think you liked having his hand down your bra and are hoping he'll do it again," Tiffany adds.

I widen my eyes at her. "Boundaries," I say, jerking my head urgently at Little Joey, who is now smirking into his Snapple bottle. "Ladies! Boundaries!"

"That's what I said." Ava, ignoring me, has turned her huge baby blues onto Tiffany. "She should just fuck him and get him out of her system. That's what I did when I found myself with feelings for DJ Tippycat on *Celebrity Pit Fight*."

I blink. Then I say firmly, "I am not going to *make love* to my fiancé's best friend, Ava. That is a totally ridiculous suggestion. For one thing, I would never betray Luke's trust like that. And I can tell you that if that's how you deal with your fiancé's friends—or . . . or DJ Tippycat—well, he isn't going to stay your fiancé for long. And for another thing, I happen to be in love with my boyfriend. Besides which, Chaz happens to be my best friend's ex-boyfriend—"

"Yeah, but it's not like she wants him anymore," Tiffany says in a bored voice. "Seeing as how she's gay and sleeping with a woman now."

Ava sucks in her breath. Little Joey looks as delighted as if he's just won the lottery. Snow White yawns and curls herself into a little ball and goes to sleep. Gran says, "I think I'll just TiVo today's episode of *Dr. Quinn* . . . how the hell do you work this thing?"

"Chaz doesn't even believe in marriage," I inform them desperately. "He thinks it's nothing but a slip of paper, and that marriage doesn't actually mean anything—"

"Okay, *now* we get to the heart of the matter," Little Joey says in a satisfied voice. "So *this* is why you aren't busting a move on the guy."

"Of *course*," Monique says, wide-eyed. "It all makes sense now. What's a woman who makes her living making women's wedding dreams come true going to do with a man who doesn't even believe in the institution of marriage? It's absurd."

"She can always make him change his mind," Ava says, as if I'm not even in the room. "It's hard. But it happens."

Tiffany looks dubious. "I don't know. This is a philosophy Ph.D. candidate we're talking about. He studies, like, existentialism and shit. I think it'd be hard to get him to change his *socks*, let alone his mind."

"Let's just forget I brought it up, all right?" I ask in an unsteady voice. "Let's talk about something else—"

"Nooooo!" Gran yells, so loudly that I have to hold the phone away from my ear.

"Let's talk about your gown, Ava," I say, ignoring Gran. "I think you're right to go a little more conservative than usual. After all, this is your wedding, and you're going to be marrying into a royal family. But since it's going to be a summer ceremony, I was thinking capped sleeves—"

"This is boring me," Gran threatens. "I'm hanging up."

"You're young and slender and can get away with them. And since it's Greece, I was thinking an empire waist . . . going a little Grecian. Here, let me show you what I mean."

The click echoes with startling finality in my ear. I ignore it, closing my cell phone and laying it aside. I'll deal with Gran later. *A load of coal into my steam engine?*

With difficulty, I finally steer them away from the topic of my love life and onto the subject of my ideas for Ava's gown—which she seems to like—until Tiffany bursts out, after a glance at the wall clock, "Crap! I have to go to work. I mean, my other work. Okay, you guys, don't talk about anything good while I'm gone. And, Lizzie, don't you dare make any decisions about Chaz without checking with me first. Obviously you can't be trusted about any of this. Just, you know. Call me first if anything new comes up, and we'll talk."

"I don't even know what you're talking about," I say with a sniff. "As I've said before—repeatedly—I love my boyfriend—I mean, my fiancé—and nothing is going to happen between his best friend and myself, because there is nothing going on between us."

"*Right,*" Tiffany says with a laugh, which is echoed by everyone else in the shop, with the exception of me.

After Tiffany leaves—announcing that there're still paparazzi waiting on the corner and that Ava had better continue to lay low—I declare that I, too, have to go to work—on making some sketches for Ava's dress; plus, there's the Bianchi, which I'm determined to finish up; not to mention loads of other projects to get started, given the fact that my boss is going to be out for at least the next four to six weeks, according to his wife, who'd phoned to give me a progress report—and slink into the back.

But instead of sketching *or* tweaking the Bianchi, I find myself staring into space, wondering whether or not what the others had said—that Chaz was in love with me—could possibly be true.

"I'm manically depressed because the girl I've finally realized I've always been in love with, and who I was beginning to think just might love me back, turned around and got herself engaged to my best friend, who, frankly, doesn't deserve her."

Sure. He'd *said* that. But he'd only been teasing me. And I, like the simple Midwestern fool that I am, had fallen for it. Why *did* my heart go all jumpy when he said that? I am completely and one hundred percent committed to Luke.

Of course . . . Chaz *had* said he saw nothing but me in his future . . . and that I wasn't even wearing Spanx.

Luke still doesn't know that I wear Spanx, or even what they are. I've managed to keep them a well-guarded secret from him.

How I've kept the twenty or so pounds I've managed to gain back since moving to New York City a secret from him is much more complicated. It involves never turning my back on him while undressed, and always letting him be on top during our more, er, intimate moments, so he doesn't notice my belly. Thank God for gravity.

How much longer I'll be able to carry on this facade, I don't know. It may end up to be easier to give up tandoori chicken sandwiches in exchange for salads or—God forbid—I could start working out.

But I do want to be a slender bride. Or at least less large than I am now.

But where will I find the time to work out, now that I'm running the shop single-handedly—well, not counting Tiffany and Monique—and will be doing so for at least another month and a half . . . maybe even longer, according to Madame Henri, who explained that bypass surgery recovery times can be hard to predict and depend on the individual? I don't even have time to *plan* my own wedding, let alone get in shape for it.

Funny how just thinking the words "my wedding" makes me feel a little tight in the chest. Seriously, like I can't breathe. And what is with that itchy red splotch on the inside of my elbow all of a sudden? What *is* that? Why does it keep appearing and then disappearing, only to reappear in a new spot, sometimes more than one?

Is that . . . oh my God, is that a *hive*? No. It can't be. I haven't had hives since I was in high school, when I was put in charge of the costumes for *Jesus Christ Superstar,* and the director wanted everyone in bell bottoms. This was before bell bottoms were back in style, and I realized I was going to have to slash—and insert brightly colored panels into—the pants legs of seventy-five cast members. In one weekend. I'd broken out into such bad hives that Dr. Dennis, Shari's dad, had had to give me a shot of prednisone.

Oh my God. There's another one on the inside of my *other* elbow.

Oh no, please. Don't let me turn out to be the same way over this damn wedding with Luke as I was over the bell bottoms. *Why?* Why is this *happening*? Is it Mom, and her insistence that our backyard is just as nice a place to have a wedding as Château Mirac? It can't be . . . you know, that other thing. What Monique said, about Chaz's being in love with me. It can't possibly be *that*.

No. It has to be the thing with Mom, and the whole idea of my family descending on Luke's familial estate, and how they might act when they get there. Gran, with her drinking, and Rose and Sarah, with their bickering and their picking on me, and . . .

Oh yeah, see? Another hive. Right there on my wrist. I knew it. It's because I keep seeing Rose's husband, Angelo, in my mind's eye, wandering around the château, wanting to know where he can get a Pabst Blue Ribbon . . .

And Gran. Gran, going up to Mrs. de Villiers and asking her what time *Dr. Quinn, Medicine Woman* is going to be on . . .

Oh God. Two more.

Chaz stepping forward when the justice of the peace—or whoever marries people in France—asks if there is anybody who has any reason why this couple should not be wed, because he doesn't believe in the institution of marriage, and it's just a slip of paper . . .

Oh my God! Another one on my wrist!

Okay. That's it. That is *it*. I am not going to think about Chaz— *or* my wedding—again. Whatever happened between Chaz and me, it's done, over, finished. What would be the point, anyway? There's no future for our relationship—even if we had one—since he doesn't believe in marriage.

And I'm sorry, but—call me a simple-minded fool—I do! I really do!

No. This is it. I am not going to see or speak to Chaz ever again—it's better this way, to avoid temptation—except when I have to, because he is my fiancé's best friend and our best man, and it would look weird if I didn't speak to the best man at my own wedding.

That's it. I'm done with Chaz.

And done with thinking about my wedding. For now.

Okay. Exhale.

Now. Where was I? Oh, right. The Bianchi. Okay.

That's right. I'll just throw myself into my work. That's all I need to do, and time will fly by so fast, I won't even realize it. Before I know it, it will be June . . . time to get ready for my own wedding day.

And then nothing Chaz can say or do will be able to ruin it for me . . .

By then everything will be perfect. Just perfect.

Exactly the way it's supposed to be.

See? I feel better already.

And look at that. No new hives.

Phew. Great. Okay. So . . . work. WORK!

A HISTORY
of
WEDDINGS

Everyone knows a bride needs to wear something old, something new, something borrowed, something blue. But hardly anyone knows why.

According to ancient superstition, the "something old" ensures the bride's friends will be faithful when she needs them after she's embarked on her new life with her husband and his family. The "something new" is supposed to promise success in that new life. The "something borrowed" symbolizes the love of her own family—that she may take it with her as she goes to live with the family of her new husband. And the "blue" symbolizes loyalty and constancy.

The full version of the rhyme goes on to add that the bride also needs "a sixpence in her shoe."

This was for cab fare home if things worked out badly.

Tip to Avoid a
Wedding Day
Disaster

You know the old saying—What happens when you assume? You make an Ass of U and Me. Don't assume everyone you've invited to your wedding knows their way
to the church and reception hall. Include a well-drawn,
legible map along with your invitation. Trust me, some
of your guests will be so drunk—yes, even before the
ceremony—they'll need it.

LIZZIE NICHOLS DESIGNS™

Chapter 8

To keep your marriage brimming,
With love in the wedding cup,
Whenever you're wrong, admit it;
Whenever you're right, shut up.

Ogden Nash (1902–1971), American poet

June, Six Months Later

We have a new awning."

That's the first thing Monsieur Henri says when he walks into the shop.

"Well, of course we do," I say with a laugh. "You know that. Your wife helped pick it out."

"But"—Monsieur Henri glances over his shoulder at the awning stretched over the entrance to the shop—"it's pink."

Madame Henri gives her husband a sharp rap on the shoulder.

"Don't be ignorant," she advises him in French. "Of course it's pink. I showed you the swatches. You agreed to the color yourself."

"No." Monsieur Henri shakes his head. "Not *that* pink."

"Jean, you *did*," Madame Henri insists. "Remember, you were in the garden, and I brought out the swatches, and you said you liked the salmon."

"That's not salmon," Monsieur Henri insists. "That's *pink*." He looks down, then gasps. "My God. The *carpet* too?"

"It's not pink," I rush to inform him. "It's blush. It's practically beige."

"If it's the rug he's going on about, tell him the customers like it," Tiffany says defensively as she leans over her desk to gaze at the new wall-to-wall. "It's very feminine."

Monsieur Henri glances at her.

"What," he asks in English, sounding horrified, "is wrong with your hair?"

Tiffany lifts up her hand to tug on her new, ultra-short bangs. "You like? They call it the Ava. After Ava Geck. Everybody's getting it." When she notices from his expression that he clearly doesn't understand a word she's saying, she adds, "It's all Lizzie's doing. She totally civilized her. Ava was like an animal before Lizzie got her hands on her. Seriously. She could barely formulate comprehensible sentences. And now she almost always remembers to put on underwear. Well, most days."

"Take me back," Monsieur Henri mutters. "Take me back to New Jersey," he says to his wife.

"No, Jean, don't be ridiculous," Madame Henri says, taking her husband's arm and leading him toward one of the newly uphol-stered chairs that sit by the fully stocked coffee bar. Monsieur Henri sinks onto the slick pink silk with a sigh. He has not snapped back as quickly—or as fully—as any of us hoped he would from his bypass surgery. His recovery has been fraught with complications, including a case of double pneumonia that had him bedridden for an extra few weeks, and he is only now, months later, making his first tenuous steps back to work.

But it's clear his heart—to borrow a phrase—isn't in it.

"Where did we get these chairs?" he whines, noticing the new material he's sitting on. "And what's that smell?"

"Those are the same old chairs you've always had," I explain. "I had them recovered. They were stained and ugly. And that smell is Colombian roast. I got a cappuccino maker so the mothers can have something to drink during their daughters' fittings—"

"How much is all of this costing me?" Monsieur Henri frets, looking around at the newly painted walls (also in blush), and the vintage dress pattern packets I've hung in elaborate gilt frames.

"It's not costing you anything, you old goat," Madame Henri chastises her husband, poking him in the shoulder. "I told you. Thanks to Lizzie, business is up almost a thousand percent since this time last year. That Jill Higgins—remember, from last year? All those society women are sending their daughters to have their gowns fitted by the same place that made hers such a stand-out. What's wrong with you? Don't you listen anymore? Did they forget to clean out your ears when they were cleaning out your arteries?"

Monsieur Henri hunches his shoulders. He's lost so much weight since his surgery he looks almost like a different person. He resembles his twenty-something sons much more closely now, being long and lean, like them.

Unlike them, however, he's gone entirely gray.

"I don't understand anything anymore," he says with a sigh. "Let me see the book. Lizzie . . . just give me the book."

I seize the venerable appointment book from Tiffany—despite her insisting we switch over to a computerized mode of taking appointments, we've stayed with Monsieur Henri's old appointment book.

And now I'm glad. I'm able to hand it to him, almost genuflecting as I do so.

"Here it is," I say. "All ready for you."

Monsieur Henri grunts and begins to flick through the heavily penciled—and just as heavily erased—book. His wife, meanwhile, nods her head in the direction of the curtain that still separates the front room from the back (though the curtain is no longer black, but a beautiful salmon brocade). I follow her through it.

"*Hola,* Lizzie," say the two seamstresses she finds there, sewing beading onto the organza skirt of a strapless lace A-line by hand, from the lounge chairs in which they're sitting while watching a *telenovela* on the portable television I purchased for them.

"Marisol, Sylvia," I say. "You remember Madame Henri, right?"

Marisol and Sylvia grin and wave. Madame Henri waves back.

"So they're working out, I see," she says in French.

"Fastest needles in Manhattan," I reply in her native language. "Shari gives the best job referrals."

"Yes," Madame Henri says. "Well, I suppose when given the choice between going back to their abusive husbands or working for you, they would make rather enthusiastic employees. But I still don't see why you had to tell them about the union. You could have gotten them much more cheaply."

I give Madame Henri a disapproving look. "*Madame . . .*"

She gives a Gallic shrug. "I am only saying—"

A second later, Tiffany, though uninvited, joins us.

"What the hell is *his* glitch?" Tiffany wants to know. "He's looking at the book—*my* book—and groaning."

"Postsurgical depression," Madame Henri says in English. "I'm so sorry . . . I ought to have warned you beforehand. He just has a mild case . . . mostly it's annoyance about not being allowed to eat all the cheese he thinks he ought to be able to, and do the things he used to be able to do without discomfort. He gets so bored being home all day, I thought bringing him to the shop . . . well, I just thought he might perk up, seeing it again. I guess I was wrong. You've done such a wonderful job running it while we've been gone, Lizzie. Really. Please don't take his criticism the wrong way."

I shake my head. "I won't," I say. "I'm not—"

"The place looks beautiful," Madame Henri says. "I love the fresh-cut flowers."

"Oh, we worked out a deal with the floral shop down the street," I say, tucking a loose strand of hair behind my ear. "I recommend them to brides who haven't picked out a florist yet, and they deliver a fresh arrangement to the shop every week—"

"Brilliant," Madame Henri said. "And I hope you're getting a discount on your own wedding. Oh, but then I suppose you and Luke are getting married in France—"

Tiffany starts to laugh, then, seeing my raised eyebrow, turns it to a discreet cough. Madame Henri glances at me. "Oh no," she says. "Don't tell me. Trouble in paradise?"

"Of course not," I say indignantly. "We're doing fine. Luke and I have just been so busy, him with his classes, and me here at the shop, we haven't had time to plan anything—"

"But she's going to start now," Tiffany says firmly. "Especially since, what with Marisol and Sylvia's help, she's practically caught up with all the dresses for the June wedding rush. *Right*, Lizzie?"

"Um," I say, shooting Tiffany a warning look. "Right. Totally."

"What's this?" Monsieur Henri thunders from the outer room of the shop. "*What is this?*"

"Oh, Lord," Madame Henri mutters, rolling her eyes. "What now?"

We duck back out beneath the brocade curtain to find Monsieur Henri on his feet, clutching the appointment book to his chest and looking apoplectic.

"Jean!" Madame Henri, going deathly pale beneath her neat and tasteful makeup, rushes to her husband's side. "What's wrong? Is it your heart?"

"Yes, it's my heart," Monsieur Henri cries. "I think it must be breaking, because I feel so betrayed. Tell me I'm seeing things, please . . . or is it true that Mademoiselle Nichols here has been using *my* shop to peddle her own *bridal gown design line*?"

I stare at him, my jaw sagging. I've never seen Monsieur Henri so upset . . . and I've seen him lose his cool over many a Long Island bridezilla, ripping his careful work apart with verbal abuse.

But this is something different.

"I—I just did it a couple of times," I stammer. "For a few select clients, after the Jill Higgins wedding. It's generated a lot of really positive word of mouth for the shop . . ."

"For the shop?" Monsieur Henri echoes. "Or for *you*?"

"Oh, Jean, keep quiet." Madame Henri looks annoyed. "Such theatrics! You should be grateful to Mademoiselle Elizabeth, not shouting at her. If you don't stop this nonsense, I will make you go and sit in the car like I used to do with the boys when they were young."

"I *should* go back to the car," Monsieur Henri says, his shoulders sagging again. "What's the point of my even being here? No one needs me."

My heart swells with pity for the older man.

"Of course we need you, monsieur," I cry, going to put my arms around him. "I've been running this place without you for months now. But I'd love to take a break. Do you know I haven't had a single day off—not even Sundays—since you had your heart attack?"

"Yeah," Tiffany says. "And she wants to get married this summer. So how about giving her some vacation time so she can start getting ready for it? Oh, yeah, and she's gonna need time off for a honeymoon too."

I shoot her an aggravated look. I don't need any reminders about how much—okay, basically everything—I still have to do to prepare for my wedding.

"It's no use," Monsieur Henri says with a sigh. "It's not there anymore."

My arms still around his much-thinner-than-it-used-to-be neck, I look into his eyes. "What's not there anymore, Monsieur Henri?"

"The passion," he says with a sigh, and tosses the appointment book back onto Tiffany's desk.

I draw my arms away from him and stare. "Of course it is," I say with a nervous glance in his wife's direction. "This is just your first day back. You'll feel it again when you get back into the swing of things."

"No," Monsieur Henri says. His gaze has grown far away. "I don't care about wedding gowns anymore. There's only one thing I care about now."

His wife looks toward the recently repainted ceiling. "Not again."

"Oh?" I glance at Madame Henri. "What's that, monsieur?"

"*Pétanque,*" he says as he stares wistfully out the plate-glass window at the golden sunlight pouring onto Seventy-eighth Street.

"I *told* you," Madame Henri snaps. "That isn't a profession, Jean. It's a hobby."

"So?" Her husband jerks his head back around to demand. "I'm sixty-five! I just had a quadruple bypass! I can't play a little *pétanque* if I want to?"

The phone rings. Tiffany lifts it and purrs, "Chez Henri, how may I help you?" I am the only one who hears her add, sotto voce, "Get me out of this lunatic asylum."

"That's it." Madame Henri leans down and snatches up her Prada handbag. "We're leaving. I thought we could have a nice day in the city, maybe have a lovely lunch. But you've ruined it."

"*I've* ruined it?" Monsieur Henri cries. "I'm not the one who insisted on my coming back to work before I was emotionally prepared to! You know what my physical therapist says. One day at a time."

"I'll show you emotionally prepared," Madame Henri says, shaking her small fist at him.

"Mademoiselle Elizabeth." Monsieur Henri gives me a courtly bow, but it's clear his thoughts are elsewhere . . . on his *pétanque* set back home in his New Jersey garden, perhaps. "Remember . . . life is short. Each moment you have is precious. Treasure every second. Don't spend them doing anything you don't love. If being a certified professional wedding gown restorer isn't your dream—if designing them is—then go after that dream. The way I intend to go after my dream of playing *pétanque* every chance I get."

"Jean!" Madame Henri screams. "I told you! Don't *start*!"

"*You* don't start!" her husband thunders back. "Mademoiselle Elizabeth . . . Good-bye."

"Um . . . Good-bye." I blink after the bickering couple as they leave the shop, Madame Henri making a hand motion to me behind her husband's back indicating that she's going to call me later.

No sooner has the bell over the front door stopped tinkling than Tiffany hangs up the phone and declares, "Oh my God, I thought he'd never leave."

"Now, Tiff," I say. But the truth is, I'd felt the same way.

"Seriously, though," Tiffany says. "Where does he get off? It's not like you haven't worked like a dog for him. And for what? I know how much you make, Lizzie, remember? You're being robbed working here. You should totally quit and open your own place."

"With what start-up money?" I reach into the mini fridge—artfully disguised as a wood cabinet—beneath the coffee bar and pull out a Diet Coke. "Besides, I owe a lot to the Henris. And he's still not feeling his best. You heard what his wife said."

"Well, if he comes back to work here, I quit," Tiffany declares. "I'm serious. I'm not sticking around with that old coot poking into our business."

"Tiffany," I say. "This is his place. It's called Chez Henri. He's the owner, remember?"

"I don't care." Tiffany folds her arms across her chest. "He's a guy. He totally spoils the ambience we've established."

I didn't want to admit it out loud, but Tiffany was kind of right. I mean, it's a bridal shop, after all. What's Monsieur Henri doing, getting so bent out of shape about a salmon-colored awning? Besides, Madame Henri and I spent a lot of time and money on that awning. It looks totally great, sort of Lulu Guinness meets Fauchon chocolate shop. Speaking of which . . . mmmm, chocolate . . .

"Come on," Tiffany says, as usual refusing to let the subject drop well after I've tired of it. "You know I'm right. And what's with this *pétanque* stuff? What *is pétanque*?"

"It's a bowling game," I explain, "called boules or bocce here, involving a dirt lane and a small metal ball—"

"Is that all?" Tiffany asks scornfully. "Well, what does he keep going on about it for, then? Is he going to start selling *pétanque* equipment in here?"

"No, I'm sure he—"

"What are you going to do, Lizzie? He's going to ruin everything you've been working so hard for. Everything!"

Another thing Tiffany has a tendency to do is be way overdramatic about things. Monsieur Henri isn't going to ruin *everything*.

I'm pretty sure.

Fortunately my cell phone rings, sparing me from having to discuss the matter further . . . at least with Tiffany. I see that it's Luke and pick up eagerly. Things are going really well with him— well, aside from the fact that we haven't picked a date for our wedding. Or a venue. Or really even talked about it much. Or at all, actually.

Still, living in our own separate apartments is working out really well. We each have our own space, so we don't get on each other's nerves, and we totally appreciate the time we spend together. Consequently, the sex couldn't be better.

And, okay, maybe he still doesn't know about my Spanx.

And maybe I continue to refuse to be on top when we make love. Or turn my back on him when I'm naked.

And, yeah, any time Luke says he wants to spend the night at his own place—alone—so he can study for an exam, I become convinced he must be sleeping with other girls in his classes.

And, yes, every time he says he's spending a Saturday afternoon studying at the library, I'm sure that what he's actually doing is seeing some other girl behind my back, and it's all I can do to keep myself from sneaking down to NYU to spy on him (except I don't have a student ID to get into the library).

But you know. Other than that, things are total bliss!

Of course I have no reason to suspect these things of him other than, nearly a year into our relationship, I still can't believe a guy as amazing as Luke actually wants anything to do with a neurotic mess like myself. As Shari frequently remarks, it really is astonishing that a woman with as much business savvy as I have is as insecure in her romantic life as I've turned out to be.

But I blame this on my obsession with Lifetime Television. Of which I've been watching a lot more now that I live alone and there's no man in the house to groan every time I switch it on.

"Hi," I say to Luke now.

"What's wrong?" he asks right away.

"Wrong?" I echo. "Nothing's wrong. What makes you think something is wrong?"

"Because I know you. And you sound like someone just told you Lilly Pulitzer died."

"Oh," I say, lowering my voice so Tiffany, who is picking up a call, can't overhear. "Well, actually, Monsieur Henri stopped by the shop a few minutes ago, and he wasn't too pleased with some of the changes I've made since he's been out sick. He was acting kind of . . . strange."

"What?" Luke sounds adorably indignant on my behalf. "You've worked your tail off for that guy. That place is doing twice as much business now because of you!"

It's a lot more than that, really, as Madame Henri herself said. But I don't correct him. "Well," I say instead. "Anyway. I'm sure it will all be fine. He's just still adjusting to life as a recent bypass patient, you know."

"Well, he has some nerve," Luke says. "Anyway, I'm calling with good news. Something that should cheer you up."

"Really?" I can't think what he could be talking about. "I'm all ears!"

"Today's my last day of classes—"

"That *is* good news," I say. No more going off by himself to study! No more weekend trips to the library! Not, of course, that this had bothered me too much at the time (except for the whole *Is-there-another-woman?* thing) because the few weekends Luke wasn't studying, I'd been busy working on bridal gowns. In fact, I'd been sort of glad he'd been so preoccupied with his schoolwork. What kind of guy wants to hear, *Oh, I can't, honey. I have to finish the neckline on this mermaid gown by Monday* every time he asks his fiancée if she can go away for the weekend?

Fortunately, this was never an issue with Luke and me. Because he never asked me to go away for the weekend. Because he was always busy too.

"And I thought I'd take you out to dinner to celebrate," he goes on. "Someplace downtown. We spend so much time eating takeout uptown, I don't think I can handle it anymore."

"That sounds fun," I say excitedly. "I can take the subway down and meet you."

"That's what I was thinking," Luke says. "We can meet at Chaz's place."

My heart sinks immediately. This is so not what I'd had in mind.

"Chaz?" I say. "Really? You invited Chaz along too?"

I set my jaw. The truth is, I'm not exactly thrilled at the prospect of seeing Chaz. Not, of course, that there's ever been a repeat of anything like what happened in the back of that taxi on the way home from Jill Higgins's wedding. Chaz hasn't even made any more baited remarks like he did that night so long ago in the sports bar. No, he's been a perfect gentleman. Gran, Tiffany, and Monique's theory—that he's in love with me—turns out to have been completely untrue. Because if Chaz were in love with me, well, he's had plenty of opportunity to act on that impulse.

And he never has. Not even once.

But that doesn't mean I want him tagging along on one of the last nights I have Luke to myself before he takes off for France for three months.

But I don't mention this. Because the last thing I'm going to do is try to wedge myself between my man and his best friend. As I know from every women's magazine I've ever read, that's a major no-no.

"Well, it's one of the last chances I'm going to have to see him," Luke says, "before I leave for Paris for the summer. I didn't think you'd mind. You don't, do you? And I thought it would be a good opportunity for us to meet his new girlfriend."

My jaw drops. Quite literally. I sort of have to lever it back in place with my hand before I'm able to speak again.

"His . . . his *what*?"

"I know," Luke says with a chuckle. "Can you believe it? And we all thought he'd never learn to love again after Shari."

I am totally positive I didn't hear Luke right. I ask, sticking one finger in my ear, "When . . . when did this happen?"

"Oh, I don't know. Apparently they've been seeing each other for quite a while, but they've been keeping it on the down low because she's up for tenure in the philosophy department, and he's just a teaching assistant, and technically a student—even if he's a grad student—so it's all sort of clandestine. And you know Chaz was never exactly one to kiss and tell. Her name is Valencia Something. I forget. But I guess she's a real knockout. And a brainiac. Well, she'd have to be, for Chaz to like her."

I hate her. I do. I hate her already.

I also feel an extreme urge to stab myself with something. There is a pair of dressmaker's shears lying nearby. I think about plunging them into my heart. Then I think about plunging them into Valencia's heart. Really, I decide, that would be much better for everyone. Me. The world. Valencia. Anyone with a name like Valencia who is up for tenure in the philosophy department of a major private university deserves to have a pair of dressmaker's shears plunged into her heart. Doesn't she?

"So," Luke goes on. "What do you say? Dinner? Just the four of us?"

"Great," I say. "That sounds great." I don't mention that I'm going to bring along the dressmaker's shears. Because I'm not going to. Not really. I also don't mention that we—Luke and I, I mean—have never, not even once, gone out as a couple with *my* best friend and *her* girlfriend. Not that Luke would object, I'm sure. It's just that Shari has never expressed the slightest interest in doing this. I sort of wish she would. But her invitations are always expressly for me, and me alone. Luke is never included.

Which isn't very surprising, considering how many hours I spent on her and Pat's couch, crying about him.

Valencia. Isn't that a type of orange? Seriously. I'm almost sure it is.

"Great!" Luke says. "So I've got reservations for Spotted Pig at eight thirty. I said we'd meet up at Chaz's place, then take a cab over to the West Village together. Does that sound okay?"

"Sure," I say. The Spotted Pig! That's one of the trendiest restaurants in the Village! I should be excited. I should be wondering what I'm going to wear. Instead, all I'm wondering is what Valencia is going to wear. Is she prettier than me? Why do I even care? *I'm not dating Chaz.* How can Chaz have started going out with someone and I never even knew it? Is he in love with her? Is he going to marry her? No, of course not. Chaz doesn't believe in marriage. "I'll meet you at Chaz's."

Maybe Valencia will make him believe in marriage. To her. Someone with the name Valencia ought to be capable of that.

A brainiac. Of course. He *would* date a brainiac.

"Okay," Luke says. "Love you."

"Love you," I say and hang up.

"So." Tiffany has ended her own phone call and is totally watching me, her eyes slitted like a cat's. "Going to Chaz's, huh?"

I ignore her attempt to bait me. "Who was that you were on the phone with just now?"

Tiffany smirks. "Who do you think?"

I widen my own eyes. "*Ava?* I thought we were done. I thought she loved it. She should be on her way to Greece by now. What could she possibly have wanted?"

"I don't know," Tiffany says. "She wouldn't tell me. She said she could tell only you. She said she'd call back."

"Great," I say. I mean it sarcastically. I am not looking forward to hearing from Ava Geck. My relationship with the heiress has vastly improved since our first acquaintance, in that she no longer chews gum in my presence and has consistently remembered to wear panties during our last few meetings. And she seems to have benefited from our—meaning the shop's—tutelage in other ways as well, since she's abandoned her bleached-blond hair extensions in favor of a flattering pageboy and has started dressing less like a prostitute.

But there's still some speculation as to whether or not her wedding to Prince Aleksandros will actually take place. The odds in Vegas are twenty-five to one that the nuptials will be called off.

I personally think the two of them are going to be fine.

So the fact that there's been this last-minute phone call is freaking me out. Just a little.

Not more than the fact that Chaz has a girlfriend named Valencia, though. A girlfriend named Valencia who is up for tenure.

Still, Ava has my personal cell phone number. She'll call it if she needs to.

"So," Tiffany says. "Another night of romance with you, Loverboy, and Loverboy's best friend? Hey, so what's going to happen," Tiffany wants to know, "when Loverboy heads off to France, leaving you and the best friend all alone in the big, lonely city during the long, hot summer?"

"Nothing," I say, leaning down to snag two more Diet Cokes from the mini fridge for Sylvia and Marisol. "As you know perfectly well. Chaz and I are just friends."

"Right." Tiffany smirks. "I give you guys three weeks after Luke leaves before you two hit the sheets."

"Right," I say. "Do you have this week's time sheets? Because I have to do payroll."

"Oooh," Tiffany says, reaching for the phone. "Make that three days. I'm calling Mo. I bet she'll want to put money on this."

"Don't bother," I say. "Chaz has a girlfriend. Her name is Valencia."

Tiffany narrows her eyes. "Isn't that a type of orange?"

"She has a Ph.D. in philosophy, and she's up for tenure."

Tiffany snorts. "So? Does she make him laugh?"

"Tiffany!" I am practically screaming. "What does it matter?

Are you even listening to me? He has a girlfriend! And I'm engaged! Engaged to his best friend!"

"Who you don't even love," Tiffany says.

I stalk out of the front room without another word. I have no need to listen to this. I know—even if Tiffany doesn't—the truth. I love my fiancé, and he loves me. Sure, we may not have set a date yet, and yeah, okay, he's never even brought it up since New Year's, when we called our families to tell them.

And yes, whenever I think about it, I still get a tight feeling in my chest and break out in hives.

But all brides-to-be are nervous wrecks. Look at Ava Geck, on her way to marry a prince, and calling *me,* her wedding gown designer, from the private plane on her way to Greece! It's natural! It doesn't mean you're with the wrong guy! It doesn't mean that at all.

Especially when the guy everyone's been saying for months is the right one doesn't even believe in marriage in the first place. If that's not Mr. Wrong, I don't know who is.

A HISTORY
of
WEDDINGS

Weddings in colonial times were replete with customs, none of which included engagement rings. A couple intending to "tie the knot" would do so literally—the man would present his intended with a handkerchief, into which he'd tied several coins. If the woman untied the knot, it was seen as her giving the okay to get hitched. The banns—a petition to marry that was printed up and posted at a church or meetinghouse so that anyone with an objection to the union had time to say something—were posted, and the couple would wed within a few days. Women who waited to wed past the age of fourteen were pretty much considered to be old maids.

But since most of them lived to be only about thirty-five, this isn't too surprising.

You want your wedding guests to get up on the dance floor.
But they're just sitting there! Maybe it's because your DJ
isn't playing what they want to hear. Make sure your DJ
has the following songs on his playlist, which have been
scientifically proven to be irresistible to even the stodgiest
partygoers everywhere:

1. Abba—"Dancing Queen"
2. Prince—"1999"
3. Gloria Gaynor—"I Will Survive"
4. Dexy's Midnight Runners—"Come on Eileen"
5. Madonna—"Holiday"
6. Deee-Lite—"Groove Is in the Heart"
7. Kanye West—"Gold Digger"
8. The Weather Girls—"It's Raining Men"
9. The B-52's—"Love Shack"
10. Village People—"YMCA"

LIZZIE NICHOLS DESIGNS™

Chapter 9

When you meet someone who can cook and do housework—
don't hesitate a minute: Marry him.

Unknown

Chaz is late. So, for that matter, is Luke. I've buzzed Chaz's apartment, but no one has answered. I'm sitting on the front stoop of his building, having carefully spread a handkerchief from inside my purse out on the step so as not to mess up my skirt. And yes, I do carry handkerchiefs. This city is filthy and you never know when you're going to need one.

And I'm waiting.

It's a gorgeous evening, so waiting on a stoop in the East Village isn't that bad. There are a lot of people out—some still hurrying home from work, some strolling around after an early supper, some just wandering with no apparent purpose. Some of them acknowledge me with a nod or smile, but many walk on by without making eye contact, like most New Yorkers, afraid that if they look you in the face, you'll ask them for money. (Though do I look like a homeless person? This is a genuine Alfred Shaheen 1950s Hawaiian sundress with a halter-style top and a full skirt with a crinoline. Would a homeless woman really be wearing that? I'm carrying a vintage Halston bag and sporting platform espadrilles too. No offense, but I look too good to be homeless.)

A group of kids have started up a rowdy game of stickball, right in the middle of the street, calling, "Car," every time a taxi turns the corner. From a window a few floors above, I hear opera being blasted.

And I can't help thinking to myself, in spite of Valencia What-ever Her Name Is . . . *I love New York*.

I do.

I didn't always. It was grim for a while. I didn't think I'd make it here, that, like Kathy Pennebaker from my hometown, I'd have to go slinking back to Ann Arbor and end up married to my high school sweetheart (except that he's gay) and shopping at the Krog-er Sav-On with a couple of runny-nosed toddlers.

Not that this is the worst fate that can befall a girl. It's a per-fectly fine fate, actually.

Except that the last time I saw Kathy she was buying way more cold medicine than I think anybody would need for normal, every-day use.

But I did make it in the big city. At least mostly. Oh, sure, I can't afford to eat out every night, and I had to take the 6 train to get down here, not a taxi.

And I haven't exactly got a summer share in the Hamptons like so many New York singletons my age, and I don't own a single item made by Prada.

But someday I will (well, not the Hamptons thing, because I saw what they do there on MTV, and throwing up copious amounts of Bacardi and Coke and sleeping with a different guy every week-end is not for me. And who needs Prada when you can have vintage Lilly Pulitzer?). But I mean about the taxi and eating-out thing. I'll have moo shu chicken every night! And take cabs everywhere!

But until then, I'm doing fine. And I love it here. I really do. I never, ever want to leave.

And then suddenly three of the boys from the stickball game get into an argument, and a much smaller boy tries to intervene, and one of the bigger boys says, "Suck it, Shorty," and pushes the smaller boy, making him fall down, and I cry indignantly, jumping to my feet, *"Hey!"*

"Stay out of it, lady," Shorty says, springing back up, like a top. "I can handle this."

And he bursts back into the argument his friends are having, only to be knocked down again.

"Hey," I say, coming down off the stoop. "If you kids can't play nicely together, I'm going to get your mothers!"

"And they'll knife you," a man's voice informs me. "Not the kids. The mothers."

I turn around, and my heart gives a swoop inside my chest.

But it's not Luke. It's not my fiancé, standing there in the last golden rays of the setting sun, looking impossibly handsome in a charcoal suit and yellow power tie.

It's his best friend.

Chaz is the one who's just made my heart do a loop-de-loop. I'm not even going to try to figure what that was all about.

I'm so flustered, I say the first thing that pops into my head.

"Why are you so dressed up?" I ask him, my voice gruff. I don't know why I sound so unfriendly. It's not *his* fault my heart reacted that way on seeing him without a baseball cap.

But I'm so shocked at my physical reaction to the way he looks, I can't help sounding like a twelve-year-old boy suddenly going through puberty.

"Departmental cocktail party," he says as he reaches into his pocket and pulls out his keys. His dark hair—in need of a trim, as always—falls over his eyes as he does so. I take advantage of the fact that he can't see me to take in other details about him . . . the fact that he's wearing dress shoes—Italian leather, from the looks of it, in the five-hundred-dollar range, at least—and that the suit is exquisitely and expensively cut, perfectly framing his broad shoulders. He looks totally out of place on his street, which includes a run-down offtrack-betting place on the corner, a Japanese noodle shop one building in, and a dive bar next door to that. Him standing there in a suit like that? It's as if James Bond suddenly pulled into a suburban cul-de-sac.

"Sorry I'm late," he says, looking up. I glance away the second his gaze meets mine and feel my cheeks begin to burn. I hope he won't notice. "You weren't waiting long, were you?"

"No," I lie hastily. "Not at all."

Oh God. What's *wrong* with me?

"Well, at least it's not raining," Chaz says. "Come on in and let me get you a drink."

He unlocks the outer door to his building's vestibule, and I follow him as he stops to open his mailbox and pick up his mail. It's weird, but I'm feeling strangely shy. I'm not sure if it's the loop-de-loop incident, the fact that I know about Valencia, or that Chaz is looking so unlike his usual self, but I feel almost as if I'm with a stranger, and not a guy I've known since my first day of freshman year of college, who used to make me laugh so hard over my Cap'n Crunch in the McCracken Hall cafeteria that milk would come out of my nose.

"So what's going on with you?" Chaz wants to know as he climbs the stairs to the walk-up he used to share with Shari, and now lives in solo. "Seems like this is the first time I've seen you in ages without the old ball and chain in tow."

Because I've been assiduously avoiding seeing you without Luke for protection, to keep exactly what just happened—that whole heart-flippy thing—from happening.

Only I don't say this out loud, of course.

"Oh," I say airily. His building's hallway is, if anything, even more industrial looking and depressing than my own. Although at least I'm the only one who uses mine, so it's not littered with Chinese food menus and alternative press newspapers. "Well, I've been really busy. Working. This is my busy season, so things have been crazy."

"I imagine," Chaz says. We've reached the door to his sprawling—and slope-floored—two-bedroom (if you can call an alcove a bedroom), and he's undoing the many various locks. "According to Luke, you work harder than any woman in Manhattan. He says he hardly ever sees you anymore. What with your own wedding to plan and all, things must be busier for you than ever."

Where, I'm wondering, is Valencia? Are we meeting her at the restaurant? Or is she meeting us here, at the apartment? I want to ask, but at the same time, I don't want to bring her up. I can't seem to bring myself to mention her name. Valencia. God. I hate her.

"That's me," I say instead. "Busy, busy." I let out a laugh that sounds not unlike a pony's whinny.

Chaz pauses mid-lock.

"Excuse me," he says. "But did you just whinny?"

"No," I say quickly.

"My mistake," he says and goes back to work on his locks.

He finally gets his door open, and I follow him inside, pleased by the blast of cool air that greets me from his many window units. Unlike Luke's mother's apartment, which took on a sort of fetid quality to it once I moved out (Mrs. de Villiers eventually started sending around a cleaning agency, after a weekend visit to the city proved that her son couldn't be trusted to handle the responsibility of doing the dishes or cleaning the toilet on his own), Chaz's is super-clean . . . except for the stacks of books and student papers piled everywhere.

But at least they're very tidy piles.

"So what'll you have?" Chaz asks, going into the eat-in kitchen (a rarity in Manhattan; apparently it makes up for one of the advertised bedrooms being no larger than a closet) and opening the refrigerator. "I got it all. Beer, wine, soda, vodka, gin, juice . . . what do you feel like?"

"What are you having?" I ask, leaning my elbow up against the pass-through, on which are balanced several stacks of library books.

He grabs a Corona from a six-pack on the bottom shelf and looks at me questioningly. I shake my head and say, "White wine would be good."

"Coming up," he says, and pulls out a bottle of pinot grigio from inside the refrigerator door. It's already uncorked. It's probably what Valencia drinks. That bitch. He just has to pull the stopper and pour. "So I've been meaning to ask you. What did you do to Ava Geck?"

I take the glass he offers to me. "What do you mean? I didn't do anything to her."

"Yeah, you did. She's not slutty anymore. She hasn't been on the cover of *Us Weekly* with a big 'Censored by Us' over her crotch in months."

I smile and take a sip of my wine. "Oh," I say. "*That.*"

"Yeah." Chaz, to my surprise, sets a glass of ice down next to my elbow. To go with my wine.

He remembered. He remembered that I like my white wine with a side of ice.

I tell myself it doesn't mean anything, though. Just because Luke never remembers, and Chaz does, doesn't mean a thing. It's

Luke's ring I'm wearing on the third finger of my left hand, not Chaz's.

Because Chaz doesn't even believe in engagement rings. Or weddings.

"So what'd you do to her?" Chaz wants to know. "She's boring now."

"She's not *boring*," I say. I try to keep speaking in a normal voice so he won't notice how nonplussed I am by the ice. "She's classy. She's acting more the way someone who is about to be married to a prince *should* act. I'm sure his parents are pleased."

"They might be," Chaz says. "But millions of *Us Weekly* subscribers like myself aren't. How'd you do it, anyway?"

"I merely suggested to her that it might be in her best interest not to be photographed climbing in and out of cars and boats with her legs completely spread apart," I say.

"Like I said." Chaz shrugs. "Boring. You've personally robbed thousands—perhaps millions—of teenage boys who spend their time combing the Internet looking for glimpses of Ava Geck's Brazilian of their only chance at seeing one. May I just say, on their behalf, a collective and sarcastic thanks. A lot."

I tip my wineglass in his direction. "You're welcome. They can just learn about feminine hair removal by looking at their dads' *Playboy*s, the way the rest of us did."

"Oooh," Chaz says, coming out of the kitchen and into the living room, then sinking down into one of the gold couches, which are left over from his father's law offices before they got a makeover. "Is that how you found out about it? This is getting interesting. Tell me about it. What was that like for you? Did you and Shari used to look at your dads' *Playboy*s together?"

I laugh. Infuriating as he is sometimes, Chaz really *can* be funny.

"Speaking of Shari," I say, joining him on one of the matching couches. "What's going on with *you*? I hear y-you're—" Here it goes. I take a long, fortifying gulp of my wine, hoping it will keep me from stammering more. "Seeing someone."

"News travels fast," Chaz says. "Yeah, I am. A woman from my department, Valencia Delgado. She's meeting us at the restaurant tonight. I think you'll like her."

Uh, no, I won't.

Where is *this* feeling coming from? The same place the loop-de-loop came from? What's happening to me? How could I have been so good for so long—six *months*—only to start falling apart now, so close to the finish line . . . or what would be the finish line, if Luke and I had ever actually gotten around to making any wedding plans? Why am I freaking out over this Valencia Delgado person? Just because she's bound to be incredibly beautiful and well read. Not at all like me. The last book I read was—God! An Agatha Christie novel someone left in the shop! What would someone getting his Ph.D. in philosophy ever see in a girl like *me*?

But wait . . . what does that matter? *I'm* not dating Chaz. He isn't even my type! My type being the kind who actually believe in marriage.

"Wow," I say, trying to sound unconcerned, although the truth is I'm consumed with gut-wrenching anxiety over meeting this woman. Which doesn't even make sense. "That's so great. I'm glad you're not still upset over what happened with Shari . . ."

"Actually," Chaz says, "Shari and I are good now. We had lunch the other day—"

"Wait." I am so astonished I completely interrupt him. "You and Shari *had lunch* the other day?"

"Yeah. And her friend, Pat," he says. He's reached up and is undoing his tie. His lovely yellow silk tie, the one that practically caused my heart to stop. "Sorry," he says when he notices the direction of my gaze. "But this thing is driving me insane. I have to go change into real clothes. Do you mind?"

I shake my head. "Go ahead," I say. Then, as he disappears down the hall, I call after him, because I can't stand not knowing more, "You had lunch with your ex-girlfriend and her new girlfriend?"

"Yeah." Chaz's muffled voice floats toward me from his bedroom. "Only Pat's not really Shari's new girlfriend, is she? They've been together, what, like half a year now. Or more, actually."

I am having trouble absorbing all of this. I dump some ice into my wine and stare at a pile of student papers sitting on the coffee table in front of me.

"So you guys are like . . . *friends* now?" I ask.

"We were always friends," Chaz calls back to me. "We just had a period where we didn't talk as much as we used to. And, of course, we no longer make the beast with two backs."

"So anyway," Chaz says, coming back into the living room. He's changed into jeans and a University of Michigan Wolverines T-shirt. One of his many baseball caps is back in its usual place. I know I should feel relieved that he's out of his heart-fluttering finery, but strangely, all I feel is confused.

This is mainly because he looks as good to me in the baseball cap as he had earlier in the suit.

"She seems good," Chaz goes on. "Shari, I mean. And Pat's nice. For someone who clearly considers me one of the hetero male oppressors."

"So," I say, unable to stop myself. I try. I really do try. But before I can clamp my mouth shut, words are pouring out of it—words I'd give anything to stuff back inside it. "I know it's none of my business, but I was just wondering if you had told Valencia your opinion on the whole marriage thing—"

"Lizzie."

It's no good, though. As usual, the words are just streaming out of me, like water from a fountain. And nothing can plug it, not even me.

"Because it really isn't a good idea to lead her on," I prattle away. "I'm just warning you for your own good, you know. I imagine a female tenure-track philosophy professor scorned is not a pretty—"

"Lizzie."

For the first time in my life, something in another human's voice actually causes my own to dry up. I close my mouth and stare. His eyes, for some reason, seem bluer than normal. His gaze blazes into mine from where he stands, looking at me from behind the pass-through.

"What?" I ask, my throat suddenly going dry. I realize, from the intensity of his gaze, that we've somehow passed from ordinary— or, in my case, anyway, mindless—conversation to something much more serious.

And, incredibly, I feel myself blushing to my hairline, my cheeks flaming hot as the asphalt outside had been before when Chaz had come walking up.

Anything, it seems, might be brought up at such a moment. The fact that for the past six months we've barely talked . . . except politely, and always in the presence of someone else (Luke).

Or the fact that six months ago, we had our tongues down each other's throats.

Is he going to bring up one of those things? And if so, which one? I'm not sure which I dread him bringing up more—the fact that I've been trying so assiduously *not* to be alone with him so we can't have a repeat performance of what had happened on New Year's Eve . . . or discussing what *actually* happened on New Year's Eve . . .

What if he comes out from behind the pass-through and tries to reenact what happened on New Year's Eve? Will I try to stop him?

Wait. Of course I will. Won't I?

Yes! Yes, of course I will! I'm engaged! To his best friend!

Except . . . his eyes are so blue right now . . . I feel as if I could go swimming in them . . .

"I swore I wasn't going to ask this," Chaz says.

I gulp. Oh God. Here it is. I try not to remember that loop-de-loop my heart gave when I saw him coming toward me down the street. I swear I don't even know what that had been about. I am not in love with Chaz. *I am not in love with Chaz.*

"Are you—"

Then I jump as the buzzer to the front door to Chaz's building goes off.

My shoulders, which I'd clenched with nervousness, sag. Whatever it was he was going to ask me, he evidently decides to drop the subject, since he says, "Huh, speak of the devil."

And he goes out into the hallway to buzz Luke in without another word.

I find that I've been clutching the sofa cushions. Slowly I release my fingers . . . as well as the breath I've been holding. I'm sweaty, as if I'd just been running a mile.

Not that I've ever *actually* run a mile. But *as if* I have.

What's going on? Why am I such a bundle of nerves? This is dinner with my boyfriend and his best friend. And his best friend's new girlfriend, the woman I'm going to murder. Nothing to worry about. What is *happening* to me?

And when is this evening going to end, so I can go home and kill myself?

A HISTORY
of
WEDDINGS

eddings farther west in postcolonial America were short on ceremony and heavy on the partying. It was around this time that the shivaree, or charivari, became popular, a tradition based on an old French custom that included the wedding guests gathering beneath the bride and groom's bedroom window on the first night of their honeymoon and banging on pots and singing drunkenly, allegedly to drive away evil spirits . . . but mainly with the intention of forcing the groom to throw money down to them in order to make them go away. Occasionally the festivities would reach such a fevered pitch the groom would be pulled out the window, and the bride would be forced to pay a ransom if she actually wanted to enjoy her honeymoon in the company of her new husband.

They didn't call it the Wild, Wild West for nothing.

Tip to Avoid a Wedding Day Disaster

Do you need a wedding planner? While they can often save you a bundle by getting you discounts, not every bride needs one. If you're planning a large wedding, have a demanding job, or don't have a mom or sister to whom to delegate the many tasks involved in planning your dream nuptials, then hiring a wedding planner might make sense. Look for one who does wedding planning as a full-time job, who has insurance and good references, and be sure to ask how much she charges (hourly, fixed fee, or a percentage of your wedding budget).

Your wedding planner isn't supposed to be your best friend . . . but she could just save your sanity—not to mention your life!

LIZZIE NICHOLS DESIGNS™

Chapter 10

A successful marriage requires falling in love many times, always with the same person.

Germaine Greer (b.1939–), Australian-born feminist writer

'm having a hard time picturing *The Office*'s Jim Halpert dining at the Spotted Pig, which he allegedly did once on a date with Karen. I know it's just a TV show and fictional and all, but this place is super-trendy, and part of what makes that show so endearing is that everyone on it is so tragically *un*hip.

But there are people here with the kind of glasses they wear only in Scandinavian countries and tattoos all up and down their arms and I heard a guy at the bar telling another guy that he just got late admission to Harvard Law School, and saw a girl lifting up her skirt to show her friends her new thong. Plus everybody standing outside smoking in their camouflage cargo pants with their carefully messed up—but really loaded down with product—hair is also checking their e-mail on their BlackBerries.

"*Why* are we here again?" Chaz keeps asking. We got a table only because someone Luke knows from one of his classes—a girl, Sophie—knows the guy who is seating people tonight.

"It's supposed to be good," Luke says cheerfully. "Oh, look. Sweetbreads."

"That's guts," Chaz says. "I had to stand for an hour outside to sit at a bench at a tiny table at a place that's going to serve me guts. We could have gone to the Polish place in my neighborhood and gotten guts for five dollars and no waiting. And I could be sitting in a chair and not on a bench."

"But then you wouldn't have seen that girl's thong," Valencia points out cheerfully.

"True," Chaz agrees.

I shoot Valencia a dirty look. It's not her fault, of course, that she's so perfect—tall and tan and thin with perfect straight dark hair that she's caught up in a classy single silver barrette—a lovely complement to her ruby red sleeveless sheath dress. She can't help that she's witty and charming and intelligent too. Even her pedicure is perfect.

I want to reach across the velvet banquette we're sitting on and grab her by that perfect hair and pull until her face hits the tabletop and then keep pulling until I've dragged her across the restaurant and then maybe when we've reached the bachelorette party at the table next to ours (when did the city become so full of bachelorette parties that you couldn't seem to go out without encountering one?) I'll turn her loose and say to the bachelorettes, "Have at her, girls—oh, and by the way, she's a tenure-track professor at a major private university." Then maybe, when they're done with her, I'll give her back to Chaz—if he still wants her.

Oh, wait—did I think that?

No, I didn't. Because I'm way too busy exchanging text messages with Ava Geck to think things like that.

Ava: LIZZIE, WHERE R U?

Me: *I'm at the Spotted Pig in the West Village. Why?*

Ava: I'M COMING.

Me: *What? Ava—Why aren't you in Greece?*

No response. Calls to her cell phone go immediately to voice mail. I'm not sure her "I'M COMING" actually meant that she was coming to the restaurant. Knowing Ava, it could just as easily have meant she was *coming*...literally, in the throes of passion, and also happened to be texting me.

It's not something I'd put past her.

"So I've been meaning to ask you guys something," Chaz says as the waitress brings the dozen oysters Luke has ordered. I'm not eating oysters tonight. Not because I don't like them, but because it's June and I can't risk a bout of food sickness. I've got twenty gowns to get to twenty nervous brides, or my name will be mud in this town.

I mean, Chez Henri's name.

"Hit me," Luke says. He's in a good mood because his classes are over. He's not sure he exactly aced his exams—he thinks he might have tanked his bio final, actually—but that doesn't seem to be bothering him too much. He's just relieved they're over, and that he's going to be getting on a plane for Paris in a couple of days.

If I weren't feeling so guilty over the fact that I've barely had two minutes to spend with him all month anyway—and won't for the next two days he's in town, either—I'd be a little miffed over just *how* excited he is to be leaving me for the summer.

"So, are you guys ever actually going to set a date, or is this just going to be the longest engagement in the history of mankind?" Chaz wants to know.

I choke on the sip of white wine I've just taken. I can't believe he asked that. I mean, it's refreshing, on the one hand, that some-one is actually asking Luke *and* me—instead of just me—about the engagement for a change. Luke's the one who always seems to escape this kind of questioning—and who also seems so perfectly content with how things are going, him living in his mother's doorman building on Fifth Avenue and me living in my hovel on East Seventy-eighth, where I have to answer the door with a lighter and a can of hair spray just in case it's a rapist and not the UPS man after all.

And okay, true, I still can't even think about my own wedding without telltale hives showing up—oh God! There's one on the inside of my elbow now!

But still. Why is it that when it comes to the wedding planning, people always ask the bride how it's going and never the groom? My family's been hounding me for months. I haven't heard a peep out of the de Villlierses about it. Are any of them throwing me showers or engagement parties? Um, no. At least my family's offered. Even though I've turned them all down, since I'm too busy with work even to think about that kind of thing.

And I seem to break into hives at the mere mention of the word "engagement."

"Charles," Valencia says.

That's the other thing about Valencia. She calls Chaz *Charles*. No one calls Chaz *Charles*. Except his parents.

Chaz can't stand his parents.

"No, no, it's okay," Luke says, after slurping down one of the Caraquets. "Of course we're going to set a date. We were thinking September, right, Lizzie?"

I stare at him in total astonishment. This is—literally—the first I've heard of this. "We were?"

"Well, that's when there's an opening in the rental schedule at Mirac," Luke says. "And it won't be too hot then. And that's when most of my parents' friends will be back from their summer places. We want to make sure they can come, because they're the ones who are going to pony up with the best gifts." He winks at me.

I continue to stare at him. I have no idea what he's talking about. I mean, I do, but I can't believe he's saying it. Out loud.

"And that should give you plenty of time to start planning things," he goes on. "Three months is enough time, right?"

I look down. It's amazing. But there's another hive popping up inside my other elbow.

"I . . ." I can't stop staring at the angry red welts in the romantic restaurant lighting. The walls are red. Just like Valencia's dress. Just like my hives. "I don't know. I guess. But . . . don't you have to be back for school?"

"I can miss the first couple weeks of classes," Luke says with a shrug. "It's no big deal."

Something in his tone causes me to look up from my hives— there are two new ones—and into his face.

"Wait," I say. "You *are* going back to school in the fall. Aren't you, Luke?"

"Of course." Luke grins at me, that handsome, easy smile that so enchanted me from that first moment I met him on the train to Sarlat. "Lizzie . . . you look like something just went down the wrong way. Is everything all right?"

"She's been working too hard," Chaz says, speaking for the first time since popping his most unwelcome question. "Look at her. She's got those dark circles under her eyes."

I fling my hands to my face, horrified. "I do not!"

"Charles," Valencia says again, grinning. Her teeth are perfectly white and even. I wonder how she has time for tenure-tracking between flossing.

"Does she even sleep anymore?" Chaz wants to know.

"She's like a machine," Luke says. "I've never seen anybody work so hard."

"Of *course* I'm working hard," I say, flinging open my handbag and digging through it for my compact mirror. "It's June! What do you think happens in June? That's when people get married. Normal people, I mean, who actually *talk* about when they're going to get married, instead of avoiding the subject like it's a ticking bomb that has to be defused the way *we* do, Luke. I've been working on twenty gowns, all at the same time. I'm trying to start a name for myself, you know. Single-handedly, I might add, since my boss has been out sick for the past half a year. And having you guys tell me I have circles under my eyes and that I work too hard totally doesn't help!"

"Lizzie," Chaz says. I can see him staring at me from behind the compact, which I hold up to check on the circles. "I'm totally teasing you. You look beautiful. As always."

"Really, Lizzie," Luke says. He picks up another oyster and swallows it without chewing. "What happened to your sense of humor?"

"She's terribly solipsistic, isn't she?" I hear Valencia murmur, though I know she hadn't meant me to. I'll have to look up the word "solipsistic" later.

I feel tears prick the corners of my eyes. I don't know what's wrong with me. But I do know I want to kill everyone at the table. I really do.

Starting with Valencia.

"And the only reason I don't talk about the wedding," Luke goes on, "is that you always seem to stress out about it so much whenever I bring it up. I know your family wants to have it at their house. I also know you'd rather die . . . but you can't seem to figure out how to tell them that. So I thought it would be better for me to leave it alone until you figure it all out for yourself. That's it. It's not that I don't want to marry you anymore, or anything like that, you knucklehead."

Luke reaches over, drags me toward him, and kisses me on top of my head. I keep my gaze on the tabletop. I'm afraid that if I look up, everyone will see the tears—and shame—in my eyes.

I can't believe I wanted to kill him.

Also that I still sort of want to.

I don't even know why. Or what's wrong with me. Oh God. *What's wrong with me?*

"Aw," Chaz says about the kiss. "That is just so sweet."

"Shut up, Chaz," I say, still not meeting anyone's gaze.

"Yeah, shut up, Chaz," Luke says. He's grinning again and helping himself to another oyster.

"So, September," Valencia says. "That's quite soon, isn't it?"

"I don't know about September," I say, digging through my purse again. I'm looking for my lip gloss. "I have a couple of gowns due in September. I don't know if I'll have them ready in time . . . let alone my *own* gown." The words "my own gown" cause my stomach to give a lurch. If there'd been anything but wine in it, I'm pretty sure it would have come up.

"Lizzie," Luke says in a warning voice.

"Well, what do you want me to do, Luke?" I ask, knowing I sound petulant, but not caring. "I'm just saying, things are going really well at the shop and if it keeps up like this, September should be a busy time for me as well—"

"When *isn't* a busy time for you?" Luke wants to know. "I feel like I hardly ever see you anymore."

"Well, you're not exactly Mr. Availability yourself, taking a job in *Paris* for the summer," I snap.

"Hey now, kids," Chaz says. "Can't we all just get along?"

"I took that job for *us*," Luke says. "To pay for our wedding."

"Oh, right," I say. "A wedding we're having at your house, appar-

ently. Which is a *vineyard*. The booze and venue are already paid
for. How much can it cost? Stop using the cost of the wedding as
an excuse for why you're leaving."

Luke stares at me. "Hey," he says, looking hurt. "Where'd *that*
come from?"

The truth is, I have no idea. I really don't. I just know the words
are out there, floating around, already said.

And there's nothing I can do to stuff them back into my
mouth.

And I don't really feel like apologizing for them this time.

"Has it ever occurred to you," I demand instead, "that I might
rather have a smaller wedding, one that doesn't require my fiancé having to be gone for the whole summer, working in France,
to pay for it?"

"Is that really what you want, Lizzie?" Luke asks, a bit of acid in
his tone. "Because I think that can be arranged. I think your mother already said we could get married in your family's backyard,
with your sisters fighting over who can make the tackiest Jell-O
mold, or whatever it is, and your grandmother passed out on the
lawn for the entertainment."

For a second, it's as if all activity in the restaurant freezes. I suck
in my breath.

Then Chaz groans, dropping his face into his hands, "Tell me
you didn't just go there, man."

But Luke only glares at me across the table, his expression defi-
ant. He's not backing down.

I am, though.

Because suddenly, I know what's going on with me. I know
exactly what's going on with me.

And what's going on with me is that I'm done. I can't take it
anymore.

I snatch up my bag, scoot out from behind the table, and say,

"You don't even *know* my family. Because in all this time, you've still never even bothered to come home with me to meet them."

Luke's expression has lost some of its defiance.

"Lizzie," he says. "Look—"

"No." I thrust a heavily callused finger in his face. I may not have a pretty manicure like Valencia, but I bet my fingers have created way more lace ruching than hers ever have. I've worked my ass off for these calluses. And I'm damned proud of them. "No one disses my grandmother. Especially if they've never even met her."

"Lizzie," he says, his expression contrite. "I'm—"

"No," I interrupt him. I can barely see him, my vision is so cloudy with tears. But I'm hoping he isn't noticing that part. "If that's how you feel about my family, Luke, why don't you just go marry *yourself*? Since that's who you're obviously so in love with anyway."

Okay, not the wittiest of comebacks. But it's all I can think of in the heat of the moment, what with the tears and all.

I do see Chaz raise his eyebrows, as stunned as I am by my outburst. Valencia can't seem to raise her gaze from her wineglass, she's so embarrassed to be seen with me. But I can't back down now. I don't *want* to back down. Instead, I turn on my heel and stalk out of the room, ignoring Luke as he stands up and says, "Lizzie. *Lizzie*, come on."

Fortunately a waitress bearing a huge tray of Cosmopolitans swoops past me, blocking his path, and I hurry downstairs and outside, toward Perry Street . . . where a black stretch limo is pulling up just as I step off the curb to look for a cab to flag down. As I peer past the limo, hoping to see a cab with the TAXI sign lit up, meaning it's available, one of the limo's rear smoked windows rolls down and a familiar voice calls, "Lizzie? Oh my God."

And Ava Geck, wearing a spangled pink tube top beneath a pair of what appear to be white rubber lederhosen, leans out the window and says, "Get in, quick, before anyone sees me."

"Ava, what are you doing here?" I am not unconscious of the fact that everyone has already seen her. Everyone gathered in front of the Spotted Pig has looked up from his or her BlackBerry and is whispering, *Oh my God! It's Ava Geck! You know, Get it at Geck's!*

"Why," I ask, thoroughly confused, "aren't you in Greece, Ava?"

"I'll tell you in the car," Ava says. "Please. Just get in."

"Ava." I rub at the tears still sliding around in the corners of my eyes. "What happened? You're supposed to be getting married *tomorrow*."

"I know," Ava says. "Just get in, and I'll explain."

"Lizzie!"

I throw a frantic glance over my shoulder and see Luke coming out the door of the Spotted Pig, his napkin still in one hand.

I'm surprised—I really hadn't thought he'd follow me—but I don't hesitate a second longer. I fling open the closest door to Ava's limo and dive in.

"Go," I yell to the driver. "Please, just go!"

"Hey," Ava says as I scramble over her in my haste to grab a seat. "Is that your boyfriend? He's cute."

"Yes," I say. "Please, can we go? I have to get out of here."

"Lizzie." Luke hurries up to the limo's still-wide-open window. "Where are you going?"

"Please go," I beg Ava's driver, who surprises me by doing just that.

And soon Luke, the Spotted Pig, and all the hipsters standing outside it, busily texting with their BlackBerries, are just tiny specks in the distance.

A HISTORY
of
WEDDINGS

The Victorians were the ones who took weddings—as they did almost everything—to a whole other level. The industrial revolution proved that just about anything could be mass-produced, and soon savvy merchants realized that they could convince their wealthier customers not to be content with mere home-baked wedding cakes and homespun bridal gowns . . . no!

Now, instead of needing bridesmaids to trick evil spirits or as armed warriors, the modern bride needed them to help with invitations, choosing the cake, floral arrangements, her gown, *their* gowns—you name it.

Pretty crafty of those shop owners, huh?

And so the wedding as we know it today was born. Alleluia . . . or curses, as the case may be.

Tip to Avoid a Wedding Day Disaster

Wedding costs breakdown, or—who pays for what (Remember, this is traditionally. With today's more modern couples opting to pay for their weddings themselves, things are changing. But up until recently, the norm was the following):

The Bride:

Thank-you gifts for the maid of honor, bridesmaids, and hostess

The wedding gown, headpiece, and accessories

The groom's ring

Flower-girl basket and ring-bearer pillow

Hotel accommodations for any attendants who will be arriving from out of town

The Groom:

The marriage license

Thank-you gifts for the best man and groomsmen

The bride's engagement ring

The bride's wedding ring

Clothing (tuxedo rental) and accessories

The bride's flowers

Corsages for mothers/grandmothers and boutonnieres for groomsmen

Clergyman/officiant fee

Limousine service/transportation to and from the wedding and reception

Hotel accommodations for any groomsmen who will be arriving from out of town

The Bride and Groom:

Wedding pictures

Miscellaneous accessories (wedding favors, goblets, napkins/printed items)

Thank-you gifts for the flower girl and ring bearer

Thank-you cards

Any overnight accommodations for themselves

Their honeymoon arrangements, unless another relative or friend offers to pay for it as a wedding gift

Parents of the Groom:

Dress/suit and accessories

The rehearsal dinner

Their hotel accommodations

Bridesmaids:

Dresses and accessories

Wedding shower

Groomsmen:

Clothing (tuxedo rental) and accessories

Bachelor party

Parents of the Flower Girl/Ring Bearer:

Dress, suit/tuxedo rental, and accessories

Hotel accommodations if arriving from out of town

Parents of the Bride:

Everything else

LIZZIE NICHOLS DESIGNS™

Chapter 11

Marriage is the perfection of what love aimed at, ignorant of what it sought.

Ralph Waldo Emerson (1803–1882), American essayist, poet, and leader of the Transcendentalist movement

hat are you and Luke fighting about?" Ava wants to know. She's cradling Snow White on her slim, tanned thighs. Besides the tube top and white rubber lederhosen, she is also wearing pink suede platform boots. I suppose I should be grateful that both her boobs and crotch are completely covered for once, but rubber *and* suede . . . in late June?

"Just wedding stuff," I lie to her, although I know I should be nicer and tell her the truth, since she has, in a sense, just rescued me. The only problem is . . . I don't know what the truth is, exactly.

And I actually have more pressing concerns at the moment. Like why I'm in a stretch limo with Ava Geck.

"Ava, what are you doing here?" I ask. "Why aren't you in Greece?"

"I couldn't go through with it," Ava says simply, then gasps and seizes my arm. "Oh my God! What happened to you? Lizzie—has Luke been *beating* you?"

I look down at the hives, which have now broken out all over the insides of both my arms. In a way, they do resemble bruises.

"No," I say with a laugh, because the idea of Luke ever hitting me is so absurd. I could probably knock him clear into New Jersey. "They're just hives. I get them every time I think about . . . you know."

"Butt sex?" Ava asks understandingly.

"No," I cry, ripping my arm from her grasp. "My wedding. And what do you mean, you couldn't go through with it? You mean you just . . . *canceled* your wedding to Prince Aleksandros?"

"That's about it," Ava says with a sigh, patting Snow White on the head as the poor dog trembles in the icy blast from the limo's air conditioner. "I was just boarding Daddy's private jet, and suddenly it hit me: I'm about to become someone's wife. I was like . . . are you *shitting* me? I'm only twenty-three! I haven't even been to *college*. What am I doing, becoming someone's *wife*? So I jumped back into the car and I've been riding around ever since, trying to get my head together."

I gaze at Ava, truly touched by her words. Especially since I'm twenty-three too. "So you've decided to go to college? Ava, that is so great!"

"Hell, no, I'm not going to college," Ava says, looking shocked. "Are you kidding me? I'm just saying there's so many things *like* going to college that I haven't done. I'm not throwing my life away yet on some guy, even if he *is* a prince. I have shit to do. I don't know what, but . . . like, I was thinking I should cut an album. Something classy, you know? Like Hilary Duff."

I blink at her. "Well . . . yes. Yes, that is definitely something you could do."

"And I don't even have my own clothing line yet," Ava goes on.

"My parents own one of the biggest discount department store chains in the world, and I don't have my own clothing line yet? What the hell am I *thinking*?"

"Exactly," I say. "What the hell *are* you thinking? Although, Ava . . . you can do all these things and still be married, you know. It's not like Prince Aleksandros would try to stop you. Not if he really loved you. He'd probably be proud of you."

"But that's just it," Ava says, looking down sadly at Snow White. "I don't think he would be. You know . . . this is partly your fault, Lizzie. My having to cancel my wedding, I mean."

"Me?" I gape at her, horror-struck. "What did *I* have to do with it?"

"Because since I've been coming to you, and you've been, like, helping me with my public image and stuff, Alek's kinda . . . I don't know. Lost interest in me. Like he keeps asking me how come I don't show my cootchie anymore. I think he *liked* it when I did stuff like that. Because it drove his parents completely insane. They were totally against his marrying me, you know. Which I think only made him *more* into me. But now that I've started to act a little classier, they've been a lot nicer to me. And that's made Alek completely lose interest."

My jaw sags. Although I guess I shouldn't be surprised. This explains so much about Ava's very conservative choices when it came to her wedding gown. And why she'd come to me in the first place. Sure, she could have gone to Vera Wang, but there'd been a small part of her that had still been rebelling . . . just a little.

It's all beginning to make sense. She'd wanted to please her fiancé's parents while still retaining some small part of herself.

But in doing so, it sounded like she'd turned off her fiancé.

Oops.

"So you're calling it off," I say, "before Aleksandros can?"

"That's just it," Ava says in disgust. "I don't think he ever was

going to call it off. That's how gutless he is. Like, he'll stand up to
his parents by marrying a total slut. But he would never *call off* the
wedding to that slut, because that would make him look bad in the
press."

I reach over and give her warm, bare shoulder a reassuring pat.
"Ava," I say. "You're not a slut."

"Oh, I totally am," Ava says matter-of-factly. "But that's okay. I'd
rather be a slut than a dickless hypocrite, like Alek. I'm just sorry
about your dress."

I shake my head. "My dress?"

"The beautiful wedding dress you designed for me," Ava says.

"Oh," I say, laughing. "Don't worry about *that*! I'm sure I'll find
someone else to buy it. Ava Geck's wedding dress? Are you kidding? I'll probably be able to sell it for a fortune on eBay."

Ava pouts at me. "I'm not giving it back," she says. "That thing
is mine. I was thinking maybe you could make it shorter, dye it
purple, slap some sequins on it, and I could wear it to the MTV
Video Music Awards in September. That way tons of people will
see it, and you'll still get the exposure you deserve. I should get lots
of airtime, because I'm giving out the Viewer's Choice VMA. And
Tippy asked me to go with him 'cause he's still got that restraining
order out on his wife. That was going to be a problem before—you
know, being his escort if I was married to Alek—but now that I'm
not, it should be all good."

"Oh," I say, taken aback. "Um . . . sure. I could do that. No
problem."

"Awesome." Ava looks a lot happier. The limo has made its way
uptown via Sixth Avenue, and now we're snaking our way through
Central Park, one of my favorite drives in Manhattan—which I
certainly never thought I'd be making via limo. We're gliding past
couples taking romantic horse and carriage rides, and less romantic pedicab rides. I wonder if they're looking at the smoked-glass

windows of the limo and trying to guess who the celebrity is inside.

I'm betting none of them is guessing Ava Geck and her wedding gown designer.

"So what are you going to do now?" I ask, conscious that my stomach is growling a little. There's nothing in it but white wine. I'm hoping Ava's going to say that she's dropping me off at home so I can get something to eat . . . or at the very least, that she's going to suggest the two of us grab something somewhere. I don't know how much longer I can go without sustenance of the nonalcoholic variety. Ava may be able to go for hours on just a PowerBar, but I'm not that kind of girl.

"Um," Ava says. "Yeah. That's why I was trying to reach you."

I perk up. "You want to grab some dinner? You want to get some sushi or something?" Another thing Tiffany, Monique, and I have managed to do is expand Ava's dining horizons, so that she now eats more than just cheeseburgers and protein bars. She has consequently developed an almost pathological love for sushi . . . which isn't actually unusual for someone who's never tried it before. Wasabi has known addictive qualities. "There's Atlantic Grill right over on Third Avenue. Or Sushi of Gari . . ."

"Not exactly," Ava says. "I mean, we can totally get something to eat if you want. But I actually need a favor."

"Oh sure," I say. "Anything you want."

"Oh goody," Ava says, grinning widely. "Joey, she said yes!"

Little Joey, I realize belatedly, is sitting in the front seat beside the driver, half hidden by the privacy screen, which Ava lowers to deliver this news.

"Oh, hey, Lizzie," he calls to me from the vast expanse of leather seats and twinkling halogen lights in the ceiling between us. "How you doing?"

"Hi, Joey," I call back a bit hesitantly, since I'm suddenly realizing I have no idea what I've just agreed to. "I'm good. Um, Ava?"

"What?" she asks a little distractedly, having dug out her Sidekick, into which she is tapping with some urgency.

"What, exactly, did I just promise to do for you?"

"You're letting me stay at your place, of course," Ava says with
some surprise, not even looking up from the screen.

I stare at her. "My place? You mean . . . in my *apartment*?"

"Well, I can't stay at my place," Ava says, finally looking up. Ava's
condo, which is on East End Avenue near the mayor's house, Gra-
cie Mansion, is within easy walking distance of mine (not that Ava
ever walks). Ava chose to move to the Upper East Side—to the
consternation of many a poodle-toting matron there—because
that's where she happened to find the only condo that met her
exacting standards (the aforementioned four bedrooms, three
baths, and an eat-in kitchen with at least two thousand square feet
of outdoor terrace and full southern exposure).

But she'd also fallen in love with the nearby Carl Schurz Park,
which is right by the river, and includes a dog run built especially
for small dogs.

"My place is crawling with paparazzi," she goes on. "Word's
already getting out that I left Alek at the altar. They've got all the
hotels staked out too, and my parents' and friends' places, as well.
You're my only hope, Lizzie. I figured you could just stay at
Luke's."

I'm shaking my head before the words are fully out of her
mouth. "No," I say. "No, I can't stay at Luke's." The thought fills me
with panic. I don't want to see Luke. I . . . I can't see Luke. Not
again. Not this soon.

"Well," Ava says, looking slightly annoyed. "Fine. Then I'll stay
at Luke's, and he can stay with you."

"No," I say, still shaking my head. "You can't stay at Luke's either.
Because Luke and I are . . . we're . . . we're in a fight. Remember?

Remember how he came running out of the restaurant after me just now, and I was like, *Drive? Please drive?* Remember that?" My eyes fill with tears again at the memory. Oh God. What's happening to me?

Little Joey says, from the front seat, "She did say that."

Ava screws up her face, trying to remember. "Oh yeah," she says. "Well. Can't I just stay at your apartment with you, then? It'll just be for a few days. Until all this blows over. You'll hardly know I'm there. Snow White and I don't take up much room."

I glance at Little Joey. Ava, noticing the direction of my gaze, laughs.

"Oh, don't worry about him," she says. "*He* won't be staying there. He has his own place in Queens."

I want to suggest that Joey's place in Queens might be the ideal hideout for Ava. The paparazzi would never think to look for her there.

But then I remember what she said, about all of this being my fault. And so instead, I say, "Ava, my place . . . it's just a one bed-room. There's only one bathroom. And it doesn't have southern exposure. Believe me, it's not luxurious—"

"I don't mind, I'm used to roughing it. I served forty-eight hours at CRDF, you know," Ava assures me, referring to the Cen-tury Regional Detention Facility in Los Angeles, which housed her when she did her time for driving under the influence.

"My place isn't as bad as *prison*," I say, slightly annoyed.

"Oh, I knew you'd say yes," Ava says, throwing her spindly arms around me and giving me a hug, and partially suffocating Snow White in the process. "This is gonna be so fun! Like camping out or something! We'll order in, and do our nails, and watch me on TV, and stay up all night talking bad about our boyfriends. Your having a fight with Luke makes it just perfect!"

I say in a strangled voice, since her deathlike grip is cutting off my oxygen, "I can't stay up all night, Ava. I have gowns I have to get finished."

"That's even better!" Ava cries, releasing me suddenly. "I can help!"

"Okay," I say. I massage my neck where she's squeezed it. I can't believe this is happening. "I guess."

"I'm so excited," Ava declares. "Vincent, make the turn onto Seventy-eighth. We're getting out there!"

Sooner than I could have imagined possible, Ava Geck, her Chihuahua, and seven of her suitcases are in my apartment, and her bodyguard is saying good night, while assuring me he'll be by at nine tomorrow morning to pick Ava up to take her to the New York Health and Racquet Club to meet her trainer for her workout. She's on my couch—though we've already established that she'll be sleeping in my bed, and I'll be on the couch, thanks to her sciatica—flipping channels with the remote, trying to see if news of her broken-off royal wedding is on E! yet. I'm supposed to be ordering dinner—moo shu chicken is out. Ava wants a Caesar salad and fettuccine Alfredo from Sistina, which is a four-star Italian restaurant on Second Avenue that doesn't deliver . . . except apparently for Ava.

I'm on the phone with the restaurant's maître d' when the buzzer to my apartment goes off, causing Snow White to burst into a cacophony of yips and Ava to squeal excitedly, "The food's here!"

"The food can't be here," I say. "I'm still on hold with Guiseppe."

Ava throws me a panicked look. She's changed from her rubber lederhosen into a pink velour sweatsuit. Although she has the word "Juicy" written across her rear end, I find this preferable to her many outfits that actually reveal her rear end, or at least the brown-cheeked moons of it. And so I am allowing her to wear it. But only indoors.

"It's the paparazzi!" she cries. "They've found me! Already!"

"It can't be the paparazzi," I say. "Unless you told someone you're here."

"Only my mom," Ava says. "And Tippy. And he wouldn't tell anyone. He knows what it's like to be hounded mercilessly by the press."

I still don't have the slightest idea who DJ Tippycat is, but I take her word for it that he wouldn't rat her out. I hand her the phone and go to the wall intercom and push the TALK button. "Who is it?" I ask in my meanest voice, which I reserve only for answering the intercom.

"Lizzie, it's me," Luke says. "Can I come up?"

I stare at the intercom as if live snakes have suddenly come bursting out of it. Luke? In all the excitement with Ava, I'd completely forgotten about my fight with him.

Ava hasn't, however. She bolts upright. "Is that Luke?" she asks, her bright eyes wide. "Are you gonna buzz him in? I can totally make myself scarce. You won't even know I'm here. I'll hide in the bathroom."

I continue to stare at the intercom, uncertain what to do. On the one hand, I'm still really, really mad at him. On the other hand . . . it's Luke. I love him.

At least . . . I think I do.

And yet . . . could he have been a bigger jerk?

"Unless you want me to pour water on his head," Ava offers generously. She's gotten up from the couch and gone to the window, where you can look down and see whoever is standing in the doorway—providing they aren't hiding beneath the awning, as the UPS man is wont to do when it's raining. "Because I could totally do that for you, if you want me to. Or pee. I could pour pee on him. I haven't gone yet. I could go in a cup and dump it—"

"That's okay," I say quickly. "I—I'll just go talk to him outside. You go ahead and order. I'll have whatever you're having."

Ava looks dubious. "Are you sure? Because I've been holding it all day—"

"I'm sure," I say. "And you really shouldn't hold it, Ava. You could give yourself a urinary tract infection that way. I'll be right back."

I grab my keys and hurry out of the apartment and down the stairs, a little leery of leaving Ava to her own devices in my place . . . but also a little relieved to have a moment to myself. Even if, the next minute, I know I'm going to have to be dealing with Luke.

Who says, "Oh," when I undo the many locks to the outside door and step onto the stoop into the warm evening air beside him. "I thought . . . I thought you might buzz me up."

"I can't," I say unsmilingly. "I have company."

Luke looks surprised. I'm pleased to see he isn't smiling, either. At least he's taking this thing seriously. So often, when we argue, he seems to think my anger is amusing, as if I'm a kitten who's upset about someone hiding her catnip mouse. I'm not a kitten.

And I'm tired of being treated like one.

"Company?" he echoes. *Now* he's smiling. "What, did you and that girl from the limo go and pick up some sailors while you were out cruising around or something?"

"No," I say, still not smiling. "Ava's going to be spending a few days at my place. She and her fiancé just broke up, and she can't go back to her place because it's being staked out by the paparazzi."

Luke's smile vanishes. "Lizzie," he says. "Jesus. So, you're just letting her stay with you? Why can't she stay in a hotel?"

"Because—" I break off and glare at him. "You know what? Who cares? She's not. She's staying with me. What's the big deal?"

"The big deal," Luke says, "is that she's a client. And you're treating her like she's a friend. You can't get business mixed up with your personal life, Lizzie. This is exactly what we were just talking about, back at the restaurant."

"Oh, really," I say. I'm ignoring, with effort, a man who is walking by with an Italian greyhound on a leash. The man is pretending he's not listening to our conversation, but he totally is. I don't care, really, except that the dog is distracting. It's so . . . skinny. I know it was born that way, but it's still freakish. How does it digest its food with such a tiny stomach? "And just what does my grandmother's drinking problem have to do with the fact that I refurbish wedding gowns for a living?"

Luke reaches out to grab both my shoulders in his hands and gives me a gentle shake.

"Hey," he says in a gentler tone than he's used until now. "I'm sorry about that. Okay? I know I was out of line, and I apologize. I tried to apologize there in the restaurant—I chased after you and would have told you so right there, but you jumped into that limo and were gone. If everyone standing out there hadn't told me that was Ava Geck you were with, I would have . . . well, I totally would have thought you'd been kidnapped or something."

"No, I wasn't kidnapped, Luke," I say, trying not to notice how good his hands feel on my skin. I can't let sensations like that distract me. "I just . . . we just . . . I want . . ."

What am I saying? What *do* I want?

Where am I going with this?

Why won't that man take his dog and go somewhere else? Seventy-eighth Street is really long. Does his dog *have* to pee right there in front of my shop?

"Luke . . . I've been thinking. And I think . . ." The next thing I know, words are coming out of my mouth that I honestly don't remember thinking. They just come out of my mouth. Like air.

Or vomit.

"Luke," I hear myself say. "I think we need to take a break."

Oh. My. God.

A HISTORY
of
WEDDINGS

The first hand-printed wedding invitations in the Middle Ages were done in calligraphy by monks, who were commissioned to do so by royalty. By the time metal plate engraving had been invented, engraved invitations—the kind that come with a fancy sheet of tissue paper on top, to keep the print from smudging—became more popular than calligraphy. This same kind of engraving is still used today (and is why you still get tissue paper with fancier wedding invitations). The traditional double envelope in which wedding invitations are so often sent stems from the fact that in olden times, mail was delivered via horse, and no one wanted the dainty hands of the recipient to be dirtied as she opened her invitation. It was assumed a butler would open the icky outer envelope and hand the clean inner envelope to his mistress.

How sad for us modern, butler-less mail openers, daily soiling our hands on germy outside envelopes!

Remember, your wedding invitations should never be mailed at the last minute . . . but you don't want to mail them out too early, either! The ideal time is somewhere between eight weeks and one month before the actual wedding day. Six weeks in advance is perfect.

And please, never use a laser-printed address label on your invitations. That's considered beyond tacky. Hand-written only! Yes, you can advertise for and hire an engineering student with impeccable handwriting for this task.

LIZZIE NICHOLS DESIGNS™

Chapter 12

A good marriage is that in which each appoints the other guardian of his solitude.

—*Rainer Maria Rilke (1875–1926), German poet*

uke stares at me. "You think we need to *what*?" he says, his grip on my shoulders loosening.

"*Oh!*"

I let out the sound in a whoosh. At least I think it was me. I realize I can't even be sure what sounds are coming out of my mouth anymore. That's how little control I have.

I sink down onto the top step of the stoop and hug my knees to my chest. The man with the dog, I notice, has hurried away. Apparently, he is no longer enjoying the show—the show of a girl in vintage Shaheen going crazy right in front of him.

"Lizzie." Luke sits down on the step beside me. "What do you mean, you think we need to take a break?"

"I don't know," I groan into my knees. God, what is happening to me? "I just . . . I mean, you're going to France for three months anyway . . . so we're kind of taking a break, whether we want one or not."

What am I saying? *What* is coming out of my mouth? I do not want a break from Luke. I do not. I love Luke.

Don't I?

"It's just," I hear myself saying, though at no point did I formulate the words in my head beforehand, "I know that you love me, Luke. But I don't always feel like you *respect* me. Or at least . . . not my job. It's like you think it's just this hobby I have that I'm doing for fun until something more serious comes along. But that's not what it is. This is really what I do. What I want to do for the rest of my life."

Luke blinks down at me with his gorgeous, sleepy eyes. "Lizzie, I know that. And of course I respect what you do. I don't know what would ever have given you the impression that I don't. All I meant, when I said that about Ava, was that I've worked in the business world for a lot of years, and we just never let our clients take advantage of us the way I think you sometimes do."

"It's not what you said about Ava," I explain. "It's the way you just thought I could leave with you to go to Paris for the summer. You know. When you brought it up."

Luke stares at me. "Last *January*? You're bringing up something I said in January? *Now*?"

I nod. "And maybe I do business a different way than you do," I point out. "But I'm not you. Different doesn't mean it's wrong."

"Point taken," Luke says. "Listen, Lizzie—"

"And," my mouth goes on. Why, oh, why, won't it just shut up? "I don't think you respect my family very much, either. I know they aren't as sophisticated as your family is. But you've never even met them. So how do you even know? And that's another thing. You've been going out with me for a year. For six months of that year we've been engaged. And you've never met *anyone* in my family. And yet you make remarks like the one you did tonight—"

"I apologized for that already," Luke says, moving to put his arm around me. "I know what your grandmother means to you. And if I hadn't—well, let me tell you, Chaz really let me know, back at the restaurant. But, Lizzie, you have to admit, you complain about your sisters a lot. And your grandmother . . . well, everyone talks about her drinking problem. And you know the only reason I haven't met your family is because I've been busy with school—"

"You could have come home with me at Christmas," I interrupt, "instead of going to France with your family. Or at spring break. But instead, you went to Houston to see your mother. And my family isn't rich like yours. It's not like they can go jetting off to New York to meet you like yours can."

I glance at him to see how he reacts to this. He isn't looking at me, however. He's looking at the Honda Accord parked across the sidewalk in front of us.

"Yes," he says in a quiet voice. "You're right. I probably should have."

"Because meeting my family isn't important to you," I say. I don't want to say it. It's like the words are being wrenched out of me. Like Gran, that time she got completely wasted on cooking sherry and decided to finally go after that balky kitchen pipe with Dad's giant wrench. The sherry had given her superhuman strength, and she'd managed to loosen the joint and remove all this gunk that had been trapped inside for six months. It just started spilling out.

Just like all this gunk is pouring out of me. Gunk that probably should have come out of me last January. It's all spilling out now. Even though I don't want it to. I really don't. Not on my nice clean relationship.

But I guess that's what gunk is. Stuff that sort of has to come out eventually.

"That's not true," Luke begins to protest, but I cut him off.

"Don't say you didn't have time," I say. "If it had been important to you, you could have made the time. It was important to
me," I go on. "And it's important to them. They keep asking me
when they're going to meet you. It would be nice if they could
meet you before the wedding."

Luke opens his mouth to say something, but I barrel on.

"But it's too late now. Because you're leaving for France the day
after tomorrow. And so," my voice adds ruthlessly, without my
consent, "whether you want to call it that or not, we're taking a
break. Because I need to think, Luke. I need to think about what's
going on here. What we're doing. What I'm doing."

"Right," he says.

And he removes his arm from around my shoulders.

We sit for a moment in silence. But the city isn't silent, of course.
Taxis rumble by, and a siren sounds over on Third Avenue. I'm not
sure, but I think I hear a window open above our heads. Ava is
eavesdropping.

That's all I hope she's dropping, anyway.

There's another thing I think I hear in the silence that's fallen
between us as well: the sound of my heart breaking.

· · ·

When I get back upstairs to the apartment, Ava is on the couch
again, innocently flipping channels while still holding the phone
to her ear. She looks up and smiles at me as I come in, fending off
Snow White's enthusiastic mini assault.

"So?" she asks. "How'd it go?"

"Like you weren't listening," I say, dropping my keys in the fruit
bowl I keep for this purpose on the bookshelf by the door.

"I was not," Ava says with a sniff. Then, seeing my expression,
she says, "Well, okay, I totally was. But I couldn't hear. I was all

ready to pour orange juice on his head if you started crying, though. Did you? I didn't think you did."

"I didn't," I say, and flop down onto the couch beside her. Snow White leaps up onto my lap, and I pat her distractedly. "We're taking a break."

"Really?" Ava stares at me, bug-eyed. "What does that mean?"

"I don't know." I shrug. "I just heard the words coming out of my mouth, and I went with them. That happens to me sometimes." Try all the time.

It hadn't made any sense, either. I mean, that I had said what I had to Luke. What had I been thinking, asking for a break? I love Luke. At least . . . I'm pretty sure I love Luke. I know I love waking up in the morning before he has and just staring at him and his incredible eyelashes, resting so dark and sooty against his cheekbones. I love how, when he's awake, those dark eyes still look so sleepy, like they hold the promise of a thousand secret dreams.

Most of all, I love that I'm one of those dreams, me, Lizzie Nichols, who no boy in my high school ever even asked out, because I just wasn't the kind of girl you asked out in high school . . . unless you were a gay boy and you didn't want anyone to know that, of course.

Oh yeah. I forgot. Gay boys asked me out. A lot. I was always the fat girl gay boys asked out to make their mothers happy.

So what was I doing? What was I doing telling this guy—this guy that I love so much, and who, more important, loves me back—that I wanted to take a break? Am I crazy?

Why couldn't I, for once in my life, have kept my mouth shut?

But the words just came out, and once they were spoken, I couldn't stuff them back. Well, I mean, I *could* have, but . . .

I didn't want to.

And that was maybe the weirdest part of all.

"Oh my God," Ava gasps. "How did he take it?"

"He was okay with it, I think," I say. Actually, maybe *that* was the weirdest part of all. "I mean, he says he understands that my work has to come first right now, and that I don't have time to be planning a wedding at the moment. But . . . he's still leaving for France. It's not like he offered to stay. Even though I told him I'd be happy with a much smaller wedding that didn't cost as much, so he wouldn't have to go work there. He's still going." Is it wrong that this bothers me as much as it does?

Ava makes a face. "Men are all such dicks."

Yeah, okay. So . . . not wrong.

"Tell me about it," I say. I look at the phone Ava is holding to her ear. "Are you still on hold with Sistina?"

"Oh, no," Ava says. "They'll be over with the food in half an hour. This is your grandmother. She wanted to know how to record something with a season pass on TiVo. So I told her how to do it. It *is* tricky, after all. Then when she told me how much she likes Byron Sully from that old show, *Dr. Quinn, Medicine Woman,* I told her how to do a Wish List for the actor, so that anything with him that comes on will be recorded. She seemed really grateful. I told her you were downstairs with Luke, so she said she'd hang on till you got back upstairs. Do you want to talk to her?"

I take the phone from Ava, feeling more stunned than ever. "Sure," I say. "Hello?" I murmur into the receiver.

"So," Gran's voice crackles into the phone. "You haven't shtupped him yet?"

I nearly choke on my own spit, I'm so shocked by the question. "I beg your pardon?"

"Sorry," Gran says. "This Chaz character. Why haven't you shtupped him?"

"Because," I say, horrified, "I happen to be engaged to his best friend."

"Is she asking about Chaz?" Ava wants to know from the couch. "I was wondering the same thing. I mean, when are you two going to get busy? Now that you're on a break."

"It's not *that* kind of break," I say, irritated.

"Well, what kind of break is it?" Ava wants to know. "I mean, if you can't fu— I mean, make love with other people, what's the point of it?"

"It's just . . . it's to . . ." I stare blankly at the television screen. Ava is watching an old rerun of *Celebrity Pit Fight,* in which Ava is wrestling with Da Brat in what appears to be an outdoor vat of pudding. "It's so that we can concentrate on our professional goals at the moment, and not be bogged down with romantic problems."

"Oh God," Gran groans over the phone.

"Oh," Ava says, brightening. "Like me and Alek. Well, like me, I mean."

"Exactly," I say. "Only Luke and I aren't broken up. We're just on a break."

"Who *is* that I was just talking to?" Gran wants to know.

"No one you know," I assure her. "Just a friend of mine. Her name is Ava."

"She sounds just like Ava Geck," Gran says with a snort. "You know, the skanky crack whore. What's Ava Geck doing in your apartment?"

"She's just staying here for a few days," I say. The call waiting goes off. I say, "Gran, can you hold on a sec? Someone's on the other line."

"What else have I got to do?" Gran wants to know.

So I pounce on the other call. "Hello?"

"Lizzie?" It's Shari. "Are you all right? I called as soon as I heard."

I blink. On the television screen, Da Brat has seized a handful of Ava's golden hair (extensions) and is using it to drag her through the pudding.

"Of course I'm all right," I say. "What are you talking about?"

"I was just talking to Chaz," Shari says. "His call waiting went off, and it was Luke saying you two are breaking up. I called as soon as Chaz told me. I thought you'd be upset. But you seem awfully calm about it."

"Because we're not breaking up," I say through gritted teeth. "We're *on a break*. Of course I'm calm about it. It was my idea."

"Oh," Shari says. "A break. I thought Chaz said a break*up*. He was talking so fast. He wanted to get off the phone with me so he could talk to Luke—"

"Oh, watch this part," Ava says, pointing at the television screen. "This is where I make her eat it. The pudding, I mean."

"Who is that with you?" Shari asks.

"That's Ava Geck," I say. When Ava makes a frantic slashing motion at me, I roll my eyes and say, "But don't tell anyone she's staying here. She's hiding out from the paparazzi. She just ditched her Greek prince boyfriend, who she was supposed to marry this weekend."

"Holy crap," Shari says. "And she's staying at *your* place? Can't she afford to hole up somewhere a little nicer?"

"Thanks," I say sarcastically.

"Well, sorry. But you know it's true. So . . . you're really all right with this break thing with Luke? I thought you'd be in hysterics."

"I'm really all right with it," I say. "Like I said, it was my idea." I pick up the orange juice container and head to the kitchen with it. "It's like all this stuff that had just been festering in me for months came pouring out. I even told him about my Spanx." My cheeks begin to burn at the memory of it.

There is silence at the end of the line. Then Shari says, "Lizzie.

Are you telling me your fiancé didn't know that you wear control top panties?"

"No," I say, opening the refrigerator door. "He didn't know. No wonder he doesn't respect me. What is there to respect? I'm a complete fake."

"Oh, honey," Shari says. "I don't think you're fake. Just . . . complicated."

"Face it," I say, slamming the refrigerator door with my foot. "I'm a fake, Shari. A big, shallow fake who would rather spend time renovating wedding dresses than with her own fiancé." I wasn't making that last part up, either. What does that say about me?

Shari sighs. "I think this break is a good idea. Both of you can spend the summer getting your heads together, putting things in perspective. Giving yourselves some space. It's been a very intense twelve months since you met on that train."

"Right," I say. I know what she's saying makes sense. I know what I've just said to Luke, out on the stoop, makes sense. It all makes perfect sense.

So why does my heart hurt so much all of a sudden?

"I have to go," I tell her. "Gran's on the other line. It's just—" My voice cracks a little. "Luke and I are breaking up, aren't we?"

"No, Lizzie," Shari says. "Not at all. I mean, I don't think so. Not necessarily. Not if you don't want to be. Do you want to be?"

"I don't know," I admit miserably. I'm so confused. I remember how he kissed me good-bye out on the stoop. Was it my imagination, or had there been something like relief in that kiss? Not relief that we weren't breaking up, either. But relief that maybe . . . just maybe . . . we were a little bit closer to doing so?

That has to have been my overactive imagination. Luke is the one who proposed, after all. I broke up with him last time, remember? He's the one who came crawling back, begging my forgiveness. He'd done the same thing again tonight. If he wants to break up so badly, why does he keep coming back, every time I give him what he wants?

Do I want to break up with him?

What is it Shari said, all those months ago in this very kitchen? *I worry that the reason you said yes to Luke is because you wanted to marry him so badly, and then when you found out he didn't want to marry you, you moved on. And then suddenly when he came back and wanted to marry you after all, you thought you had to say yes because you'd been so adamant that that's what you wanted all along. But you know, Lizzie, it's okay to change your mind.*

No. Not that . . . the other thing. That I love the *idea* of Luke, not Luke himself.

But that's ridiculous. Isn't it? I mean, how can you love the *idea* of someone, and not the person himself? Of course I love Luke. I love that he wants to be a doctor and save the children, and I love his eyelashes, and that he always looks so impeccably put together, and smells so nice when he gets out of the shower . . . those aren't *ideas*. Those are real . . .

Aren't they?

"Fights like this," Shari goes on, "can sometimes make couples stronger. They're almost always a good thing. Getting things out in the open can only make things better. Chaz says—"

"What?" I ask, snapping back into the present at the mention of Chaz's name. "What did Chaz say? I can't believe he called you. Since when are you and Chaz so chummy all of a sudden?"

"You know Chaz and I always stayed friends," Shari says. "I love him . . . as a pal. I always will. And he adores you, you know. He always has. He was worried about you. He says you ran out of the middle of a restaurant and jumped into some limo—"

"Ava Geck's," I say.

Ava, in the living room, looks up and calls, "Seriously, you have to watch this part. This is where Tippy comes in and starts shaving his legs! With pudding!"

I head obediently back into the living room. "Really," I say into the phone. "I was fine. I just got so mad at Luke. You know? He said the shittiest thing to me, and right in front of Chaz's new girl-friend, Valencia. Who's perfect by the way. You should see her, no cellulite whatsoever and tan all over. Plus, she's got a Ph.D. She called me solipsistic."

"She called you what?"

I try again. "Solipsistic."

"She *said* that?"

"Right in front of me," I say, nodding vigorously, even though Shari can't see me. "Why? What does it mean?"

"Um. I'm not sure," Shari says. I can tell she's lying. "Look, just call me back after you're done talking to Gran. Pat and I are having a Fourth of July barbecue next week, and we want you to come."

"Really?" I'm touched. "Shari, I'd love to."

"Great. It's going to be fantastic. We've got the back garden to ourselves, you know, for the barbecue, and then we've also got roof rights, so everyone can go upstairs after nightfall and watch the fireworks. We've got a great view."

"Oh, Shari, it sounds perfect. Can I bring anything?"

"Just your lovely self. Chaz is bringing a strawberry rhubarb pie, and maybe a blueberry pie too, if he can wing it—"

"Wait." I can't believe what I'm hearing. "You invited *Chaz*?"

"Of course I invited Chaz," Shari says. "You don't think I'd let him be alone on Fourth of July—or go off with that horrible Valencia—do you?"

"No," I say, thinking that there was no way, if Luke had been in town, she would have invited me to her place. Not if she thought there was a chance I'd bring him. Not in a million years. "I just didn't know you guys were *that* tight."

"Hey, I didn't break up with the guy because I don't *like* him anymore," Shari reminds me. "I broke up with him because I fell in love with someone else. He's a great guy. I just hope he finds somebody who can appreciate him, you know? He's got a lot to offer."

"I think he already found somebody," I say gloomily. I don't mention the loop-de-loop my heart gave earlier in the evening when I saw him. I still haven't figured that part out. I'm not sure I want to, either.

"I mean somebody *nice*," Shari says. "Not vile cellulite-free philosophy department skanks. Don't tell him this, but there's a cute new girl in my office I'm hoping to set him up with at my party. I specifically told him to come stag so I could fix them up together. I think they'll get along great. She loves college basketball too. I don't think she cares about baseball caps. And I *know* she's never used the word 'solipsistic' in conversation."

I feel as if Shari's just shoved a steak knife through my heart. Really. My best friend. I can barely breathe, in fact, I'm so wounded.

"Is she pretty?" I hear myself wheeze. It's surprisingly hard to talk with a steak knife in your chest.

"What?" Shari asks. "Did you just ask me if she's *pretty*?"

"No," I say quickly. "I said is she witty. Because you know Chaz likes only witty girls. Because he's so . . . smart."

Oh. God. What's wrong with me? How can I even be worried about this? I'm possibly—okay, probably—breaking up with my long-term fiancé, the man of my dreams, right now. Why am I even giving a moment's thought to the fact that Shari is setting up Chaz with some girl from her office?

I'm engaged to Chaz's best friend. Even if we *are* on a break.

"That's great," I say with forced enthusiasm.

"I know. Anyway, so we'll see you on the Fourth, around seven?"

"I'll be there," I say, and after Shari asks me one more time if I'm okay, and I assure her that I think I am, even though I'm pretty sure I'm not, we say our good-byes, and I hang up.

"Oh shit," I say, remembering Gran when I hear her breathing.

"Yeah." Her cranky voice fills my ear. "Still here. Remember me? The grandma?"

"I'm so sorry," I say. "That was Shari."

"Of course it was," Gran says in a bored voice. "You still haven't answered my question. Why haven't you shtupped him?"

"I did answer your question," I say. "Because I'm engaged to his best friend. And where did you learn a word like 'shtup'?"

"TV," Gran says, sounding wounded. "Where else? And what should it matter who you're engaged to? When it's right, it's right. And with that one, it's right."

"Gran," I say tiredly. "How do you even know?"

"Because I've been alive a lot longer than you have. Now, what are you going to do about it?"

"Nothing, Gran," I say. "He has a new girlfriend. She's really pretty and smart. Her name is Valencia."

"Isn't that a type of orange?"

"Gran. You know what I mean. She's perfect for him."

"So?" Gran sounds offended. "And you're not?"

"No, Gran," I say miserably. "I'm not. I'm just . . . I . . . I—"

I don't know how to go on, really, or what more there is to say. I find myself, for one of the first times in my life, at a loss for words. How can I explain to her just why it is that Valencia is so perfect for Chaz—for any guy, really—whereas I, on the other hand, am not? So not.

Gran, however, comes to my rescue.

"Yeah, yeah, yeah," she says. "I know. You're engaged. I heard. Engaged isn't married, you know. Engaged isn't dead. Listen, I gotta go. My show's coming on. I've seen it before. I've seen them

all before. But that's one of the good things about getting old. I
can't remember how a single one of these goddamned episodes
turns out. I'll talk to you later."

She hangs up. I do the same and turn around to find Ava looking up at me with a wounded expression on her face.

"You're going somewhere on the Fourth of July?" she asks
sadly.

It takes me a minute to register what she's saying. Then I shake
my head.

"Just to a barbecue," I say. "At my best friend's house. In Brooklyn." When Ava continues to look stricken, I add, "Ava . . . you can
come, if you want to. But . . . won't you have other plans? I mean,
the Fourth of July isn't for another week. You'll probably have gotten a better invitation by then." And, please God, you won't still be
staying at my place.

"I don't know," Ava says. "Maybe. Chaz is going to be there?"

"Yes," I say slowly, wondering what she's getting at.

"I kind of have been wanting to see this guy," Ava says. "You talk
about him so much. Maybe I'll just stop by. Oh, *there he is!*" She
points a French-manicured finger at the screen.

And I have the privilege of gazing, for the first time, at DJ
Tippycat.

He is surprisingly normal looking—a bit on the short side,
slightly balding, and wearing a shirt with the word "Wonderbread"
written on it. In fact, if Shari were here, she'd accuse him of being
a nebbish.

"Wow," I say. "He's . . . that's . . ."

"I know," Ava says with a sigh. "Isn't he *hot?*"

And I realize that there really is no accounting for taste. At least
when it comes to DJs. And, I'm pretty sure, princes.

And philosophy Ph.D. candidates.

A HISTORY
of
WEDDINGS

When, during medieval times, marriages represented not only the joining of two people but of two families, or even two countries, it was necessary for the bride to dress to impress, meaning layering on the bling . . . not just jewels, but the costliest furs and materials that could be found, as she was representing her noble lineage.

So were introduced the first wedding gowns . . . the richer and more powerful the bride's family, the wider the sleeves and the longer the train.

Obviously, those on the lower social rungs attempted to copy the richies until . . . well, *everyone's* wedding gowns were long and flowing.

It wasn't until Queen Victoria chose to wear white to her wedding to Prince Albert that the color became the most popular choice for wedding gowns. Until then it wasn't thought to represent brides or purity—blue was!

But white has stood for brides ever since, and we have the Victorians to thank for it . . . along with the concept of evolution, free public education, and don't forget Jack the Ripper!

Tip to Avoid a
Wedding Day
Disaster

While starlets such as Sarah Jessica Parker might be able
to get away with a black wedding gown, a touch of white
to acknowledge the special nature of the day is generally
appreciated. Wearing all black on your wedding day is
actually considered bad luck. While it hasn't appeared to
affect Sarah (as of this writing), really—why risk it?

LIZZIE NICHOLS DESIGNS™

Chapter 13

There are three things that last: faith, hope and love, and the greatest of these is love.

I Corinthians 13:13

I wake the next morning to the sound of a horrified gasp.

I spring from the couch—ignoring the crick in my neck, brought about by having spent the night on a less than comfortable sleeper sofa that does not, in fact, fold out—and lunge for the window, where Ava is standing.

"What?" I demand, expecting to find a dead body, at the very least. But all I see are a few dozen paparazzi lying in wait below.

Ava points a trembling finger at them. They haven't yet noticed that she's spotted them; they are leaning against parked cars, smoking cigarettes and sipping coffee from Starbucks cups.

"*How,*" Ava demands, in a sleep-roughened voice, "*did they find me?*"

I blink down at the rough-and-tumble cameramen, with their beards and their cargo pants and their multiple lenses.

"How should I know?" I ask. I try not to sound as cranky as I feel. I'm not really a morning person, and feel even less so after my night on the couch. "I didn't tell anyone you were here."

"Well," Ava says. She's scooped up Snow White and is clutching her to one silk pajama–ed breast. "*I* certainly didn't tell anyone I was here."

"Little Joey?" I ask.

Ava shakes her head. "No way. Are you sure you didn't tell anyone?" Ava has begun tearing about the apartment, gathering up her things and stuffing them back into her seven suitcases—as much as she can do so one-handed, since she's still hanging on to her dog. "What about Luke? Could Luke have told anyone? Maybe he's mad at you for breaking up with him."

"We're not broken up," I remind her. "I told you, we're just on a break. Besides, he doesn't even know who you are."

I notice Ava's lower lip jut out a fraction of an inch, but she chooses to ignore this ill-timed reminder that not everyone is addicted to Google Entertainment News.

"Well, what about your friend Shari?" she asks. "You told her not to tell anyone I was here, didn't you?"

"Of course I did," I said. "She'd never say a word. What about your limo driver? Would he have told anyone?"

"Absolutely not. They all sign a confidentiality agreement with the company they work for. He'd never breathe a word, not if he didn't want to lose his job." Ava pauses as she's jabbing numbers into her cell phone. "What about your grandmother?"

I immediately begin chewing my lower lip. Gran. I'd forgotten to tell Gran not to tell anyone that Ava Geck was staying in my apartment. But surely she wouldn't—

"Yeah," Ava says, looking away from me. "That's what I figured." Someone picks up on the other end of the line she's dialing. "Joey?"

she barks into the phone. "Code one. We're compromised. Come *now*."

"But she wouldn't have told anyone," I insist, trailing after Ava as she heads into the bathroom. "I mean, Gran didn't even know for sure it was you. And she wouldn't have known who to call. She doesn't exactly have TMZ or whoever on speed dial!"

"Yeah," Ava says, looking tight-faced. "Well, she sure seems to have caught on fast, hasn't she?"

It's all I can do not to burst out with, *You're the one who picked up the phone! You're the one who taught her how to program the season pass on her TiVo!*

It's not Ava's fault, though, I know. It's mine. Me and my big mouth. As usual.

"Ava," I say. "I'm so sorry. I'm really just so, so sorry."

"Whatever," Ava says, with a shrug of her slim shoulders. I notice she can't seem to make eye contact with me. "I'm going to take a shower. When Joey gets here, will you buzz him up? He'll buzz three times quick in a row, then twice, real slow, so you'll know it's him. Okay?"

I nod. I feel terrible. "Ava—"

"Just let him in," Ava says. "Okay?"

I nod again, then back out of the bathroom so she can close the door. A second later, I hear the water turn on.

I can't believe this. What a disaster! The integrity of Chez Henri has been totally compromised. Not to mention my own personal integrity. Not that I had much of it to begin with.

Still, I can't believe Gran of all people had been the one who'd called the paps on Ava. She wouldn't even have known how to do it. It's not as if it matters—the damage is done, obviously—but I have to know. I have to know if it's really my fault. I pick up the phone and call my parents' house. Gran picks up on the first ring.

"What?" she demands.

"Gran," I say. I keep my voice low, in case Ava hasn't gotten into the shower yet and is eavesdropping, as she is all too wont to do.

"Who is this?" Gran demands. "Lizzie? No one's here. Your dad's at work, and your mom's at the Y. Your sisters are all God knows where—"

"That's okay, it's you I want to talk to, anyway," I say. "Did you say anything to anyone about Ava Geck staying at my place?"

"Well, good morning to you too," Gran says. "Did you shtup him yet?"

"Gran," I whisper. "I'm serious. Did you tell anyone about Ava?"

"Of course not," Gran says, sounding annoyed. "Who would I tell? No one talks to me except you. I'm just crazy old Gran, too drunk for anyone to take seriously—"

I feel myself begin to relax. It hadn't been my fault after all. For once in my life, it hadn't been me—

"Although," Gran says, in a different tone, "your sister Rose was skulking around last night while I was talking to you."

I feel my blood run cold. If it had been Sarah, I wouldn't be worried. But Rose is a different story.

"Do you think she heard you?" I ask.

"I *know* she heard me," Gran says. "She asked a lot of questions after I hung up, like why I was asking about Ava Geck, and what Ava Geck was doing at your place. I just told her what I knew—"

I let out the worst curse word I know. Gran, being Gran, is unimpressed.

"Well," she says. "You can't exactly blame her. It's not like she doesn't need the money, the way she's maxed out her credit cards on clothes over at the discount places . . . especially that T.J. Maxx. Plus that no-good bohunk of a husband of hers got laid off again, and he's not exactly impartial to the jewelry counter over at JCPenney. You should see how many gold neck chains I saw him wearing at the pool the other day."

I close my eyes, trying to summon the strength I need not to burst into tears on the spot. I'm sure Rose is swimming in debt.

That doesn't mean I don't want to hop on a plane to Ann Arbor and strangle her.

"If you see Rose today, Gran," I say, "can you give her a swift kick in the pants for me?"

"Don't worry," Gran assures me, relishing, as usual, being in the middle of a cat fight between me and one of my sisters. "I'll remind her of how fat her arms looked in that slutty dress she wore for her senior prom. That always makes her cry. Like goddamned Niagara Falls."

"Thanks," I say, and hang up feeling only slightly better. Really, could things get any worse?

And yet they do when, a half hour later, Ava emerges from my bathroom looking perfectly coiffed in a purple animal-print cat-suit with bright orange stilettos, and finds Little Joey and me waiting for her on the couch.

"Ready?" she asks him, not even glancing at me.

"Ava," I say, leaping up. "I'm sorry. It was me. I mean, I told my grandma. But it wasn't her fault. My sister—"

"It's okay," Ava cuts me off. But I can tell from her pinched expression it's not. It's not okay. It's far from okay. "We're going now. Right, Joey?"

Joey heaves his three-hundred-pound girth up from the sofa. "You got it, Miss Geck. I already took down the suitcases."

"Ava," I say, trying again.

"It's *okay*, Lizzie," Ava insists.

But I know it isn't. Nothing is okay.

Nothing is ever going to be okay—at least between me and Ava—again.

I watch them leave through the living room windows. The paparazzi throw down their cigarettes and coffee cups—I'm going to have to sweep them all up before the shop opens—and surges forward to virtually attack Ava the minute she walks through the front door of my building. Little Joey shields her the best that he can, using his elbows and sizable belly to forge a path for her to the waiting limo. Ava climbs inside, Little Joey follows, and they speed off, the photographers in hot pursuit.

And then my street is quiet again. If it weren't for all the litter on the sidewalk—and the wad of blond hair in my drain—it would almost seem as if they hadn't been there at all.

But I know I've just messed up an important client relationship. Worse, I've messed up a budding friendship.

And honestly, I have no one to blame for it but myself. Just like all the other messes in my life at the moment. Great.

Just great.

• • •

I had never been up to Shari and Pat's roof before, but it turns out they've built a little garden oasis there. On a redwood deck, surrounded by overflowing flower boxes bursting with geraniums and delphiniums, you can stand and look out at the skyline of Manhattan, rising in all its glory out of the East River. It's an amazing view. And it's all theirs.

Well, along with all the other tenants in their building. And all the other neighboring rooftops along their street. All of whom are having Fourth of July parties at the same time as theirs.

But they aren't about to let all the dueling stereo speakers bring them down. Shari, at least, has a lot of other issues to worry about.

"I can't believe he brought her," Shari keeps saying, casting dark looks in Chaz's direction.

"I told you he would." I'm downing ice cream like there's nothing else being served, which isn't true, because there are also burgers, hot dogs, chips, about ten different kinds of pasta salad, and, of course, the two pies Chaz brought.

But somehow, the only thing that is making me feel better is ice cream. It's been a long week. A loooooooong week.

And the sight of Chaz sitting over there with Valencia—who is looking cool and serene, in spite of the ninety-degree heat, in white linen gauchos and a black tank top that shows off her perfectly toned arms—isn't doing much to make me feel better.

"So, is that the girl?" I ask between gulps of rocky road.

"What are you talking about?" Shari wants to know.

"The girl you're trying to fix Chaz up with. Is that her?" I point to a pretty girl who has joined Chaz and Valencia over by the beer cooler they're both sitting beside.

"Yeah," Shari says, looking annoyed. "See how cute they look together? They'd be a perfect couple—if he hadn't brought that ice bitch with him. And what's Tiffany doing over there with them? She's totally monopolizing the conversation, it looks like."

I take an enormous bite of my ice cream. "I don't know," I say, my mouth too full to say more. Fortunately.

I don't mention that Tiffany, in the car service her fiancé, Raoul, insisted we share on the way over, had sworn to me that she was going to keep Chaz from making a love connection with "that ho from Shari's office, because he's totally right for you. And, furthermore, I am going to split him and that orange-name lady up too."

I didn't bother reminding her for the millionth time that it doesn't matter to me who Chaz dates because I'm actually engaged to someone else, because she'd just have brought up, as she usually does, that I'm "on a break," and people who are happily engaged don't tend to ask for one of those.

"Hey, so what's up with Ava Geck?" Shari asks, distracting me from my gloomy thoughts. "Is she still mad at you for outing her to the press?"

I wince. The fallout from the Ava situation turned out to be worse than even I could have imagined. The Henris had not been too happy to see the front of their shop in photos plastered all over the press the morning after it was announced Ava Geck's high-profile royal wedding had been canceled. I'd tried to convince them there was no such thing as bad press, but they hadn't really gone for it. They couldn't understand what Ava was doing spending the night in my apartment in the first place. Like Luke, they didn't think an employee inviting a client to stay with her was particularly professional.

In retrospect, maybe they were right. But then, Ava had pretty much invited herself.

"Yeah," I say. "She's not speaking to me. Which I can understand."

"Well, she's the only person I know who *doesn't* want to be a member of Lizzie Nichols's entourage these days." Shari points at the small cluster of people gathered around Chaz's pies—he'd brought both a strawberry rhubarb *and* a blueberry—running their fingers around the empty tins and then licking them, and then running them around the rims again. Tiffany's fiancé, Raoul, and Monique and *her* fiancé, Latrell, have already handed out the bottles of champagne and boxes of sparklers they brought along with them, to contribute to the festive party mood. And to make up for the fact that they hadn't exactly been invited.

"Okay," I say sheepishly. "I realize four people is a lot. But they all *really* wanted to come." I don't mention that Shari's fantastic view of the fireworks—and the fact that the Fourth of July happened to fall on a Wednesday this year, making it hard to go out of town—had something to do with it.

"I'm not complaining," Shari says. "It's just that if you get any more popular, I may have to move to someplace bigger in order to accommodate all your fans every time I have you over."

"I'm not *popular*," I say, abashed. "I'm just . . ."

"Admit it," Shari says with a smile. "They're the misfit toys, and you're the island. How are things going with Luke, anyway?"

I shrug. "Fine," I say, speaking around the red plastic spoon hanging from my mouth. "I mean, as well as can be expected, seeing as how he's in Paris and I'm here and we're on a break."

Shari points at the ring finger of my left hand. "You're still wearing it."

"Well," I say, neurotically shoveling more ice cream into my face, "we're still engaged. He's acting like everything is fine."

"Ooooh!" shrieks Tiffany suddenly, jumping to her four-inch stilettos and pointing into the twilit sky. "They're starting!"

We hear a muffled boom, and the next thing I know, a huge carnation of light is exploding in the sky.

"Zee One Hundred," Shari screams. "Switch it to Zee One Hundred! We're missing the musical accompaniment!" She dives for the radio while two dozen people look at her as if she's lost her mind.

A second later, Tiffany sidles up to me and says, "Okay, so here's the L.D."

I screw up my face at her in confusion. "The what?"

"The L.D.," she says. "The *lowdown*?" When I nod, she goes on, "Don't look at me. Look at the fireworks. *Pretend we're talking about the fireworks.* Her name is Mae Lin, and she's got some kinda like master's degree in like social work or something. She lives in Alphabet City and she loves the Buckeyes—that's a basketball team—and collects vintage Fiesta Dinnerware. You are so fucking dead."

I look at Tiffany. "Tiff," I say as the fireworks boom along the skyline behind me, "I told you. I don't care. I don't like Chaz that way."

"Yeah, right," Tiffany says with a hoarse laugh and takes a swig of her champagne. "*Whatever!* If he were the marrying kind, you would so have screwed him already. Just admit it."

Z100 is blasting "Born to Run." Shari's girlfriend, Pat, is saying, "No. Just . . . no. Are you kidding me with this?" While Shari says, "Honey, it's the Boss. What are you gonna do?"

"Here's what you do," Tiffany says, taking my empty ice cream bowl from me and setting it on a nearby picnic table. "Go over there—both Mae Lin and Valencia are gone now, it's okay, they went downstairs to dry off. I 'accidentally' spilled my bottle of champagne on them—and tell him his pies were good."

"Tiff." She's pushing me toward Chaz. I lock my knees, refusing to budge. "No. I'm engaged. And he doesn't . . . what you just said. About marriage. Remember?"

"God!" Tiffany gives me another shove. "Why are you being so fucking stubborn? You can *change* him! I know all your *other* girl-friends are always telling you men can't change, and in general it's true. But not in this case. With you. And him. *Believe me. I know.* Come on, Lizzie. You're always helping other people. Why won't you let *us* help *you* for once?"

"Because you aren't helping me," I say from between gritted teeth. I have to raise my voice a little, because the boom of the fireworks—and the swell of Z100, playing from so many rooftops—is so loud. I notice two leather-braceleted men looking over at us in amusement.

I turn my back to them. "I told you, Tiffany, I love Luke. *Luke,* not Chaz."

I almost completely believe this as I say it too. To the point that I even manage to convince myself that I have not spent the whole of the party trying not to look over to where Chaz is sitting and wondering how he's managed to get such a dark tan so early in the summer, or why he insists on wearing khaki shorts. They're so undignified for the urban male.

Although with muscular legs like his, he can, of course, get away with it . . .

"I don't think you do," Tiffany insists. "And I'm sorry, but I don't think Luke loves you, either. He wouldn't have gone to France—or agreed to your stupid fucking break idea—if he did. I think you two are both just afraid to admit it's been over between you for a long time already. You had a summer fling that's gone on way, way too long. Believe me, Lizzie, I know what real love is, and I see it standing over there by that fuckin' beer cooler in a baseball cap. Now go . . . over . . . there . . ."

Tiffany shoves me with a strength surprising in so thin a person—well, she *does* work out—and I find myself stumbling in my lace-up platform espadrilles . . . only to end up stumbling practically *into* the beer cooler. I'd have fallen inside it if Chaz hadn't reached out and grabbed my arm.

"Hey," he says, looking concerned. "You okay?"

"Yeah," I say, turning beet red. "I'm fine. Tiffany wants me to tell you that, um. She liked your pies."

Chaz stares down at me, his dark eyebrows raised.

"Oh," he says. "Well, that's nice."

"Yeah," I say, trying to regain my composure. "I did too. Good . . . pie. Both of them."

Am I? I ask myself. Am I *really* the stupidest human being on the face of the planet? Or does it just feel that way sometimes?

"Great," Chaz says. "So. How's the break going?"

"The break?" I echo lamely.

"Yeah," Chaz says. "The break you and Luke are on."

"Oh, the *break*!" Behind Chaz's head, fireworks are exploding into amazing shapes, like apples and kissing lips. And he's not even looking. His gaze is riveted to my face. Which I hope he can't tell is still burning as brightly as the lights of the skyline behind him. "Um, fine. I guess. Luke really seems to like it over there. It's a lot of work. But then he knew it would be."

"Well," Chaz says, picking up his beer and taking a sip of it, "he's always had a thing for numbers."

"Yeah," I say. "Well, he's just doing this as a favor for his uncle."

"Yeah," Chaz says. "Right."

I glance up at him sharply. "What do you mean by that?" I snap.

"What do you mean, what do I mean?" he asks defensively. "I don't mean anything. I just said you were right."

"You sounded like you were being sarcastic," I say.

"Well, I wasn't being sarcastic," he says.

"You think he was desperate for any excuse he could get," I say, clarity breaking over me suddenly like a crystal ocean wave, "to leave town and get away from me. Because I'm smothering him."

Oh my God. It's happening again. My mouth, I mean. Running away without me. What am I even talking about? I mean, I know, of course . . . it's what I stay up nights—when I should have fallen asleep hours before, exhausted from adjusting seams all day with Sylvia and Marisol—worrying about.

But why am I mentioning it to *Chaz*, of all people?

Chaz seems to be wondering the same thing.

"How much wine have you had?" Chaz asks, laughing with disbelief.

"None," I say. Amazingly, it's the truth. Also, I'm wishing I'd shut up. But my mouth keeps on moving without me, as usual. "And you're wrong. I don't smother him at all. If anything, I don't pay *enough* attention to him. And besides, that would completely fly in the face of what you said that day."

"What day?" Chaz asks, looking more confused than ever.

"The day I told you he proposed. You said he was proposing only because he's so scared of being alone, he'd rather be with a girl he knows isn't right for him than be by himself."

Shut. Up. Lizzie.

Chaz blinks at me. "Well . . . I still think that's true."

"But you can't have it both ways." In the distance, the fireworks are still going off, in much quicker succession than before. *Boom. Boom. Boom.* Each blast seems to be timed to go off with my heart-beat rather than the Bon Jovi song that's now blasting from the radio around us. I'm standing so close to Chaz that I can see his chest rising and falling in the same rhythm through the front of his short-sleeved polo. It's hard not to put my hands on his chest to see if his heart is beating in time to mine as well.

God, what is *wrong* with me?

"Either I'm smothering him or he's scared to be without me," I blurt out instead. "Which is it?"

"You are completely insane right now," Chaz says to me, still laughing a little. "You know that, don't you?"

The truth is, I do know that. But knowing it doesn't help.

"You're his best friend," I point out. "You've known him longer than I have. And you seem to have so many opinions on our rela-tionship. Or at least you used to. I realize we haven't talked about it in a while because you've been so busy with *Valencia*, but I assume you must have some new theories on the matter. Go ahead. Let's hear them."

"Not now," Chaz says, looking down at me with a grin I can only call suggestive. "Too many people around. Why don't you come back to my place after this? I'll be happy to tell you every theory I know. And illustrate them, as well."

The grin has caused my breath to catch in my throat. Not that I'm about to let him know that.

"Oh, you'd like that, wouldn't you?" I demand. I'm standing so close to him now that our faces are just inches apart. "Is that the only way you can relate to women? As sexual objects?"

"As you know perfectly well," Chaz says, looking mockly offended, "no. What is the *matter* with you tonight? Is this about Valencia? Are you jealous or something? I don't think I should have to remind you that you're the one who's engaged."

"Right. To your *best friend.*"

"Hey, he's *your* fiancé. As you seem to feel the need to keep reminding yourself."

"At least I *have* a fiancé," I say. "At least I'm not an emotional cripple who is afraid to commit myself to someone just because the girl I liked turned out to like girls."

"Oh yeah?" Chaz's blue eyes flash more brightly than any of the fireworks that have exploded in the night sky so far. "Well, at least I didn't get myself engaged to the first guy who asked me to marry him just because I'm in the wedding gown business and I couldn't stand seeing all my clients getting pretty diamond rings on their fingers and not have one for myself."

I suck in my breath, outraged—just as my cell phone vibrates in the pocket of my gingham sundress. I have to keep the stupid thing on all the time these days because of bridal gown emergencies. Although I have no weddings scheduled for today.

"That," I snap at Chaz, "is so untrue. I happen to love Luke. And I want to spend the rest of my life with him."

"Yeah," Chaz sneers. "Keep telling yourself that. Maybe someday you'll even start to believe it."

I slide the phone out, thinking maybe Luke is calling—although it's close to two in the morning in France—then see that it's my mom.

"And I suppose," I say to Chaz, "you think you're so much better for me than he is."

"I'll tell you one thing," Chaz says. "I wouldn't be stupid enough to go off to *France* for the summer and leave a girl like you on your own with guys like me around."

Flustered by this, I fumble with the phone, nearly hanging up on my own mother in my attempt to answer her call.

"Mom?" In the background, the fireworks are reaching their crescendo. It's the show's grand finale. "I can't talk right now. I have to call you back—"

"Oh, Lizzie, honey," my mom interrupts. "I'm so sorry to bother you. I know you're at Shari's party"—we'd talked earlier in the week, and I'd mentioned that I'd be attending a party at Shari's today—"and I don't want to spoil it for you. But I wanted to tell you before you heard it from anybody else: Gran died."

The fireworks are so loud, I don't think I've heard her correctly. I put one finger in my ear and yell, "WHAT?"

"Honey, GRAN DIED TODAY. Can you hear me? I just wanted to make sure you didn't hear it on your machine or from the Dennises or anything like that. Honey? Are you there?"

I murmur something. I don't know what.

I think I'm in shock.

What had she said?

"Lizzie?" Chaz is looking down at me with a funny expression on his face. "What is it?"

"Can you hear me now?" Mom is asking in my ear. The ear I can hear out of. When I say yes, she says, "Oh good. Anyway, it was very peaceful. She went in her sleep. I just found her there this afternoon, in her chair. She must have dozed off watching *Dr. Quinn.* You know she figured out how to TiVo it. She had a beer in one hand, I don't know how she got hold of it. Well, we had a Fourth of July barbecue, she must have sneaked one . . . Anyway, I just wanted to let you know, we're planning a memorial service for this weekend. I know how busy you are, but I hope you'll be able to come. You know how fond she was of you. It wasn't right that she played favorites with you girls, but you really were always the one she liked best out of all the grandkids—"

The world seems to have tilted. Suddenly, I can't stand up anymore. I feel my knees give out . . . but it's all right, because Chaz has his arm around me and is steering me toward the beer cooler, the lid of which he's snapped closed. He sits me down on it, then sinks down beside me, one arm around my shoulders, going, "It's okay. Take it easy. I've got you. Just breathe."

"Gran's dead," I say to him. I can't see him very well.

Then I realize it's because I'm looking at him through a veil of tears. I'm crying.

"I'm sorry," he says. "Lizzie, I'm so sorry."

"She was watching *Dr. Quinn*," I tell him. I don't know why. It's all I can think about. "And drinking beer."

"Well," he says. "If you're Gran, and you have to go, that's the way to do it."

I let out a hiccupy sound, halfway between a sob and a laugh.

"Lizzie?" Mom's voice sounds in my ear. "Who's that with you?"

"Ch-Chaz," I say with another sob.

"Oh, honey," Mom said. "Are you crying? I didn't think you'd be so upset. Gran was ninety, you know. It wasn't as if this was entirely unexpected."

"It was by *me*," I wail. I realize dimly that the booming of the fireworks has ceased, and that it's grown very quiet all of a sudden. I realize, as well, that the pale blobs I can see through my tears are faces . . . the faces of everyone at Shari's party. And that they're all turned toward me. I fight to regain my composure, reaching up and trying to wipe away my tears with the back of my wrist.

But they won't stop. They just seem to come faster.

Chaz, seeming to realize the problem, pulls me into a hug. And suddenly I'm weeping against his chest.

"Oh," Mom says comfortingly into my ear. I'm clutching my cell phone tightly in one hand, and the front of Chaz's shirt with the other. "Good. I'm glad Chaz is there. He's a good, old friend and will take care of you." I don't mention that my "good, old friend" not five minutes ago was making lewd suggestions about "theories" he was going to illustrate to me back in his apartment.

"Yeah" is all I can manage to choke out.

Because the truth is, until she'd called, I had pretty much been going to accept his invitation.

"Mom," I choke. "I'm gonna go now."

"Okay, honey," Mom says. "I love you."

And then she's hung up, and I've hung up, and Chaz is saying, "Shhh," into my hair, and Tiffany has come over and is asking what's wrong, and Shari is stroking my arm and going, "Oh, Lizzie. It's going to be all right."

But it isn't. How can it be?

Gran is gone.

I never even got to say good-bye.

A HISTORY
of
WEDDINGS

Why is the third finger of your left hand considered the ring finger? Ancient Egyptians and Romans both believed that a vein from that finger led directly to the heart, so it seemed like the logical position for the placement of the wedding band. Science has since proved this not to be strictly accurate.

But tradition lives on, and that finger is still universally known as the ring finger. And isn't it romantic to think that our wedding rings are linked to our hearts? Well, by a creepy vein of blood, anyway?

*It may sound obvious, but try on your rings—both bride
and groom—in the days leading up to your wedding. The
last thing you want to be doing during your wedding ceremony is squeezing a ring that won't fit over fingers that
have swollen due to nervous last-minute binge eating.*

LIZZIE NICHOLS DESIGNS™

Chapter 14

You were born together, and together you shall be for ever-
more . . . but let there be spaces in your togetherness. And
let the winds of the heavens dance between you.

Kahlil Gibran (1883–1931), Lebanese-American artist, poet, and writer

Here's another one," my sister Rose says, dropping the casserole plate down on the kitchen table in front of me unceremoniously. "I think it's green bean. Or something green, anyway."

My other sister, Sarah, looks up from the notebook into which she's recording the names of everyone who has brought something over for us to eat, since we are supposedly so consumed with grief over Gran's death that we can't cook. For some of us, this is actually true. The kitchen table is covered with casserole dishes.

"Who's it from?" Sarah wants to know.

"I don't know," Rose says crabbily as she digs through her purse, which she's left on the kitchen counter next to the sliding glass door to the deck. "I found it on the front porch. Check the card, nimrod."

"Suck my dick," Sarah says, snatching the card off the top of the casserole dish.

"Do you kiss your husband with that mouth?" Rose wants to know. Then she lets out a tinkly laugh. "Oh, that's right. He left you. So where's Luke, anyway?" Rose turns her attention to me.

"Don't talk to me," I say to Rose.

Rose looks at Sarah. "What's her glitch?" she wants to know.

"She's not speaking to you," Sarah says. "Because you called TMZ on her client. Remember?"

"Oh, please," Rose says with a laugh. "You're not still mad about that, are you? That should be water under the bridge. Our grandmother is dead. Now, come on. Where's Luke? Your fiancé? Isn't he going to come to your own grandmother's funeral? Or is he too busy with school or whatever? As usual."

"He's in France," I say from between gritted teeth.

"Oh, *France*," Rose says with another laugh. "Sure. Why not. *France*."

"He *is*," I say. Why can't I not speak to people I've resolved never to speak to again? "He's helping his uncle set up a new investment office. Not that it's any of your business. He wanted to come. He's really sorry. But he can't leave right now." And besides. We're on a break. I don't mention this to Rose, who doesn't deserve to know any of my personal business. But it's true.

"Of course," Rose says. "You know, we're all starting to wonder if this Luke guy even exists, or if he's just some guy you've made up to make us think you finally got a boyfriend. As if." Still laughing, Rose opens the sliding glass door and steps out into the cool evening air, not bothering to close it behind her, so all the mosquitoes come buzzing in.

"I hate her too," Sarah informs me matter-of-factly as soon as Rose is out of earshot. "Don't pay any attention to her. You have no idea how lucky you are you got out of here. Seriously."

I am sitting with my arms crossed in front of my chest, holding on to both my elbows. I have been sitting like this since I got home.

I just can't believe she's really gone. Gran, I mean. The thing is . . . I knew she was old. I did.

I just never thought she was *that* old.

"Well, she just died, Lizzie" is what Shari's dad had said when I'd asked him how it had happened when he stopped by to drop off a plate of Mrs. Dennis's Heath Bar Crunch cookies a little while ago. "She was old."

"But—" I'd been going to ask if there was going to be an autopsy. But a warning look from my mother had stopped me. Mom doesn't want people talking about cutting up his mother in front of Dad. Which I guess I can understand.

And okay, Gran *was* ninety, after all. I guess *how* she died isn't any big mystery.

But why *now*? When I need her most? I mean, not to be selfish or anything. But couldn't she have waited a month or two, for a time when I wasn't so . . . confused?

Everyone seemed kind of relieved when Dr. Dennis gave me a little bottle of pills.

"Shari asked me to prescribe you these," Shari's dad said, uncomfortably handing them over. "They're to make you feel better. Now, remember . . . no drinking alcohol while you're on those, Lizzie!"

Everyone laughed like Dr. Dennis had made a great joke. And looked at me expectantly, waiting for me to take one of the pills. Which I pretended to, just to get them off my back.

But if they think doping me up is going to keep me from asking the hard questions—like are they going to play Gran's favorite song, "Highway to Hell," at the funeral, or aren't they?—they can just think again. I'm not going to be dismissed that easily. Gran might have been happy to ride through life in an alcoholic haze— she might even have been good at it—but not me.

Never me.

"Really," Sarah is going on. "You wouldn't believe what a bitch Rose has turned into. Well, not turned into, because she was always a bitch. But she's gotten worse with age. You think that thing with her calling the paparazzi on your friend is bad? Just wait. Maybe it's perimenopause. I saw something about it on *Oprah.* So Chuck and I are having some problems? He didn't *leave* me. He's just taking some time to work through a few things. Like Rose and Angelo have it so perfect. He doesn't even have a job. She's still supporting both of them."

"Huh," I say. I still can't believe my own sister thinks my fiancé is made up. Like I would even go to the trouble. For *her.*

And, okay, so Luke didn't even *offer* to fly back and meet me here for the funeral. But I'm the one who asked for the break. Maybe he thinks he wouldn't be welcome. That's a natural assumption, right? It's my fault, really. The poor guy probably thinks I don't want him anymore.

Besides, he doesn't have any living grandparents. They all died when he was little. He doesn't know what it's like to lose a grandparent as an adult. A grandparent I was as close to as Gran. Luke doesn't have any idea what that's like.

Neither do I, actually. I'm just going through it now for the first time. Without my fiancé's shoulder to lean on.

"And you should see what she's doing to her kids," Sarah goes on. "You have never seen kids so overextended. Ballet, tap, karate, gymnastics, French—*French,* for Christ's sake. They live in Michigan. When are they going to need to speak French? Except maybe at your wedding, if it ever takes place. They never have a minute to themselves, just to be kids. No wonder they're so weird."

At that minute Maggie, Rose's eldest, wanders into the room, holding a reporter's notebook, a pencil poised in one hand.

"Excuse me," she says. "I'm starting my own newspaper. Do you have any news?"

Sarah and I blink at her.

"What?" I say.

"*News,*" Maggie yells. "I'm starting my own newspaper. A kid's newspaper. I need some news to put in it. Do you have any *news*?"

"Your great-grandmother just died, for Christ's sake," Sarah says. "That isn't enough news for you?"

Maggie looks at me. "Aunt Lizzie," she says. "How do you feel about Gran being dead?"

Tears prick my eyes. Trying not to weep openly in front of my niece, I say, "I'm very sad about it. I'm going to miss her very much."

"May I quote you on that?" Maggie wants to know.

"Yes," I say.

"Good. Thank you." Maggie turns around and leaves the room without another word.

"See?" Sarah says as soon as she's gone. "There's something wrong with that kid."

Rose chooses that moment to reenter the kitchen, reeking of cigarette smoke. She closes the sliding glass door behind her and drops a pack of cigarettes and her lighter back into her purse.

"Something wrong with what kid?" she asks.

"Your kid," Sarah snarls. "Maggie. She just came in here and announced she's starting a newspaper and asked us if we had any news."

"At least," Rose says mildly, peeling the aluminum foil back on a peach cobbler someone has brought over and plunging a spoon into it, "she's not an unimaginative, nose-picking moron like some people's kids I could mention."

Sarah sucks in her breath, but before she can say anything, I ask, "So what did you do with the money, Rose?"

Rose looks up from the cobbler. "Excuse me?"

"The money you got from spilling the fact that Ava Geck was

hiding out in my apartment." I stare at her. "What did you spend it on? It couldn't have been liposuction for your upper arms, because they're looking as enormous as ever."

Rose's shriek of outrage causes Mom's china collection to tinkle. I take that as my cue to get up and leave.

"What's going on back there?" Mom asks me as I drift into the living room, where she and Dad are meeting with Father Jim, who'll be conducting Gran's memorial service.

"Nothing," I say and collapse onto the couch beside her. "Just sister stuff."

Mom gives Father Jim an apologetic smile and says, "I'm so sorry. Go on, Father."

I sit and listen to their conversation, barely able to register what they're saying through the miserable haze into which I've sunk. I can't remember ever feeling quite so horrible. I want to die. I do. Why won't someone just kill me already? How can everyone just go on talking like nothing is wrong when it's the end of the world, already?

"Well," Father Jim says. "I was thinking a mass would be a lovely gesture."

"Oh, a mass," Mom says, looking over at Dad. "Yes, that would be lovely."

Dad looks skeptical. "I don't know," he says. "A mass. That'll make it an hour longer." I wonder if Father Jim caught the fact that my mom kicked my father under the coffee table. "Ow. What I mean is, my mother wasn't a particularly religious woman."

Even through my misery, I'm able to register the fact that Gran wasn't religious. She'd want a Byron Sully tribute at her memorial, not a tribute to God. Because to her, Byron Sully *was* God. I feel myself perking up. Just a little. Because I'm starting to feel something besides sadness. And that's anger.

"That just makes it all the more important," Father Jim goes on, "to have a mass. Your mother's attendance at our church was, especially in her later years, sketchy at best. But I know, had she been in full possession of her faculties at the end, this is what she'd have wanted."

She *was* in full possession of her faculties, I want to shout. Fuller possession of her faculties than any of you.

"Now," Father Jim continues. "About the musical selections—"

"Her favorite song was 'Highway to Hell,'" I surprise myself by saying.

My mom glares at me. Dad bursts out laughing, but stops when my mother transfers her glare to him.

"Er," Father Jim says. "Yes. Well, be that as it may, I find a more traditional selection tends to please parishioners—"

"But it's her favorite song," I interrupt. I don't blame my mother for glaring. She's right. Why am I interfering? At the same time, though— "Surely you'd want to play someone's favorite song at her *funeral*."

"Well, maybe not *that* song," Mom says, looking flustered. "It's about . . . well, going to *hell*, Lizzie."

"Maybe we could find an instrumental version," Dad says thoughtfully.

Mom gives me a "see what you started" look. Then she says, "Lizzie, Mrs. Brand said she'd be stopping by with a Brunswick stew. Could you wait on the porch for her? She twisted her ankle recently and I don't want her trying to get out of the car while holding a large pot. It would be lovely if you could meet her in the driveway and take the stew from her directly."

I stare at my mother as if she's lost her mind. When it becomes clear from the unblinking way in which she stares back, however, that she's not kidding, I sigh and get up from the couch. I'm almost all the way out of the house when I overhear her say, sotto voce, to Father Jim, "Lizzie and her grandmother were very close. I'm not sure having her here while we plan the service is really the best idea. Lizzie's always been the most . . . well, *emotional* of my children."

Tears fill my eyes. I stagger out onto the night-darkened porch—no one has thought to flick on the light—and sink down onto the steps, burying my head in my knees. *Emotional?*

Well, I guess that's me. Is it *emotional* to be sad that my grandmother is dead? Is it *emotional* to wish that the person who was conducting her funeral was someone who actually knew her, who could maybe say a few words about her that might actually *mean* something?

Is it *emotional* to feel as if I'm a stranger in my own family, as if these people I've known my whole life don't actually know me—or care about me—at all? Gran was the only one—the *only one* of them—who ever said anything to me that was actually worth a damn.

Not that I ever told her that.

And now she's gone. And I'll never have the chance. Never have the chance to talk to her again.

No wonder I'm so *emotional.*

God. Maybe I should take one of those pills Dr. Dennis prescribed after all. I can feel them, rattling around in their bottle in the pocket of my jeans. Will they make me feel less *emotional?* Will they stop me from feeling anything at all? Because right now that's what I'd really, really like.

Headlights flash, and I raise my head. Mrs. Brand and her Brunswick stew. I swipe at my cheeks with my wrists. I don't want Mrs. Brand—whoever she is—to see me looking like such an unholy mess.

But the car doesn't turn into the driveway. It pulls over and parks down the street. It's so warm and humid outside, a sort of mist has settled over the street, making it look as if a fog has rolled in. I stare at the red taillights through the fog, breathing in the summer air, so familiar and yet so strange after so many months in the city. The smell of fresh-cut grass, the whine of cicadas, the chirp of crickets . . . these are summer scents and sounds that are almost foreign to me now, I haven't experienced them in so long.

Someone gets out of the parked car. Even though it's pretty dark out, and the mist is pretty thick, I can see it's not a woman. It's a man, tall and broad-shouldered. I look away, through the fog, into the dark sea of our yard—the yard where Rose and Sarah forced me to hose off Mom and Dad's bedspread that time Gran was babysitting us and ended up vomiting cooking sherry all over it.

Yeah, that hadn't been much fun.

But before that—before the vomiting—Gran had told me the story about working in the munitions factory during World War II, while Gramps had been off fighting the Nazis in France (every single man in his platoon had died when they'd found a bottle of wine in an abandoned farmhouse in Marseille and drank from it, not knowing it had been poisoned by Nazi sympathizers. Gramps, being a teetotaler, was the only one to survive), and how she and the other girls had painted black lines on the backs of their legs to make it look like they were wearing stockings with seams when they went out on Saturday nights, because all the silk had been used up for parachutes.

That's the kind of thing we should be talking about at her funeral. The happy times. The incredible sacrifices her generation made—without complaint. Not some stupid biblical passages that have nothing to do with Gran and never did.

I notice through the fog that the man is walking toward our house. I also notice he's the same shape and size as . . . my fiancé.

My heart seems to freeze inside my chest.

But what would Luke be doing here? I mean, it's true my grandmother—the family member I cared about most in the world although I might not have realized it until it was too late—is dead. And it's true I'm really disappointed in him because he's made no effort during the course of our relationship so far to meet anyone in my family.

But he's in France. He wouldn't have flown all the way to Ann Arbor just for the funeral. *We're on a break.*

And then, as the mist swirls and tumbles around the man's legs as he turns into our driveway, I see something that causes my heart, which a moment ago was frozen, to explode into what feels like a million tiny pieces of flame—like fireworks, only inside my chest, instead of up in the night sky: *he's wearing a baseball cap.*

A second later, I'm on my feet and I'm running. I'm running toward him through the fog, and a second later, I skid to a halt in front of him. He stops too.

So, it seems, does time. All I can hear, in those few heartbeats, is the sound of the cicadas. And our breathing.

"What are you doing here?" I demand. My voice sounds gravelly for some reason.

"What do you think I'm doing here?" Chaz shoots back. His voice sounds gravelly too. "I came to see how you're doing."

I scan the street behind him. I see no one else in the mist.

"Where's Valencia?" I ask him.

"Fuck Valencia," he says.

"I'd assumed you already took care of that," I say.

"You know what?" Chaz says, starting to turn back toward the car. "I can leave, if that's what you want."

My heart gives a twist, and I take a quick step forward, laying my hand on his arm.

"Don't go," I say. "I'm sorry. I just . . ." A sob catches my throat. "Oh, Chaz. Everything is so screwed up."

"I know," he says. I can't see his eyes because they are hidden in the shadow of the brim of his baseball cap.

"No," I say, my own eyes swimming in tears. "I mean, it's not just—it's not just Gran. It's a lot more than that."

And then, just like that, it happens. My mouth takes over from my brain, and the words just come spilling out before I can stop them.

"It just sucks," I hear myself saying in that same strange, gravelly voice, "because . . . because I think I'm in love with my fiancé's best friend."

"So?" Chaz says without skipping a beat and sounding completely unsurprised. "I've got it worse. I'm in love with my best friend's fiancée."

For a moment there's no sound at all. Neither of us seem to be breathing, and even the cicadas have fallen silent.

I'm not sure I heard him right. His best friend's fiancée? But that . . . that's *me*! Chaz means he's in love with *me*!

That's what he's doing here at my parents' house on this foggy summer night. That's why he's standing here in front of me with his arms at his sides, palms open, nothing to hide, no more sarcasm, no more biting remarks, no more Luke, no more Valencia, no more nothing. Just us.

All it took was a few thousand miles of separation, the stripping away of all but the rawest of emotions, and the death of one of the people I love most in the world.

Then, as if by some unseen cue, we both take a step forward until our chests collide, and he says, "Oof," and then, "Lizzie—" and I throw my arms around his neck and drag his head down so that I can press my lips to his.

And then neither of us says anything for quite some time.

A HISTORY
of
WEDDINGS

he first bridal registry was established by the department store Marshall Field's in Chicago in 1924. It was created in an effort to help couples keep a list of wedding gifts they desired for their households and soon caught on in shops worldwide.

The first electronic or online registry was introduced by Target in 1993.

When the first jealous ex logged on to mock the bride's choice of flatware in front of all her coworkers was not recorded.

No one ever wants to think that a wedding could be canceled. But these things happen. That's why proper wedding etiquette calls for wedding and shower gifts never, ever to be used before the wedding actually occurs. That way, if the wedding does not actually take place, these things can be easily returned to the giver, as is the appropriate action in such a case.

LIZZIE NICHOLS DESIGNS™

Chapter 15

Come live with me and be my love,
And we will some new pleasures prove
Of golden sands and crystal brooks,
With silken lines and silver hooks.

John Donne (1572–1631), English poet

This is so wrong," I say as I sprawl naked across Chaz's equally naked chest.

"Is that why it feels so right?" he wants to know.

"If there's a hell," I say, "we're going straight to it."

"At least we'll be together," he says. "And I'm pretty sure Elvis will be there. And Einstein. He was an adulterer too, right?"

I groan and turn my head only to find that I'm looking at a mural on the wall of a castle on a hill. It's not even a very good mural.

But I don't turn my head again because on the other wall is an even worse mural of a knight riding a white horse. Chaz is staying at the Knight's Inn, which has windows with imitation diamond panes and a turret to make it look like a castle. When I asked him why in God's name he would choose to stay at a Knight's Inn out of all the hotels in Ann Arbor, he'd said, "Lizzie. I've got a *turret* in my room. How can you even ask me that question?"

"And Shakespeare," Chaz says now. "He was an adulterer. So at least hell won't be boring."

"I'm not an adulterer," I say. "I'm not married. I'm just engaged. And we're on a break."

"Did you specify the parameters of the break?" Chaz asks. "Did it include rampant monkey sex with your fiancé's best friend?"

"Stop it," I say. "You took advantage of me when I was in a weakened emotional state."

"Me?" Chaz starts to laugh, his stomach muscles causing my head to bob up and down. "You assaulted me in your parents' driveway. I was just coming by to pay my respects, and the next thing I knew, your tongue was in my mouth, and your hand was down my pants. I was so scared, I almost called nine-one-one to report a sexual predator on the loose."

"Seriously," I say. "What are we going to do now?"

"I can think of a few things," Chaz says, lifting the sheet that's covering us and looking under it.

"We can't let animal lust get in the way of our friendship," I say.

"I don't want to be friends with you," Chaz says matter-of-factly. "I stopped wanting to be friends way back last New Year's Eve. Remember? You're the one who had to go and ruin everything by getting yourself engaged to someone else. While I was sleeping, I might add."

I roll off him and lie on my back, staring at the ceiling, which is made out of that hideous stuff that has sparkles in it. There's an overhead light that has been crafted to look like an old-fashioned lantern. I wouldn't be surprised to learn that it has a lipstick camera in it that has been videotaping our every move for the past two hours. The Knight's Inn seems like it might be that kind of hotel.

Which makes it the perfect place for my tawdry affair with my best friend's ex-boyfriend and my fiancé's best friend.

"You don't even believe in marriage," I wail miserably to the lipstick camera. If there is one.

"Well, if I did, I certainly wouldn't marry you, that's for sure," Chaz says. "You'd just go around sexually assaulting my best friend behind my back while I'm in France and you're at your grandmother's funeral. You'd make the worst wife ever."

I lean over to hit him, but he rolls over on top of me, pinning my arms down beneath the sheet. A second later, he's staring deeply into my eyes.

"Lizzie," he says, looking serious for a change. "You need to stop beating yourself up about this. You and Luke have been over for a long time. You should never have said yes when he asked you to marry him. I told you that that morning in your apartment. If you had listened to me then, you could have saved everyone a lot of heartache. Especially me. And yourself."

I glare at him. "Do you think I don't know that?" I demand. "But you didn't exactly go out of your way to act like Prince Charming that morning, you know. You could have just told me you loved me then, you know."

"I seem to recall that, number one, you never gave me the chance . . . you were already engaged to someone else by the time I woke up, and that, number two, I did tell you I love you, and you took it as a joke and walked out."

I blink. Then say indignantly, "You mean at the *sports bar*? But you were so nasty! I didn't think you were serious."

He looks hurt. "I bared my soul to you, and you thought it was nasty. Nice."

"Seriously," I say. "You were horrible. You couldn't possibly have expected me to think you meant a word that you said—"

"I was mortally wounded!" Chaz insists. "The woman I loved, and whom I thought loved me in return—don't lie, you even said at Jill Higgins's wedding the night before that we were going to try taking things to another level—had just pledged herself to another!"

"Now you're just being ridiculous," I say. "Agreeing to take things to another level and saying that I'm in love with you are two completely different things."

"*If* I was nasty, like you say, I had a right to be," Chaz says. "You were acting like a crazy woman. Getting yourself engaged to a guy who is so completely wrong for you—"

"You didn't seem to have any objections when Luke and I got together last summer," I point out.

"Sure, I had no objections to your sleeping with him," Chaz says. "I never thought you'd want to *marry* the guy. Especially when I knew perfectly well you weren't in love with him."

Still pinned beneath his body weight and the sheet, I can only glare at him some more. "I beg your pardon," I say. "But I most certainly was."

"*Before* the Great Christmas Sewing Machine Incident, maybe," Chaz says. "But not after. It just took you awhile to admit it to yourself."

I blink at him, trying to figure out if what he's saying is really true. There's a part of me that's sure it isn't.

But there's another part of me that's equally scared it is.

"But you finally came around to admitting you're in love with me now," Chaz says as he reaches for the room service menu. "So what does it matter? Now I need sustenance. All of this cuckolding makes a knight hungry. What should we have? Beef nachos supreme? Or . . . ooh, bacon and cheddar potato skins with sour cream. Such fine fare this establishment offers . . . oh, wait. Cream cheese and turkey pinwheels. Who could resist?"

"I can't tell him," I burst out.

Chaz stares down at me. "About the cream cheese and turkey pinwheels?"

"No," I say, poking him through the sheet. "Get off me, you weigh a ton." Obligingly, Chaz slides off me. "Luke. He can never know."

Chaz leans up on one elbow, his head in his hand. "I can see why," he says, regarding me, his blue eyes expressionless. "Who eats turkey with cream cheese? That's a disgusting combination."

"No," I say, sitting up. "About us. He can never know about *us*."

Chaz's tone doesn't change. "You're going to marry Luke and keep me around as a boy toy? How twenty-first century of you."

"I . . . I don't know what I'm going to do," I say. "How can I . . . I mean, he loves me."

Chaz taps the menu. "Lizzie. Let's just order. We don't have to figure it all out tonight. And they stop serving at eleven."

I chew my lower lip. "I just," I say. "I . . . I'm not very good at this. At being . . . bad."

"Oh, I don't know," Chaz says with a grin. "I think you did an exemplary job of it earlier."

I lift up one of the flat, uncomfortable Knight's Inn pillows and smack him with it. He laughs and tugs it away from me, then wrestles me back down to the mattress.

We barely order our nachos in time to make the eleven o'clock cutoff.

• • •

"Where were *you* last night?" Sarah wants to know when I come tromping into the house the next morning.

"And aren't those the same clothes you were wearing yesterday?" Rose asks cattily.

Their eyes light up a second later, however, when Chaz follows me through the screen door.

"Chaz!" my mom cries, looking genuinely delighted. "What a surprise!"

"I'll say." Rose shoots me a look so laser sharp, it might have melted steel. "When did *you* get into town, Chaz? Don't tell us . . . last night?"

"How sweet of you to come," Mom says, going to give Chaz a hug. Having dated Shari for so long, he's an old family favorite. Well, with my parents. My sisters don't play favorites. Except among their kids.

"Of course I came," Chaz says as my mom releases him and my dad wanders in from the den, his reading glasses perched on top of his head and the newspaper dangling from his fingers. "I was a big fan of Mrs. Nichols."

"Well, my mother was something of a character," Dad says, shaking Chaz's hand. "Good to see you."

Rose and Sarah, meanwhile, are taking in the beard burn that no amount of foundation on my part has so far been able to cover up. Chaz's five o'clock shadow starts growing at approximately ten in the morning, and any kissing after that takes its toll. Conscious of their scandalized yet delighted gazes, I check out the new offerings—a pie from one of the neighbors, a floral arrangement from Gran's dentist—while Chaz accepts Mom's offer of coffee and a piece of the coffee cake the Huffmans brought over.

As soon as they're out of earshot Rose takes two quick steps toward me and hisses, "Sssssslut," in my ear while giving me a quick pinch on the butt as she heads into the kitchen to refill her own coffee mug. I let out a yelp—she always gives the most painful pinches.

Then Sarah moves in to whisper, "I always did think he was cute. You know, not, like, traditionally cute, but tall, at least. A little too hairy for me, though. But isn't he still in school? Does he not have a job? How's he going to support you without a job? Are *you* going to have to support *him*? I'm all for being a feminist, but not *that* feminist. Look what happened to Rose."

My eyes are still filled with tears from Rose's pinch. I have to sit down because I can't see to navigate the living room furniture, which my mother has rearranged to make space for all the floral arrangements that have been arriving. The next thing I know, a sheet of paper is thrust into my hands.

"Here," a child's voice says.

"What's this?" I ask.

"It's my newspaper." When my vision clears a little, I see that my niece Maggie is standing in front of me. "That will be one dime, please."

I reach into my pocket, find some change, and give Maggie a dime. She walks away without saying thank you.

I look down at the sheet of paper. It is printed in sixteen-point type and arranged to look like the front page of an actual newspaper. She's clearly had someone's help with it, since, being in the first grade, she'd only just learned to read and write. The headline, which is in twenty-six point, screams, "*GRANDMA NICHOLS DIES!!!!*"

Below that, the article goes on to describe Gran's death in grisly detail, with a line about how Elizabeth Nichols is quoted as being "very sad."

"Now, Lizzie," Mom says, coming out of the kitchen with Chaz in tow, holding a steaming mug of coffee and a plate of coffee cake. "I wanted to let you know, we've selected a reading for you to do at the service this afternoon."

"A reading?" I look up from the paper. "What kind of reading?"

"Just a passage from the Bible that Father Jim picked out," Mom goes on as Rose drifts out from the kitchen and takes a seat by the piano. "I'll get you a copy so you can practice. Each of you girls is doing one."

"Gran never read the Bible," I say, "in her life."

"Well, you can't have a funeral without Bible readings," Sarah says.

"And these are very tasteful Bible passages, honey," Mom says. "Don't worry."

"Tasteful Bible passages," Chaz says, putting his plate of coffee cake down on a side table. When Mom looks at him, he grins and raises his mug of coffee toward her in a salute. "Great coffee, Mrs. Nichols!"

Mom smiles. "Why, thank you, Chaz."

I'm too miserable to smile. "Mom," I say. "This funeral . . . it's like it doesn't even have anything to do with Gran. We should be having a celebration of her life. The things in it should represent things she really loved."

"Like what?" Mom asks with a tiny snort. "*Dr. Quinn, Medicine Woman* and beer?"

"Yeah," I say. "Exactly."

"Don't be ridiculous, Lizzie," Rose says. She shoots a look at the kitchen door, through which my dad hasn't reappeared, apparently still being busy getting his own coffee and cake to go with it. She drops her voice to a whisper as she hisses, "Grandma embarrassed us enough while she was alive. Let's not have her embarrass us in death too."

I widen my eyes and swing my head around to look at Chaz, who's choked a little on the mouthful of coffee he's just swallowed.

"So, Chaz," Dad says as he comes into the room, followed by Angelo, Rose's husband, who is wearing a black suit with no tie and a black shirt unbuttoned almost to midchest. "Are you still in school?"

"Yes, sir," Chaz says. "I have about three more years of course work left, then I have to start writing my dissertation, and then I'll have to defend it. I hope after that I'll be able to find a job and start teaching."

"Oh?" Mom makes room on the couch for Dad to sit down beside her. "And where are you hoping to find a position? Back here in the Midwest? I know how you feel about the Wolverines. Or out East?"

"Doesn't matter," Chaz says with a shrug. "Wherever Lizzie is."

Mom pauses with her coffee mug halfway to her lips, looking as if she's not quite sure she's heard Chaz correctly. Rose narrows her gaze and directs it pointedly to the ring on my left hand, while Angelo looks confused. Sarah coughs. Dad just grins affably and says, "Well, that's nice," and shovels the rest of his coffee cake into his mouth.

"I don't get it," Angelo says. "I thought Lizzie was engaged to that Luke guy. Chaz, weren't you goin' out with that lesbo friend of hers?"

"Who's Luke?" Dad wants to know.

"Oh, you remember, dear," Mom says. "We talked to him on the phone. That nice boy Lizzie met in France."

"I'm still engaged to Luke," I say quickly. "Things are just . . . complicated right now."

"Are they ever," Rose says, getting up and grabbing Chaz's and Dad's empty plates. "Too bad Gran's gone. She'd have *loved* this."

And I realize, a little belatedly, that Rose is right. Not only would Gran have loved what's going on between me and Chaz, but she'd have been rooting for it. She was the one who'd urged me not to get engaged. She was the one who always thought Chaz was my boyfriend all along.

And a hunk too, if memory serves.

Gran had been right.

About a lot of things, it turns out.

A HISTORY
of
WEDDINGS

The first wedding rings were worn only by brides, not grooms. That's because the first brides were considered possessions by their husbands and once "ringed" (or captured), they were considered their husbands' property. The ring—though still worn on the third finger of the left hand, the finger with the vein thought to lead to the heart—was a symbol of the husband's ownership. It wasn't until World War II, in fact, that it became popular for men as well as women to wear wedding rings, and not until the Korean War that it became standard.

Why is this? Why, so women could be sure that their menfolk, when away from home, were reminded that they were not available!

When canceling a wedding, it is appropriate, but not mandatory, to send out formal announcements. Informing friends and family verbally that your plans have changed is fine. If, however, you are postponing the wedding, it is necessary to send out a card simply stating the rescheduled date and location of the wedding. If calling all the guests on your list to tell them that your wedding is canceled is too painful for you, have someone else—such as your wedding gown designer—do it for you. That's what we're here for! Well, what our receptionists are here for, anyway.

LIZZIE NICHOLS DESIGNS™

Chapter 16

I have spread my dreams beneath your feet;
Tread softly because you tread on my dreams.

W. B. Yeats (1865–1939), Irish poet and dramatist

Honey, where have you been?" Mom demands as Chaz and I enter the church, late. This was a deliberate ploy on Chaz's part to spare me what he'd declared to be a barbarous practice—the viewing, which had been scheduled for the hour prior to the funeral.

Unfortunately, I discover as Mom grabs my hand, they've kept the casket open just for me.

"Hurry," she says, tugging urgently. "They're about to close it."

"Uh, that's okay," I say. "I'm good."

"No, honey," Mom says. "You, more than anyone, need the closure of seeing Gran at peace."

"No," I say. "I really don't, Mom."

But Mom evidently doesn't believe me, because she rips me from the safety of Chaz's protective embrace and drags me to the side of Gran's coffin, which is at the back of the church, waiting to be wheeled to its place of honor up front. The lid is open, and Gran, looking incredibly small and frail—and completely unlike her normal self—is inside. I stare in horror.

"See?" Mom says in comforting tones, pulling me toward it. "It's all right. They did an incredible job. She looks like she's just sleeping."

Gran does not look like she's sleeping. She looks like a wax dummy. For one thing, whoever did her face put way too much rouge on her. And for another, they've put her in a blue dress with a collar that's too high and lacy—something she'd never have worn in life—and clasped her hands across her chest over a rosary.

A can of Bud would have been entirely more appropriate.

"You can kiss her good-bye if you want," Mom says to me soothingly.

I don't want to insult anyone, but the truth is, I'd sooner kiss DJ Tippycat.

"No," I say. "That's okay."

"*Maggie* kissed her," Mom says, looking a little affronted.

I look around for my niece, expecting to find her huddled in a corner of the church, rocking gently and telling herself everything's going to be all right. But she's over by the doors trying to fill a Snapple bottle with holy water and telling her cousins it's okay, she drinks it all the time.

"Uh," I say to Mom. "I'm good. Really."

I don't care if my six-year-old niece did it before me, and I don't care if it *is* Gran: No way am I kissing a dead body.

"Well," Mom says as the funeral attendant, obviously fuming about having been kept waiting this long, takes this as his cue to lower the lid to the coffin. "I guess it's too late now."

But in a way, I realize, it isn't. Also that Mom's right. And that the half hour Chaz spent driving crazily around town, insisting we not get to the church until he was certain the casket would be closed, had been for nothing.

Because seeing Gran like this—this empty shell of a body, this statue of her former self—has given me a form of closure. It's proven to me that the essence of Gran, what made her . . . well, Gran, is really and truly gone.

And when the funeral attendant snaps the casket closed, I suddenly don't feel sad anymore. At least, not as sad. Because that isn't my grandmother he's shutting up inside that box. I don't know where my grandmother is.

But she isn't there.

And that's a huge relief. Wherever Gran is now, I know she's finally free.

I wish I could say the same for me.

"Let's go," Mom says, taking Dad's arm and pulling him away from the wall of church bulletins, which he's been assiduously studying this whole time (Dad's always been powerless in the face of flyers). "Girls." She snaps her fingers at Rose and Sarah, who are trying to gather their progeny. "It's time."

And like magic, Father Jim appears with a few altar boys holding candles, and then we all fall into our places behind the coffin, which is wheeled to its place of honor before the congregation, almost none of whom I recognize . . . except Shari, whose gaze locks with mine as Chaz leads me down the aisle. She's standing with her parents, and at the sight of her I realize, guiltily, that I really ought to have checked my cell phone, which has been vibrating angrily all day, no doubt with messages from Shari, telling me she's arrived.

Well, I know it now. And she knows I know. And she knows something else too, judging from the expression on her face . . . she knows I've got beard burn from making out—and more—with her ex-boyfriend.

Honestly, I can't think about that right now. I look away from her, my cheeks on fire—and not from beard burn—and slip with Chaz into the front pew with the rest of my family as Father Jim goes up before the altar and the mass begins.

It soon becomes obvious that exactly what I feared was going to happen has happened: This isn't a funeral for my grandmother. It's a funeral for some woman with the same name as my grandmother.

But it could be any woman with that name. Because Father Jim didn't know my grandmother. He didn't know she hated tomatoes and mustard. He didn't know she liked television dramas and AC/DC. He doesn't know anything about Gran. She didn't care about any of the things Father Jim is talking about. She certainly never went to church (except on Christmas Eve, to see her grandchildren and great-grandchildren perform in the nativity, and even then she kept a flask in her purse until Mom found it and confiscated it. And then she begged everyone to buy her beer afterward).

It's not that the service isn't nice. It is. The flowers are beautiful, and the sun slanting through the stained-glass windows in the sanctuary is lovely. Father Jim gives off an air of good-humored sincerity.

It's just that none of this is about Gran. That reading Sarah just stood up and gave from the Gospel according to Luke? Nothing to do with Gran. At all. That nice song the choir just sang? So not something Gran would have liked.

But it won't embarrass Rose. And I guess that should make her happy.

But it doesn't say anything about the person whose life we're allegedly gathered here to celebrate. It's like the wax figure inside the coffin. It's not Gran. Gran, like Elvis, obviously left the building a long time ago.

Which is good for Gran. But it's not the way to memorialize her. It's just not.

But as I look at the faces of my family around me, I can see that they're all pleased with the way things are going. And why shouldn't they be? This is probably the first family event we've ever had that Gran hasn't ruined somehow. She wasn't exactly the easiest person to live with . . . as I know only too well. As fun as she could be—how many times did she show up at my school, saying I was wanted urgently at home, only to take me to the movies in the middle of the day because some big blockbuster was opening that she wanted to see before everyone else did and spoiled the ending for her?—she could also be a huge pain in the butt. I should know . . . I'm the one who cleaned up after her enough.

And I'd already heard Mom and Dad talking about how they were going to turn Gran's bedroom into a playroom for the grand-kids. Which I can completely understand them wanting to do.

Still. It just seems like *somebody* could say *something* personal . . .

A hand settles over both of mine, which I'm clasping tightly together in my lap, and I look up to see Chaz smiling sympathetically at me, as if he's reading my thoughts. He's wearing a suit—the same one he'd been wearing that day outside his apartment building, when my heart had reacted so violently to seeing him. He left the baseball cap back in the hotel room. He'll never be as handsome as Luke—at least, not in the conventional way that the rest of society thinks of as handsome. He doesn't have Luke's long eyelashes, and his eyes aren't dark and sleepy-looking.

But my heart does another loop-de-loop as I look at him.

I'm gone. I know it now. I am in such deep, deep trouble.

And the worst part of it is, except for the trouble I know this is going to cause the people I care about—Shari, and of course, Luke—I don't even mind.

Suddenly Rose is elbowing me, saying, "Your turn," and I realize it's time for me to take my place behind the lectern beside the altar. I slip my hands out from beneath Chaz's and stand up, conscious of his whispered "Go, champ."

Then I'm walking to the lectern, the sheet of paper with the words Father Jim and Mom have picked out for me to read—the Gospel according to John—printed on it crumpled in my slightly sweaty hands. I climb the steps to the lectern and mess around with the microphone until it's the correct level, and then I look out at the sea of faces before me.

Wow. I had no idea Gran had so many friends.

Then I realize that she didn't. These are Mom's and Dad's friends. I see Dr. and Mrs. Dennis, Shari's parents, and even, way in the back, the Pennebakers, Kathy's parents. I see my childhood dentist and, more embarrassingly, my gynecologist. Nice.

The one face I notice I don't see is my fiancé's.

But that's okay. Because we're on a break.

And I'm sleeping with his best friend, anyway.

"Um," I say. My voice reverberates throughout the church, sounding amazingly loud. I unfold the piece of paper Mom gave me. "A reading from the holy Gospel according to John." What's my *gynecologist* doing here? I mean, it's true she's Mom's gynecologist too. And maybe Rose's and Sarah's also, for all I know. But did she know Gran? Was she Gran's gynecologist? Did Gran go to a gynecologist? That is totally weird. I never thought about my grandmother's vagina before. I don't want to be thinking about my grandmother's vagina. Not here, at her funeral. In a church. While I'm doing a reading from the Bible.

"Jesus said to his disciples . . ."

Wow, my voice sounds loud. Why am I reading about Jesus? Gran couldn't have cared less about Jesus. I mean, if there's any justice in the world, she's with Jesus now, but chances are, she's with Elvis, like Chaz said, in hell. I mean, if there is a hell. And if Elvis went there, which I'm not saying he did. Hell probably is a lot more interesting than heaven. Less boring. I bet Gran would *rather* be in hell.

"'Do not let your hearts be troubled.'"

I'd rather be in hell. I mean, if Elvis is there. And Shakespeare. And Einstein. And Gran. And Chaz.

"You know what?"

Oh God. Everyone is looking at me. Mom looks like she's about to have a coronary. Oh well. She shouldn't have asked me to do a reading. She had to have known this was going to happen.

"My heart *is* troubled," I say, laying down the sheet of paper with the Gospel of John written on it. "It's troubled because I don't think any of this is what my grandmother would really have wanted to hear at her funeral. Don't get me wrong, I think it's very nice," I assure Father Jim, who is looking alarmed (although I can't help noticing that the altar boys seem delighted by this unorthodox turn of events—beneath their crisp white robes, their sneakers are filthy). "I just don't think anything that's been said so far actually has anything to do with my grandmother. Which is why I took the liberty of preparing an alternative reading earlier this morning." From the pocket of the black vintage jacket I'm wearing, I pull another slip of paper, on which I've penned a set of lyrics. "This is from a song I know my grandmother actually did enjoy. Don't worry—I'm not going to sing it." I see my sisters visibly relax. "But I think it's important that we honor the memory of those we've lost by actually mentioning a few things they really did enjoy . . . and this is something I know Gran really did like. So, Gran . . . this is for you. Wherever you are."

And then, unfolding the slip of paper, I read: "'Season ticket, on a one-way ride . . .'"

I risk a brief glance up. I notice that the assembled congregation are staring at me, most with open mouths. My mother, in particular, looks stunned. Dad, however, has a slight smile on his face. It grows larger as I read this next part:

"'Nobody's gonna slow me down . . . I'm on the highway to hell.'"

Now a few more smiles have joined Dad's. Angelo is smiling too. So is Chuck. Even Sarah has cracked a small one.

But that's pretty much it.

Except for Chaz. Chaz is grinning broadly. And giving me a thumbs-up.

I grin back at him.

"Thank you," I say demurely to the parishioners. And then I step down from the lectern.

• • •

"That was quite an interesting reading you gave," my former gynecologist, Dr. Lee, says an hour later, once we've all returned to my parents' house for refreshments after the funeral.

"Thanks," I say. I'm holding a plastic plate, on which I've piled as many different kinds of cookies as I could find. Thanks to the number of concerned friends and neighbors who've dropped off baked goods in the past couple of days, this turns out to be quite a lot of cookies.

I am not sharing these cookies with others. I am eating them all myself.

"Was that the Kinks?" Dr. Lee wants to know.

"AC/DC," I say.

"Oh, of course," Dr. Lee says. "How silly of me."

She drifts away, and Chaz ambles over to take her place. He's holding a plastic plate containing two different kinds of samosas, Korean barbecue, chicken satay, and cold sesame noodles. I can tell he's been visiting the table where my dad's grad students have plopped down their offerings.

"How's it going?" he wants to know.

"Great," I say. "My gynecologist liked it."

"That's two," he says.

"Two?"

"I liked it," he says, gnawing on chicken satay.

"Oh," I say. "Right. Dad liked it too. And Chuck and Angelo. And Sarah, I think."

"So five," Chaz says. "Out of two hundred. Not bad."

"So when do you think we can get out of here?"

"I was going to ask you the exact same question."

"Give it another fifteen minutes," I say. "Mom hasn't had a chance to really ream me out yet."

"Okay. And we're sticking around for that why?"

"To make her feel better?"

"You're a really good daughter," Chaz says. "Have I told you that you look hot in that skirt?"

"About twenty times."

"You look hot in that skirt."

"Twenty-one."

"You'd look hotter with it off. You know what you'd look hottest in? One of those really tiny Knight's Inn bath towels."

"Make that ten minutes," I say to him.

"I'll go make sure no one's blocked in the rental car," he says and abandons his plastic plate.

Not ten seconds after he's gone, Sarah and Rose corner me by the piano that all three of us loathed being forced to learn to play (and none of us succeeded in learning to play well).

"All right, spill," Rose says. "What's the deal with Shari's ex? And don't try to deny there's something going on. You reek of cheap motel shampoo."

"He can't take his eyes off you" is Sarah's more charitable contribution to the conversation.

"I don't know," I say to them. "Look, I don't have time for this. I have to go get reamed out by Mom."

"Mom's got a migraine," Rose says. "She's in her room with a wet washcloth over her face. You already killed her. So just give it up. What are you going to do about that Luke guy? Isn't he, like, Chaz's best friend?"

"Are they going to *fight* over you?" Sarah wants to know. It's been her dream since seeing *West Side Story* that two guys might one day fight over her.

"I really don't want to talk about it," I say, stuffing a whole chocolate chip cookie into my mouth so that, no matter what they say next, I won't be *able* to talk about it.

"Does this mean you're not getting married in France?" Sarah wants to know. "Because I was going to take some French lessons over at the Y. But if I don't have to, let me know. Because there are way cuter guys in the Italian class."

"If you think Mom's dead now," Rose says, "wait until she finds out you're not marrying this Luke guy. She's already told everybody in her scrapbooking class that you're engaged to a prince. This will totally finish her off. What AC/DC lyrics are you going to read out loud at *her* funeral, I wonder?"

I cannot speak, due to all the cookie in my mouth. This, I think, can only be a good thing.

"Lizzie?" I turn my head and see Shari standing there. My heart sinks. Not that I'm not happy to see her. I'm just not looking forward to what I know is about to follow.

I swallow. "Hi, Share," I say. "How are you?"

"Oh, fine," Shari says, eyeing my sisters with distaste. "I was wondering if I could have a word with you—alone—for a moment."

"No problem," I say. But of course it's a problem. I can tell from the expression on Shari's face that I'm not going to like whatever she's got to say.

I follow her up the stairs to my old room—which has been turned into a guest room—nonetheless, and sink down onto my old bed, trying to avoid the accusing stares of the Madame Alexander dolls my mom's parents sent me over the years. Jo March looks particularly disappointed in me as she glares down at me from my childhood bookshelf.

"Lizzie," Shari says, closing the door behind her. "What are you doing?"

"I don't know what you mean," I say, keeping my gaze on my feet.

"Yes, you do," Shari says. "Are you on those drugs my dad prescribed you? Because if you are, I want you to stop taking them. I thought they'd help, not send you into a complete break with reality. I mean, sleeping with Chaz? Have you lost your mind? What about Luke?"

Tears fill my eyes. I look up, only to find that Jo's mom, Marmee, is staring down at me with an even more accusing look than her daughter. Why, oh, why, had Grandma and Grandpa insisted on sending me a Madame Alexander doll for every birthday and Christmas until I turned sixteen? There are just so many of them, all looking down at us.

"It's . . . it's not like that," I say, my voice catching. "I never even took any of those pills."

"Then what the hell is going on, Lizzie?" Shari demands. She crosses the room in a single step and sinks down on the bed beside me. "Because this isn't like you. And don't try to deny it's going on, because it's written all over both your faces—beard burn not withstanding. I mean, don't get me wrong, I've always thought you and Chaz would make a great couple. I'll admit the whole Mae Lin thing was to make you jealous. I knew you'd never realize how great Chaz was until you saw him with another girl—a real girl, not a fembot like Valencia. I knew how he felt about you—it was totally obvious. He couldn't talk about anything but you. It's true you were the one thing he and I still had in common, but no guy talks about a girl that much unless he's crazy about her. Which he all but admitted to me. *You* were the one I wasn't too sure about."

I shake my head. "What do you mean, Mae Lin was to make me jealous? What are you talking about?"

"Well, it worked, didn't it? You were jealous, right? I couldn't believe how you stomped over there and picked a fight with the poor guy the minute Mae Lin and Valencia went downstairs. He had *no* idea what was going on. Oh my God, I nearly wet my pants I was laughing so hard."

Now I'm a little mad. Also a little stunned by Shari's under-handedness. She's been my best friend since forever. But I had no idea she was capable of this kind of duplicity.

"Shari," I say. "That's so mean. You were plotting all along to fix me up with your ex, when you knew perfectly well I'm *engaged*? To his best friend? And you used some poor girl from your office to do it?"

"Oh, whatever," Shari says, making a pooh-poohing gesture. "Mae Lin's dating a hot paramedic. She was willing to play along. But I never thought you'd actually fall into bed with the guy before *breaking up with your fiancé. At your grandmother's funeral.* What are you doing? Have you completely lost it?"

I glare at her. I'm pretty sure I look every bit as accusing—and disapproving—as the Madame Alexander dolls above our heads.

"For your information," I say, "I was *not* jealous of Mae Lin. And who I sleep with behind my fiancé's back at my grandmoth-er's funeral is my business."

"Well, excuse me," Shari says, looking taken aback. "I just don't want to see you get hurt. You or Chaz."

"Oh," I say, unable to keep from letting out a bitter laugh. "*Now* you're worried about Chaz's feelings?"

"Hey." Shari narrows her eyes at me. "That's not fair. You know I loved him."

"Well," I say. "So do I."

"Do you?" Shari wants to know. "Well, then why are you still wearing Luke's ring on your finger?"

"I have some things I still need to figure out," I admit, uncomfortably pressing my left hand into the mattress so neither of us can see my ring finger. "I'm not saying I have all the answers just yet, Shari. I feel like I'm barely hanging on, as a matter of fact. But I know I love him, and I think I always have."

"What about Luke?" Shari demands.

"I'm doing the best I can, okay? Luke's in France," I say. "I'll wait until he gets back to figure out what's going on—or not—between the two of us. In the meantime . . . well, engaged isn't married, you know," I add. "Or dead." I'm a little startled to find myself parroting Gran's words. But what more appropriate place to do it, I realize, than after her funeral.

Shari looks at me as if she were seeing me for the first time. Maybe in a way she is. She shakes her head and asks, "Did you ever look up what solipsistic means?"

"Yes," I say indignantly. "And it's not true. I'm *not* extremely preoccupied with indulging my own feelings and desires. If I were, I'd never have moved out of Luke's Fifth Avenue apartment, much less looked twice at Chaz. He's a poor graduate student, whereas Luke's a rich prince, remember?"

Shari, to my relief, lets out a laugh. The Madame Alexander dolls look startled.

"That's true," she says. And she reaches over and takes my hand, the one with the engagement ring still on it. "Oh, Lizzie. Be *careful*. You're playing with fire here."

"*Me?*" I raise my eyebrows. "You're the one who just admitted you hired a girl from your office on purpose to flirt with Chaz to try to make me jealous!"

"But I thought you'd do the right thing and break up with Luke first," Shari cries. "Not start sleeping with Chaz during your grandmother's funeral. Not that it isn't a fitting tribute to her, one she'd have gotten a huge kick out of. Still. I'm just worried someone's going to get hurt. And I'm afraid it's going to be you."

I squeeze her hand. "I'm a big girl now, Share," I say. "I can take care of myself."

But as we make our way back downstairs, I wonder if that's really true. Can I? It's true I'm living on my own for the first time ever. I'm supporting myself, running my own business (well, practically), and at any given time spinning a dozen plates in the air at once. If I dropped just one, the whole thing would come tumbling down in a mess like no one would believe . . .

So what am I doing, having this torrid affair with my fiancé's best friend?

And it *is* torrid, I realize when I walk into the living room and notice him standing there waiting for me, and my heart slams into my ribs as it always seems to whenever I see him. I'm not going to escape from this unscathed. None of us are, I know.

But when Chaz lifts his head and I feel that electric shock that always seems to go through me lately when I look in his direction and his gaze meets mine, I realize I don't care. I don't care what's going to happen. As long as we can be together . . .

For now.

For however long now lasts.

A HISTORY
of
WEDDINGS

Flowers have always played an important role in weddings, since the very first recorded marriage ceremonies in ancient Greece, where they were used to make a crown for the bride to wear as a gift of nature. Floral wreaths and garlands were often used in ancient ceremonies to bind couples together in lieu of rings.

Different herbs and flowers—such as garlic flowers as well as bulbs—were often carried to ward off evil spirits. Evil spirits, of course, are not the only ones who'd be warded off if brides today started carrying garlic bulbs.

It's traditional to give your wedding guests a favor by which to remember the day. This is a centuries-old practice that stems from the French habit of giving bonbonnieres, or sugared almonds, to departing guests. Today's couples tend to choose candles or, if you really want to bring on the bling, rhinestone sunglasses.

LIZZIE NICHOLS DESIGNS™

• Chapter 17 •

In all of the wedding cake, hope is the sweetest of plums.

Douglas Jerrold (1803–1857), English dramatist

$\mathcal{I}$ am standing with my forehead resting against the wide glass window overlooking the planes landing and taking off on the tarmac in front of me. Chaz and I have flown commercially out of Ann Arbor and are waiting for our connecting flight to LaGuardia from Detroit.

What I hadn't prepared myself for is Luke's unexpected phone call midway through the screwdrivers Chaz and I were downing at the Fox Sports Bar while waiting for boarding.

"How *are* you?" Luke had wanted to know. "I'm so sorry I couldn't be there for you, Lizzie. I know it must have been really, really hard. But you know I couldn't get away from the office. Uncle Gerald really needs me here."

I'd had to leave the bar and wander the concourse. I couldn't talk to Luke in front of Chaz.

"Of course," I'd said. "I know. And I'm good, I'm fine."

There are thunderheads gathering along the horizon. They're what's causing our flight to be delayed. Just a half hour so far. But who knows? We could be stuck in Detroit overnight.

And yet somehow the thought of being stuck in Detroit—or anywhere—with Chaz doesn't bother me. At all.

It's wrong that I'm talking to my fiancé on the phone and thinking about how much I don't mind being stuck in an airport with his best friend. Whom I can't seem to stop touching. Every time I'm away from him I feel something akin to a physical pain until I can get back to his side and lay my hand on his arm or touch his shoulder or slip my fingers into his . . . It's totally bizarre, and something I've never experienced before. Not even with Luke, the man to whom I'm engaged.

Rose is right. I *am* a slut.

"But I've been doing a lot of thinking," Luke is saying.

"You have?" I've completely lost track of the conversation. Behind me, one of those people movers is going *beep-beep-beep* as it tries to shuttle some elderly passengers to their gate, and no one will move out of its way.

"I have," Luke says. "How would you feel about coming to Paris for a week?"

I shake my head as if there were a bee inside it.

"Me?" I ask. "You mean . . . ?"

"Right. I want a break from our break," he says.

"Um," I say. "You want me to come visit you? In Paris?"

My God! He can tell! He can tell about me and Chaz! I hadn't mentioned that Chaz had shown up to the funeral. And Chaz obviously hadn't spoken to Luke since he'd arrived.

This is horrible. Luke's going to break up with me now, over the phone. Oh well. I deserve it. I'm a horrible person. I'm on the highway to hell.

I close my eyes, in preparation for being broken up with.

But all Luke says is "It's just, I've really been enjoying my time here. I know I shouldn't say that, considering what you've just been through. But it's true. I forgot how much I love Paris. And working with Uncle Gerald has been great. I'm really having a blast."

I open my eyes. Wait. This isn't breaking up with me. This doesn't sound like breaking up with me at all.

"I forgot how much I love working in the business world," Luke goes on. "It's really been fantastic. And I think you'd love it too. You know what a great time you had here last summer. It's such a shame you didn't come with me."

"Well," I say. "I really couldn't afford the time away from work." Each word sounds foreign as it falls from my lips. Except that I'm speaking in English.

"Sure," Luke says. "I know. Your job is important to you. I know that now. This break has taught me that. Really, Lizzie. It has."

I sneak a peek over at Chaz. He's watching the television over the bar. It's broadcasting a golf game. Based on his television viewing habits back in the hotel room—the few times we actually turned it on—I'm starting to realize there really isn't any sport Chaz won't watch.

"That doesn't freak you out, does it?" Luke asks. "I mean, that I'm enjoying it here so much?"

"Why should that freak me out?" I ask. What's freaking me out is that I'm sleeping with my fiancé's best friend, a guy who *also* happens to be my best friend's ex-boyfriend. Yeah, my best friend who's a lesbian now. *That*'s what's freaking me out.

Not that I'm going to mention this to him.

"Well, that's a relief," Luke says. "I mean, I haven't given up on the medical school thing yet. Not completely. I'm just . . . I'm not totally sure it's for me, and Paris . . . well, Paris is so incredibly great. I just think you'd really love it—"

Okay. Now I've officially freaked myself out. I have to get off the phone. I have to get off the phone *now.*

"Uh-oh, they're calling my flight," I lie. "I have to go. I'll talk to you later, Luke."

"Oh, right," Luke says. "Love you!"

"Love you too," I say and hang up.

What just happened? *What just happened there?* I don't even know if I can deal with it. I hurry across the crowded concourse to slide back onto my bar stool at the Fox Sports Bar, pick up my screwdriver, and drain it.

"Slow down, there, slugger," Chaz says, observing me with some alarm. "They have more vodka back there than just what's in that glass, you know."

I set down my empty glass and lay my head down upon the bar. "He wants me to come to Paris to see him," I say to the beer nuts that have fallen to the airport floor.

"The bastard," Chaz says. "Next thing you know, he's going to want to set a date for the wedding."

I lift my head and look at him. He's wearing a Wolverines baseball cap and is looking adorably—and sexily—rumpled, as if he's just rolled out of bed.

Which, in fact, he has. With me.

The guilt over what we've done slams me—as it does a hundred times a day—yet again.

I drop my head back onto the bar. I want to start sobbing. I really do.

Chaz lays a large hand on the back of my neck. "Cheer up, sport," he says. "It could be worse."

"How?" I demand of the bar top.

"Well," he says after stopping a moment to think about it. "At least you're not pregnant."

This doesn't have the comedic effect Chaz apparently intended it to.

"Chaz," I say miserably. "Everything you said that morning after Jill's wedding is true. I know it. Luke really did ask me to marry him only because he was scared of being alone. I realize that now. He doesn't care about me. I mean, he does, but not . . . not the way you care about me. If he did, he'd have shown up for Gran's funeral. *You* did. But even so. Now look at the mess I'm in. I've got a fiancé I don't love who wants to marry me. And a lover I do love who doesn't. Why *don't* you want to get married, Chaz? *Why?*"

"I've told you why," Chaz says. "And if you won't accept me as I am, warts and all, then maybe you're better off with Luke. He's the one offering you the ring, the investment banker's bonus, and the place on Fifth Avenue. You'd be crazy not to go with him. All I've got is a walk-up in the East Village and a low-paying teaching assistant's salary. Oh, and no ring. I don't know what you're doing sharing this bowl of beer nuts with me in the first place."

I stare blearily down into the nut bowl. He's not, I know, referring to beer nuts. At least entirely. I can't help remembering that cold night when we'd sparred so unpleasantly at O'Riordan's, and I'd asked myself afterward what, if you didn't end up getting married, the point was.

The crazy thing is, with Chaz, I'm sort of starting to see. I mean, the point is just to be together. Who cares about a stupid piece of paper?

Wait—did *I* just think that? What is happening to me? Who am I even turning into? Can I actually be turning into that kind of girl? The kind of girl who doesn't care about marriage?

I guess so. I mean, I'm already the kind of girl who cheats on her fiancé—with his *best friend*.

I groan aloud suddenly. "How can I do this to him? How can *we* do this to him?" I cover my face with my hands. "I'm going to throw up. I swear."

"Please do it in that trash can over there," Chaz says. "And stop beating yourself up. He hasn't exactly been a Boy Scout himself while you two have been together."

I blink at him from between my fingers. "What are you talking about?"

"Nothing. Do you want another drink? They just delayed our flight by another hour. I think you need another drink." He signals the bartender. "This young lady would like another screwdriver. Ketel One."

The bartender nods and takes away my old glass to make a new drink.

"I'd rather have a Diet Coke," I say to the bartender. I've lowered my hands and am gripping the bar in an effort to stay upright. The vodka I've just downed so quickly has made me light-headed. "What do you mean, Luke hasn't exactly been a Boy Scout while we've been together?" I ask Chaz.

"I told you, nothing. Look, I've always wanted to ask you. What's with the garter?"

"*What?*" I stare at him in an alcohol-befuddled daze.

"The thing with the garter," Chaz says. "At weddings. You know, when the groom peels the garter off the bride and throws it to the guys."

"Oh," I say. The bartender has delivered my Diet Coke, and I take a grateful swig. "That's from olden times, when people in the court were required to follow the newly wedded couple to their bedroom after the ceremony to make sure they consummated the marriage. They'd demand the royal bride's garter or stocking as proof that the defloration had occurred. Since peasants like to imitate the behavior of nobility, it became standard practice to demand that *all* brides give up their stockings or garters after the ceremony—sometimes the wedding guests would take the garter by force, so it became traditional for the groom to take it off during the reception so people wouldn't follow the bride and groom back to their bedroom, and also so that the wedding guests wouldn't rip it off her."

Chaz makes a face. "Now, see," he says. "That right there is reason enough why the institution of marriage ought to be abolished."

I stare at him, comprehension dawning. "It's not *marriage* you're against," I say. "It's *weddings.*"

"True," Chaz says. "But you can't have one without the other."

"Yes, of course you can," I say matter-of-factly. But it doesn't, I realize, matter. Not really. Not considering the grave we've already dug ourselves. "Do you really not feel guilty about what we're doing?"

Chaz finishes off his screwdriver. "Not in the least," he says. "I've done a lot of terrible things in my day, Lizzie. But loving you is not one of them. I don't know what's going to happen when Luke gets back in the fall. But I intend to enjoy the weeks I have left with you to the fullest. Because as I know from my study of the philosophy of time, whatever is going to happen in the future is already unavoidable."

I blink at him. And say the only thing I can think of to say. Which is, "So?"

"So . . . what?" he asks me.

"So . . . what next?" I am really hoping he has the answer. Because I feel completely lost. And sort of scared. In a heart-pounding, excited way. The way I felt when Shari and I got off the plane from Michigan and were standing in the line for taxis at LaGuardia Airport, not knowing what we were going to find when we got into Manhattan. I didn't have the slightest idea where I was or what I was doing.

But that didn't mean I was in the wrong place, exactly.

"Next," Chaz says, signaling the bartender, "I'm going to have another drink. And I suggest you do the same. Because there's a lady I know who deserves to have her memory toasted, and *not* with Diet Coke."

I give him a somewhat watery smile. "I'm not good at not knowing what's going to happen," I say when our screwdrivers arrive, and we lift them to clink.

"Are you kidding?" Chaz says. "That's what you're best at. You take the road less traveled and turn it into gold every single time. Why do you think Luke's still hanging on so tight when he's half a world away? You've got the magic touch. And everyone knows it."

"I don't know," I say uncertainly.

"Lizzie." Chaz looks me dead in the eye. "Why do you think it was you, out of all the people in your family, your grandmother connected with so well? You, and no one else? You were the only other person in your family who, like her, would never take no for an answer, and just did whatever the hell you wanted. Now raise your glass."

I do, chewing my lower lip a little.

"To Gran," Chaz says, clinking the rim of his glass to mine. "A fine old drunk with some damn good taste."

"To Gran," I say, blinking back sudden tears. But they're happy tears. Because finally someone is saying what I've been wanting to say about Gran all along.

Gran, I know, would approve of what Chaz and I are doing. Whatever that is, exactly.

I lift my glass. And I drink.

To Gran.

A HISTORY
of
WEDDINGS

The first toasts were performed back in the sixth century B.C., when the ancient Greeks would pour wine for their dinner guests from a communal pitcher. The host would drink first to assure his guests that the wine wasn't poisoned (a common practice at the time for getting rid of pesky in-laws or neighbors). Later, the clinking of vessels at weddings became a popular method of keeping demons away from the newly wedded couple.

At a traditional modern reception, the first toast is always to the bride, usually by the best man. The last toast is generally from the father of the bride. After he has made a weepy spectacle of himself, the reception can officially begin. Only at a nontraditional modern reception does the bride get to give her own toast, thanking her wedding party and guests (who, after sitting through so many toasts, truly deserve thanking).

Keep your toasts short. Please, no crib sheets. The point of the toast is to wish the happy couple well and invite all the other guests to join you in doing so, not to embarrass the couple or show how witty you are. You should also thank the parents for hosting the wedding and the couple for bestowing the honor of allowing you to be their best whatever-you-are. Lift your glass, ask others to do so as well, congratulate them, then get your butt back in the seat, for the love of God, so the rest of us can eat our cold rubbery chicken.

LIZZIE NICHOLS DESIGNS™

Chapter 18

To love someone deeply gives you strength. Being loved by someone deeply gives you courage.

Lao Tzu, fourth century B.C., Taoist philosopher

I'm late for work Monday morning.

There is only one explanation for how I can be late to work in a place that is precisely two floors below where I live: Chaz.

It turns out there *is* a disadvantage to living two floors up from where you work . . . if you don't want the people you're working with to know you're sleeping around behind your fiancé's back, anyway.

I told Chaz that if he wanted to spend the night at my place he had to get out *before* anyone else showed up at the shop in the morning. I couldn't have Tiffany and the other ladies seeing him leaving. Which meant he had to be out of there before nine . . . preferably before eight thirty.

He would have made it too, if it hadn't been for my own insufferable weakness when it comes to men who bring girls breakfast in bed. It isn't a weakness I ever knew I had before. Because no guy has ever brought me breakfast in bed before.

And it wasn't just that he brought me breakfast in bed, either, but that he got up way before I did and must have crept around super-quietly so as not to wake me, and gone to the store—since there was seriously nothing in my refrigerator—and then made scrambled eggs and bacon and toast and brought it all in on a tray with a single red rose in a bud vase next to an icy cold Diet Coke still in the can . . . just the way I like it.

What girl wouldn't have melted? And then jumped his bones (as soon as she was done with her eggs . . . I didn't want them to get cold, after all)?

So I'm a little bit . . . frazzled . . . when I finally get downstairs to work. Frazzled in a good way. A highly relaxed, but still slightly disoriented and dazed way. It's how I've been feeling since I first kissed Chaz . . . good, but almost as if I had gone ahead and started taking those pills Shari's dad had given me, instead of flushing them down the toilet back at the Knight's Inn, like I actually did. The world seems . . . different. Not better, not worse, just . . . different. Suddenly, things that used to bother me—men who wear baseball caps indoors, for instance—don't bother me at all anymore. Fears that used to consume me—that I might end up shopping for vast amounts of cold medicine at my hometown grocery store on weekends like Kathy Pennebaker—no longer seem likely . . . in fact, they seem improbable. Instead of obsessively eating in one sitting the entire bag of cheese popcorn that I bought at the airport, I ate only a handful.

And I didn't even *think* about buying a Cinnabon.

Something is happening to me. I've even stopped wearing Spanx. I just don't care if my bulges show. Maybe because Chaz actually *likes* my bulges?

I never have to worry about being on top with him, or making sure I walk backward out of the room when I'm naked so my butt doesn't show. In fact, I'm pretty sure if I did this, Chaz would ask me what the hell I was doing, something Luke never seemed to notice. Or wonder about.

Maybe this is what comes from being a loose woman. When you give up your morals, they *all* just go, inhibitions too.

Anyway, I'm not the first person into the shop. Sylvia and Marisol are already there, working on the lace-and-tulle I. Magnin & Co. 1950s cocktail-style number we'd gotten from a punky bride whose mother had worn it and who wanted to squeeze into it as well . . . only she was a size 12 and her mother had been a size 8. We'd assured her we could handle it.

But from the way Sylvia and Marisol start staring, their mouths hanging open, when I walk in, I'm not sure we can handle much of anything, let alone retrofitting a size 12 I. Magnin cocktail dress to an 8.

"What?" I demand, staring right back at them.

They know. I don't know how they know, but it's obvious they do. I might as well be wearing a big scarlet letter *A* on my chest.

Great. The boss is a slut. In an hour, when Tiffany gets here, everyone in Manhattan (and parts of North Dakota, where Tiffany is from) will know it.

How do I handle this? There was never an article about this in *Fortune Small Business*. What to do when all your employees know that you're sleeping with your fiancé's best friend. At least I don't think so. Damn, I knew I should have paid more attention to that magazine and less to *Us Weekly*.

"This is looking good," I say about the dress the two women are working on. They've ripped all the stitching from the waist and bodice and will be inserting stretchy lace panels—the big girl's friend—in discreet locations. Yeah, that's it. Maybe I can distract them by complimenting their work!

The two women exchange glances.

"I was sorry to hear about your grandmother, Lizzie," Marisol says.

"Yes," Sylvia says. "I'm very sorry too."

I blink at them for a moment, then realize . . . they don't think I'm a slut at all! They weren't being weird before. They just didn't know what to say because I've just come back from my grandmother's funeral.

God! I'm such an idiot!

"Oh," I say, smiling. "Thank you so much. She . . . she had a good, long life."

I'm feeling much better about things—less disoriented, and actually caught up on the things I've missed, including phone messages, of which there weren't too many, due to the holiday weekend—an hour later when Tiffany walks through the front door, takes one look at me, and goes, "Oh my God. You had sex this morning."

I nearly choke on the Diet Coke—my second of the day—I'm sipping.

"Wh-what?" I cry, trying not to spill all over the appointment book I have open in front of me. "What are you talking about? No, I didn't."

"Oh, don't even try," Tiffany says in disgust as she sashays into the shop in her four-inch lace-up stilettos. "You think I can't tell by now when you've had morning sex? And whoever it was, he did you *good*. Who was it? It couldn't have been Luke. I've never seen you *glowing* like that before. It's kind of revolting." She halts midway across the shop and stares at me owl-eyed. "Oh my God, Lizzie. Did you and Chaz—"

"NO!" I leap up from the reception desk and begin to wave my arms at her like a madwoman. "No, of course not!"

"Holy shit." A slow smile begins to spread across her face. "You screwed your fiancé's best friend. You slut."

"I *didn't*," I cry. "I swear I didn't!"

"And now you're *lying* about it." Still smiling, Tiffany reaches into her Marc Jacobs bag and pulls out her Sidekick. "Monique needs to hear about this. So does Raoul. In fact, I can't think of one person I know who doesn't need to hear about this. This is sick. Little Miss Prudy Pants got her rocks off this weekend with her fiancé's best friend. Oh shit, her best friend's ex!" Tiffany laughs to herself as she types into her Sidekick. "Even better! Man, you are going to burn in hell for true!"

I reach up and lay a hand over her keyboard. "Tiffany," I say earnestly. "Please. Look at me."

Tiffany looks down from her towering six feet two inches (with the heels) and blinks her heavily mascaraed eyes. "What?" she asks. She's still grinning like the Cheshire cat.

"It's not what you think," I say. There's a knot in my stomach. All the yummy eggs and toast and things I put into it an hour ago feel as if they're about to come back up. "The thing is . . ."

"Oh, what?" Tiffany demands sarcastically. "You *looooooove* him?"

"Yes," I say tightly. I am so close to vomiting I don't know what to do. I don't want to throw up all over Tiffany's pretty Laundry sundress, but I'm not sure how much longer I can hold it in. "As a matter of fact, I do."

Tiffany lowers her Sidekick, leans down until her face is level with mine, and says, enunciating very clearly, "*Duh.*"

Then she straightens back up, yanks her keypad out of my grasp, and, prattling on as she keeps her gaze on what her fingers are doing, says, "Jesus, Lizzie, do you think we don't know that? Frankly I think the only person in all of the tristate area who *didn't* know you were in love with Charles Pendergast the Third is you. It was so fucking obvious you like him and he likes you that it was just a matter of time until you guys did something about it. And you know what? I'm glad, because I am so fucking over Luke. He was getting on my last nerve. What is this spending the summer in France thing? Good riddance, as far as I'm concerned. I don't care if he *is* a prince. There're more important things than being royal, you know. Like, did he go to your grandmother's funeral? No? But Chaz did, right? Did he? Is that how this all happened?"

When I nod, dumbly, still stunned by her outburst, Tiffany goes on, turning her attention right back to her Sidekick. "See? I knew it. Monique owes me fifty bucks. Anyway. I can tell by your face you've been completely guilt tripping yourself about all this. Get over it, Lizzie. Yeah, Luke's a nice guy, and all, and he gave you a big rock . . . but when it's counted, has he ever been there for you? No, he hasn't. You're better off with Chaz, who really does love you—anyone can tell that just by the way he was looking at you at that Fourth of July party . . . though I'll admit most of the time it seemed like he wanted to kill you. The thing is, he's the real deal." She snaps her Sidekick closed, her message apparently delivered to all of the East Side, the West Side, Brooklyn, and most of Queens as well. "And that's the kind of guy you need. I'm glad he finally banged you."

I stare up at her. My urge to vomit has passed. I'm seized by a new urge . . . to hug her.

I know better than to act on this urge, however. Instead, I hug myself, and say in a soft voice, "Thanks, Tiffany. I . . . it's been kind of . . . weird."

"I can imagine," Tiffany says, sauntering the rest of the way across the room to her chair and collapsing into it. "I mean, for *you*. You're not used to being a bad girl. But the thing is"—she reaches into her enormous bag and pulls out a chocolate croissant, then gestures for me to make her a cappuccino, which I do—"you're not really even being that bad. You know? I mean, it's not like you and Luke are married. You're engaged. And, like, barely.

You haven't even set a date. On the Bad Girl Scale, ten being really bad, and zero being barely bad, you're like a one."

I hand her the cappuccino I've whipped up, having already turned on the machine when I got in. "What are you?"

"Me?" Tiffany bites into her croissant and chews thoughtfully. "Well, let's see. Raoul's married, but his wife left him for her personal trainer. The only reason they aren't divorced is because he doesn't have his green card yet. As soon as he gets it—which should be any day now—he's going to divorce her and marry me. But we *are* living together. So, on the Bad Girl Scale, I'm like a four."

I've never heard of the Bad Girl Scale—never having done anything before to put me on it. I'm genuinely interested.

"What's Ava?" I want to know.

"Ava? Oh, let's see. She's sleeping with this DJ Tippycat guy, and *he*'s married. But, according to the tabloids, his wife came after him in an Outback Steakhouse parking lot with a chain saw, so he's got a restraining order out on her. That only puts her at about a five on the Bad Girl Scale."

"That's higher than you," I say, impressed.

"True," Tiffany says. "Tip's got a rap sheet. He tried to take an ounce of marijuana on a plane once. It was in one of his kid's stuffed animals. But still. Oh my God. I have to remember to tell Ava about you and Chaz. She's gonna be stoked. She had a fifty riding on it too. Little Joey's got a hundred on it!"

"Please," I say, raising a hand. Ava's a bit of a sensitive subject, since she still hasn't spoken to me since that morning we woke up to find the paparazzi swarming outside the shop. "Can we just keep it on the D.L. for now? There are people who don't know that I'm trying to figure out how—or if—I'm going to tell. Like Luke."

Tiffany blinks at me. "What do you mean, if? Of course you're gonna tell Luke."

I look down at the ring I'm still wearing on my left hand and don't say anything.

"You *are* going to break up with Luke, right, Lizzie?" Tiffany demands. "*Right*, Lizzie? Because, oh my God, if you don't, do you know what number you go to on the Bad Girl Scale? Like, directly to ten. You cannot string along both those guys at the same time. Who do you think you are, anyway? Anne Heche?"

"I know," I say with a groan. "But it's just going to hurt Luke so much. Not the part about me, but the part about Chaz. I mean, he's his *best friend* . . ."

"That's Chaz's problem," Tiffany says. "Not yours. Come on, Lizzie. You can't have them *both*. Well, I mean, *I* could. But *you* can't. You wouldn't be able to handle it. Just look at you. You're falling apart as it is, and one of them isn't even on the same continent, and there's no chance of you getting caught. You're going to have to decide. And, yes, one of them is going to get hurt. But you should have thought of that before you decided to become a Bad Girl."

"I didn't *decide* to become a Bad Girl," I insist. "It just happened. I couldn't help it."

Tiffany shakes her head. "That's what they all say."

At that moment the bells over the front door tinkle, and Monsieur Henri comes in, followed by his wife, looking tight-faced, and another woman I've never seen before. The woman is dressed in a summer-weight business jacket and skirt and is carrying a briefcase. She looks a little too young to be a mother of the bride, but a little too old to be the kind of bride who wears the type of gowns in which we generally specialize. Not to be ageist or anything. But it's true.

"Ah, Elizabeth," Monsieur Henri says when he sees me. "You've returned, I see. We were very sorry to hear of your loss."

"Um," I say. I haven't seen Monsieur Henri since his first—and last—venture to the city after his heart surgery. According to his wife, with whom I've spoken on the phone several times since then, he's been back at their home in New Jersey, brushing up on his *pétanque* skills and watching *Judge Judy*. "Thank you. I'm sorry I was away for so long."

I was actually gone for four days, only two of which were actual workdays. But I can't think of any other reason why Monsieur Henri should be back so suddenly, and with what appear to be reinforcements.

"Not to worry, not to worry," Monsieur Henri says, waving my concerns off as if they were nothing. "Now, Miss Lowenstein. This is the shop, as you can see. Let me take you into the back room."

"Thank you," Miss Lowenstein says, giving me the briefest of smiles as she passes by, following closely behind Monsieur Henri.

I turn my bewildered gaze on Madame Henri, who can barely look me in the eye. "Oh, Elizabeth," she says to the carpet. "I hardly know what to say."

"Oh, yeah," Tiffany says, breaking off while taking a slurp of her cappuccino. "I totally forgot to tell you . . ."

A HISTORY
of
WEDDINGS

For many years it's been assumed that the wedding veil, which was traditionally worn over the face, was used to disguise the bride, and thus protect her from evil spirits. But more recent historians argue that perhaps the veil served a more practical purpose . . . the veil may actually have been to keep her betrothed, in case of an arranged marriage, from seeing the face of his intended until after he was already committed. A less than charitable interpretation, but have you *seen* some of those twelfth-century portraits?

Make sure the color of your veil matches that of your dress! Not all whites are the same. Never choose an ivory veil to go with a cream-colored dress. You might think the difference is slight, but believe me, it will show up in the photos, and you'll notice, and slowly, over the years, looking at the photos will drive you insane. Make sure you match the color of your dress to your veil. These are two items you won't want to mix and match.

LIZZIE NICHOLS DESIGNS™

Marriage—a book of which the first chapter is written in poetry and the remaining chapters written in prose.

Beverley Nichols (1898–1983), English writer and playwright

should have told you," Madame Henri says miserably as she dumps another sugar packet into her latte. We're sitting at a table in the window booth at the corner Starbucks, and she keeps glancing nervously toward the doors of the Goldmark Realty Offices, through which her husband has disappeared with Miss Lowenstein, Goldmark's self-proclaimed top sales agent. "But it was all decided so suddenly, and you'd already had the bad news about your grandmother . . . I just didn't have the heart to pile on this bad news as well."

"I understand," I say.

I don't, actually. I really don't see how, after everything I've done for them—all my hard work these past six months—they can do this to me. I mean, I *can*—it's their business, after all, and they have the right to sell it if they want to. But it seems awfully cold. On the Bad Girl Scale, I'd give what they're doing about a five hundred.

"So . . . he really just wants out?"

"He wants to go back to France," Madame Henri says glumly. "It's so strange. All these years, before the heart attack, I was begging him to take more time off, to spend more time with me at our house in Provence, and he wouldn't hear of it. For him, it was always work, work, work. Then he has the heart attack, and suddenly . . . he doesn't want to work anymore. At. All. All he wants to do is play *pétanque*. That's all I hear about. *Pétanque* this and *pétanque* that. He wants to retire to our house in Avignon and just play *pétanque* until he dies. He's already contacted his old friends there—his schoolmates—and formed a team. They have a league. A *pétanque* league. It's insane. I suppose I should be glad he's found something that interests him. After the operation, I thought nothing would, ever again. But this . . . it's obsessive."

I look down at the Diet Coke I've bought but haven't even opened yet. I can hardly believe this is happening. How could my day, which had started out so incredibly well, be going downhill so fast?

"But . . . what about your boys?" I ask. "I mean, doesn't he want them to come with you?"

I can't imagine Provence would hold any appeal whatsoever for the two club-hopping Henri boys.

"Oh, no, of course not," Madame Henri says. "No, and they don't want to come with us. They have to stay and finish school. But that's why we need to sell the building. We'll need something to pay for that. New York University is so expensive." She sighs. Her eyeliner, usually so carefully and expertly put on, is smudged, a clear sign of the stress she's under. "And then we'll need something to live on. If he's doing nothing but playing *pétanque* all day . . . I suppose I could look for work, but there isn't much a middle-aged woman who used to manage a bridal gown refurbishment shop can do in the south of France." She sighs again, and I can see the pain the admission has caused her.

"Of course," I say. The urge to vomit that I'd felt while speaking to Tiffany earlier returns. "And you don't think you can get by just from the sale of your house in New Jersey?"

"Well, we hope to get a nice amount for it, of course," Madame Henri says. "But nowhere near what we can get for the building. Miss Lowenstein is going to send over an inspector and then get an appraisal, but she says comparable buildings in this area are selling for four to five million dollars."

I nearly choke on my own saliva.

Four to five million dollars? Four to five *million*?

So I don't have a hope of being able to buy the shop myself. I'm pretty sure you can't get a mortgage for that amount. Not if you're me, and you're making thirty grand a year, and you have exactly two thousand dollars in your savings account.

So I'm homeless *and* jobless. Great. Just great.

"It's just," I say, clearing my throat. "The shop is doing really well. *Really* well." Nowhere near four to five million well. But I don't mention that. "And since you already own your home in Provence, and you'll have the money from the sale of your house in New Jersey, it just seems like—"

"Oh," Madame Henri says. She's looking across the street. Her husband is coming out of Goldmark Realty and glancing around impatiently for her. "Here he is. Elizabeth, listen . . . I know. I feel terrible. And I am doing what I can for you. I . . . will speak to Maurice, if you wish." I stare at her in horror. Maurice? The rival wedding gown rehabilitator who was trying to run the Henris out of business when they first hired me . . . but didn't, thanks only to my efforts?

"Um . . . that's all right," I say in a strangled voice.

"I will speak to you soon. Yes? I will telephone. Good-bye for now." She kisses me on both cheeks and is gone.

I sit there, trying to figure out what just happened. Did my boss's wife really just tell me that they're selling out and moving overseas? That I am out of both a job and a place to live? Worse, that I'm going to have to fire my staff? Where are Sylvia and Marisol going to go? I'm not so worried about Tiffany and Monique. They'll find some poor sap to hire them to answer phones somewhere. But what about my seamstresses? How am I going to break this news to Shari? I promised her I'd take care of them.

Oh my God, could my day suck more?

This can't be happening. It really can't. What am I going to do?

Sighing, I pull out my cell phone and look at my contacts. Who am I going to call? In times of crisis in the past, I've always called one number . . . home. And okay, generally I've wanted to talk to my mom. But Gran is always the one who answered. And whether I liked it or not, Gran is the one who generally gave me the single piece of advice that almost always ended up helping me the most.

But Gran's not here anymore.

I think about calling Chaz. But this isn't Chaz's problem. It's mine. If I'm ever going to stand on my own two feet, I can't go running off to the man in my life every time something goes wrong. I have to work this through on my own.

Besides, I know what Chaz is going to say: "Oh, you can move in with me."

No! I can't let that happen! I have to solve this myself, without a guy helping me. Besides, that's how I ended up in this mess with Luke, when I moved in with him out of necessity when Shari and I couldn't find a place together, as opposed to because the two of us were actually ready for cohabitation.

Suddenly, my cell phone chirps . . . and when I see who is at the other end of the call, I almost sag with relief.

"Hi," I say, picking up.

"Hey," Shari says in the gentle tone that I've begun to notice people use with the newly bereaved. "How *are* you? I've been meaning to call."

"Not good," I say. "I really need to talk. And not on the phone. There's—" I clear my throat. I am so phlegmy lately. Well, when you've been crying as much as I have, I guess it's only natural. "Something I need to tell you. Can you take a break and meet me somewhere?"

"Sure," Shari says, sounding concerned. "How about the bubble tea place down here near my office?"

Where Shari told me all but the real reason why she was leaving Chaz. How appropriate.

"I'll see you there in half an hour," I say and hang up, then start hurrying toward the subway. At this time of day, a taxi down the FDR would be quicker. But I'm about to be unemployed. I need to save every penny I've got.

. . .

Shari calls to say she'll be late, of course. A crisis at the office arises, and she's the only one, as usual, who can handle it.

Fortunately she calls just as I'm exiting the subway, so I'm able to use my sudden windfall of spare time to window-shop. Her office is so far downtown that it's actually on the fringes of Chinatown, and as I wander around, blindly going from window to window, I find myself walking past shops displaying wedding gowns. Some of them have Mandarin collars and toggles down the front, and yet the mannequins are wearing veils.

Despite the fact that they are being sold in shops that are right next to fish markets or restaurant supply stores, the gown's prices are right up there with those at Kleinfeld's. I overhear two women in front of one window speaking in rapid Chinese while pointing at a particularly gorgeous gown, and while I can't understand exactly what they're saying, the meaning behind the words is clear: eight hundred dollars for the pretty white sheath with lace overlay is too much . . . especially for something any talented seamstress could make at home for a fraction of the price.

I agree with them. Bridal gown shopping is a bitch.

I find a table at the bubble tea place and end up waiting only five minutes before Shari comes bursting in, effusing apologies and sliding into the chair opposite mine before saying kindly, "Now, I've told everyone at the office that I'm not to be disturbed. I've turned off my phone *and* beeper, and I have all the time in the world. So tell me. How are you? What's going on?"

I surprise both of us by bursting into tears. I try to hide my face in a napkin, but the few students and other scruffy-looking, writer-looking types working on their fancy laptops at nearby tables still glance over at us in annoyance. The waitress, who was approaching to take our order, decides to give us a wide berth instead and goes off in the opposite direction.

Shari is so shocked she can't help laughing a little.

"Lizzie," she says. "What is it? Is it your grandmother? I'm so sorry. I know you miss her, but she died happy, Lizzie, in her sleep, with a beer in her hand. She's probably in heaven right now, watching *Dr. Quinn* all the time. And every single episode has Sully in it!"

I shake my head so violently that my hair falls out of the sloppy ponytail into which I've pulled it. Strands of it stick to my now-wet cheeks.

"I-it's not that," I hiccup.

"What is it, then?" Shari wants to know. "Is it Chaz? Did he do something to upset you? I'll kill him. Just say the word and I'll go cut his wiener off—"

"No." I shake my head some more. "It's not Chaz. It's not Gran, either—"

"Oh." Shari nods knowingly. "I get it. You told him. Luke. Oh,

Lizzie. I'm sorry. But, you know, it's for the best. I mean, the truth is, you're better off without him. I never could stand him. He was just so . . . *perfect*. Do you know what I'm talking about?"

I sit there staring at her in horror. I don't think I could have spoken if I'd tried.

"I mean, with the château and the good looks and the doctor thing and the apartment on Fifth Avenue," Shari goes on. "There was something almost creepy about it. Like . . . what lucky star was *he* born under? Then when he was so mean to you last Christmas . . . Seriously, I couldn't believe it when you said yes when he asked you to marry him. I pretended like I was happy for you because that's what best friends do, but now . . . When are you going to dump him? Because I so want to buy a Carvel cake." When she notices that I'm staring at her without having said a word, she explains, "To celebrate."

"Shari," I say when I can finally summon the ability to speak. "I didn't break up with Luke."

It's Shari's turn to stare at me for a while. Finally she says, "Oh. You didn't?"

I shake my head.

"So . . ." She chews on her lower lip. "So I just really put my foot in my mouth, didn't I?"

I take a deep breath. Then I release it. Because suddenly the tears are back.

Only this time I'm not going to let them win.

Then I say, "Shari. The Henris are selling the building I live and work in and moving to France. I'm losing my job, my apartment, and, basically, my life. Plus, even though you apparently think Luke is too perfect, I wouldn't exactly jump to that conclusion, because unlike Chaz, at least he actually wanted to marry me. Chaz most emphatically doesn't. Still, I'm really happy that you're so glad for me that I'm getting rid of him. But excuse me if I don't feel like I have too much to celebrate right now. Especially with a Carvel cake."

"Lizzie." It's Shari's turn to look horrified. "I—"

But I realize I can't sit there a second longer. I have to get out. I just have to. I push back my chair and stand up as the waitress is heading over. She gives me an annoyed look, but I keep heading toward the door.

"Lizzie," Shari calls after me. "Lizzie, come on! I didn't know. You can't just walk out of here like that! Come back here and talk to me. Lizzie!"

But I keep going. I have to. Even though my tears are blinding me and I can't see where I'm going.

A HISTORY
of
WEDDINGS

The reason brides have traditionally stood to the left of the groom is so that he'll have his sword (right) arm free to fend off any last-minute would-be gentleman callers who might still want to press their suit.

It's also for this reason that originally best men were not attendants on the groom's side, but the bride's. They were supposed to defend the bride from any unwanted male attention that was not the groom's.

Unfortunately, the incidence of brides running off with best men tended to be rather high, so the position of best man was switched to the groom's side, and a maid of honor was appointed to the bride to keep her chaste. Weddings (and wedding parties) sure used to be a lot more interesting!

Tip to Avoid a
Wedding Day
Disaster

Don't be a bridezilla! Yes, everyone is going to have an opinion on who you ought to hire and what you ought to choose for your flowers, your cake, your wedding photos. Take the advice you like, and politely ignore or laugh off the rest. Don't take it all so personally! So what if your wedding isn't as grand/expensive/beautiful/bohemian as cousin Jacqueline's? It's not a contest! It's about your joining your life—forever—to someone else's. GET. OVER. IT.

LIZZIE NICHOLS DESIGNS™

Chapter 20

Hail, wedded love, mysterious law; true source of human happiness.

John Milton (1608–1674), English poet

My cell phone won't stop ringing. I know who it is. But I won't pick up.

I am standing on Madison Avenue between Seventy-seventh and Seventy-sixth Streets. I am staring into the windows of a shop. I've stopped crying and can now see clearly. I can make out every inch of the yards and yards of creamy white silk and petal soft lace draped on the mannequin in front of me. I can see every minute detail on the stitching, so fine it's almost invisible, the delicacy of the beading, the luxuriousness of the stiff tulle crinoline that holds the skirt in place. The gown is perfection personified.

It must cost thousands of dollars. Tens of thousands, maybe.

And yet.

And yet I think I could come up with something fairly close that—though it wouldn't be quite as sumptuous—would make the girl wearing it feel just as special.

For a fraction of the cost.

I'm just saying. What I do is cheap—yeah, okay? I'll admit it. But it's still pretty good. People like it. Ava Geck liked it. Jill Higgins liked it. Hundreds—well, okay, dozens—of other brides have liked it. It was good enough for them.

Okay, maybe it wasn't Vera Wang.

But it was good enough for their wedding day. It made them feel special. It made them look beautiful.

And that ability—that talent for taking something not so great and making it into something pretty, for not a lot of money—it's all I have.

I realize this as I stand there on the busy sidewalk, as the summer heat beats down on me and busy New Yorkers rush by.

The reality is, that's all I've got to contribute to the universe.

It's true. Shari helps women who've been abused. Chaz is going to teach philosophy, probably to students as snotty about it as he is. (But hey. That's important. Probably.) Luke is going to save the children—or help already rich people get richer, depending on what he decides. Tiffany models and answers phones, and Ava Geck . . . well, Ava does whatever she does, while Little Joey protects her.

And I make old wedding dresses pretty again. Sometimes I create new ones. For a fraction of what a designer gown at the shops around the corner on Madison Avenue would charge to do it.

It's an okay thing to do.

It has to be. Because it's all I've got.

And there's nothing wrong with that. Right?

My phone rings again. This time, when I glance at the display screen, I see that it's not Chaz, but Luke. Unable to imagine why he could be calling, I pick up.

"I heard," he says in a grim voice after I say hello.

My heart seems to stop. For a second, all the sounds of the busy street behind me—the honking, the sirens, the squealing of brakes—seem to fade away. All I can hear is my own breathing. And that seems shallow and irregular.

"You . . . heard?" I manage to wheeze.

"About the shop closing? Yeah," he says. "I called there first. Tiffany told me. Lizzie, I'm so sorry."

And my heart begins to beat again. And all the sounds of the city come floating slowly back.

"Oh," I say.

God. I am so stupid. Also, I am the worst Bad Girl ever to grace the Bad Girl Scale in the history of Bad Girls.

"Right. Yes. It's awful. I don't know what I'm going to do."

"I do," Luke says. "You're going to move to Paris with me."

I am trying not to be run over by all the people who are hurrying along the sidewalk. For the most part, they are stepping around me. But every once in a while, a harried Upper East Side mom on her way to some important lunch appointment uptown doesn't see me and almost barrels her Bugaboo baby carriage into me, and I have to move. This happens now, and in the confusion, I think I've misheard Luke.

"I beg your pardon?" I say to him.

"I know what you're going to say, Lizzie." He is thousands of miles away, but he sounds as if he were standing right beside me. Except for the car horns and occasional police siren down Madison Avenue, which makes him slightly difficult to hear. I put my finger in my nonphone ear, just to be sure.

"But just listen for a minute," he goes on. "I tried the medical school thing. I did. You can't say I didn't give it a fair shot. But . . . I just don't think I'm cut out for it. I can't hack another five or six—or more—years of school. I can't do it. I think it will kill me. I really do."

I watch as another young mother, this one pushing a newborn, walks by, a seven- or eight-year-old skipping by her side, an ice cream cone dripping all over his hand, down his arm, and onto the front of his shirt. Neither he nor his mom seems to care.

"Oh," I say.

"But since coming to work for Uncle Gerald—Lizzie. It's been great. I love it. I really do. I know when you first met me I was doing the same thing, and I said I didn't like it, and I seemed burned out . . . but this is different. Gerald's offered me my own department. I'll have people working under me." I've never heard Luke sound so enthusiastic. About anything. He sounds like his father sounds when he talks about wine. He sounds young. He sounds . . . *happy.* "There's just one catch."

"What's that?" I ask.

"It's here," Luke says. "In Paris. I'd have to move to Paris. Permanently."

"Oh," I say.

"But that's why when I heard what happened today at the shop," he goes on excitedly, "I thought, it's a perfect opportunity. You're out of a job, and I just got offered a great one. Lizzie, you can come here, to Paris. You can start over, like I'm doing. You can open a new shop here. A bridal shop. I walked by one the other day, and your dresses are a thousand times nicer. And much more afford-able. Everything here is so expensive. There's a real demand for affordable fashion. That's where your niche is, I think, Lizzie. That's what you need to do. Open your own shop here in Paris. A shop that offers beautiful couture for the ordinary girl, at prices she can afford. For brides."

"I already have a bridal shop," I say, sniffling. "In New York."

"I know," Luke says. "But that shop belongs to someone else. And they're selling it. I'm talking about a shop of your own."

"But . . ." I say, looking at the display window in front of me. "In *France?*"

"Look," Luke says. "You speak French. My family can loan you the start-up income. Lizzie . . . don't you see? This is a perfect opportunity for it."

"But." I look around at the people hurrying by in all their different shapes and colors, at the buildings all around me, at the taxis and buses and delivery vans and trucks whizzing by, the sun slanting through the leaves of a nearby tree, growing, against all odds, through the pavement, in the shadow of the skyscrapers all around us.

Because that's what New York City is all about. Trees growing up out of the pavement, in the shade, where no tree should ever grow.

And I say, "I love New York."

"You'll love Paris too," Luke says. "You've been there, remember? It's just like New York. Only better. Cleaner. Nicer."

"It's so far away," I say as a kid walking by with a dog fails to clean up after it, and a woman with a Chanel purse yells at him for it.

"From what, Lizzie?" Luke asks. "Your grandmother? She's dead. Remember?" But Gran isn't who I'm thinking about.

"I can't decide right now," I say. "I . . . I'll have to think about it."

"You do that," Luke says. "You think about it. You take all the time you need. But I think you should probably know . . . I've accepted the job my uncle offered me."

"*What?*" I think I must have misheard him again.

"We'll figure something out," Luke says hurriedly. "If you decide to stay in New York, we'll just do the long-distance thing for a while. People do, Lizzie. We'll make it work. Don't worry."

Don't worry? My fiancé—on whom, it is true, I am cheating— informs me that he is going to move permanently to another country, but that I shouldn't *worry*?

"And if you need a place to stay, you know you can always move back into my mother's place on Fifth. She already said it was all right. She'll just need to use the place one weekend a month, for her—you know . . ."

He means her monthly Botox injections. But I don't say that out loud, since Luke doesn't need me to remind him about that.

I am standing there, openmouthed in astonishment, when a voice behind me says, "Hey."

I spin around, startled, and see a flash of khaki and the brim of a baseball cap.

"Luke," I say into the phone. "I have to go. I . . . I'll call you later, all right?"

"Okay," he says. "Honestly, Lizzie . . . I don't want you to worry. About any of this. I'm going to take care of it. Of you. I love you."

"I . . . y-you too," I stammer. And hang up. Then I demand, "What are *you* doing here?"

"Standing in front of Vera Wang's flagship store?" Chaz quips. "Oh, I come here most days, actually. I like to try on a few of the mother-of-the-bride gowns. They feel so smooth and slinky against my skin." He blinks down at me. "Shari called me. What do you think? And then I called the shop when you wouldn't pick up any of my calls on your cell. Tiffany told me I might find you here. She says you like to come here to clear your head." He looks at the display window. "I can see why. It's so . . . *shiny*."

I stare at the shop window too. But what I'm actually looking at is our reflection, him so tall and lanky, with his University of Michigan baseball cap perched on top of his head, and his strong, muscular legs, so tanned, unlike the tourists who occasionally walk past. And me, slightly wilted in my sundress from having run all over town in the heat of high summer, my hair hanging in a bedraggled mess from my barrette, wanting, basically, to die. We make the strangest-looking couple.

If that's what we are. Which I'm not even sure of.

And of course behind our reflection is the beautiful, perfect Vera Wang wedding gown of the week. In a size two.

"They're closing the shop," I say to his reflection. "The Henris. They're closing it. And moving to Provence."

"I know. Tiffany told me that too." He shrugs, looking infuriatingly unconcerned. "So. What are you going to do?"

"I don't know," I yell at him. "What do you think I'm standing here trying to figure out?"

God! How can I be in love with him? How can he be so different from Luke, whom I thought I loved for so long? *I don't want you to worry. About any of this. I'm going to take care of it. Of you.* That's what Luke had to say.

Whereas all Chaz has to say is: *So. What are you going to do?*

Then again, I'm the one who was so keen on wanting to stand on my own two feet.

"Well, you'll figure it out," Chaz says now, with another shrug. "I'm starving. Have you had lunch?"

Have I had lunch? *That's* all he has to say?

"How?" I demand. "*How* will I figure it out?"

He looks a bit startled by my outburst. So does the Chinese-food deliveryman hurrying by.

"I don't know," Chaz says. "You'll open a new shop."

"Where? How? With what money?" I demand, my voice breaking. Because that's what I'm pretty sure my heart is doing.

"Jesus, I don't know, Lizzie. You'll figure it out. You always do. That's what's so amazing about you."

I turn my head and look up at him. Him, and not his reflection.

And I realize—as I've been realizing over and over all summer . . . all year, actually—how hard I've fallen for him.

This is really it, I realize. There's no turning back. I think I've just gone up a notch on the Bad Girl Scale.

"Luke is dropping out of medical school," I say. "He's taking a job with his uncle's company in Paris. He's *moving* to Paris."

"Gee," Chaz says tonelessly. "I'm so surprised to hear that."

I stare at him, appalled. "You *knew*? He *told* you already?"

He shrugs yet again. "He's my best friend. He tells me everything. What do you expect?"

"You told me," I say, shaking my head in disbelief. "You told me he's never been able to stick to anything in his life. And I thought you were nuts. But you were right. You were a hundred percent right."

"Luke's not a bad guy," Chaz says mildly. "He's just . . . confused."

"Well," I say, slipping my cell phone back into my purse. "Are you going to ask me?"

"Ask you what?"

"If I'm going to move to Paris with him? He wants me to, you know. He says his family will loan me the money to set up a shop there."

"I'm sure they will," Chaz says. "And no, I'm not going to ask you."

I set my jaw. For someone I'm so crazy about, Chaz happens to be the most infuriating person I've ever met.

"Why not?" I demand. "Don't you *want* me to stay here in New York?"

"Of course I do," Chaz says. "But, like I said, what happens in the future is already unavoidable. So I'm just going to enjoy what time I have left with you."

"That," I say disgustedly, "is such crap."

"Well," he says in the same unruffled tone, "that's probably true too. What do you feel like? I feel like Thai food. Do you feel like Thai food? Isn't there a good Thai place around the corner from here?"

"How can you think about food at a time like this?" I yell at him. "Do you know—do you have any earthly idea—that every time I think about marrying Luke, I break out in hives?"

Chaz raises his eyebrows. "That," he says, "is not a good sign. I mean, for him. And, I'm guessing, for Paris."

"It's a *horrible* sign," I say. "What did you mean back in Detroit when you said Luke hasn't exactly been a Boy Scout the whole time he and I have been going out?"

Chaz rolls his eyes. "Look," he says. "I don't really want to talk about this in front of the Vera Wang flagship store, okay? Let's go home. We can change out of these hot sticky clothes and I can run you a cool bath and order some Thai food and fix us both a couple of gin and tonics and we can sip them while we discuss the vagaries of life and I give you a full body massage—"

"No," I say, resisting the arm he's put around me. "Chaz! I'm serious. *This* is serious. I don't want to—"

But I never get the chance to tell Chaz what it is I don't want to do, because at that moment, two women who were passing by stop in front of the window and gaze at the gown I was admiring.

"See, Mom," the younger woman says. "That's the kind of dress I want."

"Well, dream on," her mother says. "Because a dress like that costs twenty grand. Do you have an extra twenty grand lying around?"

"It's not fair," the girl insists, stamping her Steve Madden–clad foot. "Why can't I have what I want? Just this once?"

"You can," the older woman says, "if you want to be paying for it for the next thirty years. Is that how you want to start your married life?"

"No," the bride says, sounding as if she's pouting a little.

"I didn't think so. So get over it. We're going to Kleinfeld's."

"God," the bride says as her mother drags her away. "You're so cheap. If you had your way, we'd get my wedding gown at *Geck's*."

The mother and daughter drift away, and I find myself staring after them in astonishment. Every single nerve ending in my body is tingling. I feel as if I've just caught fire.

A shop that offers beautiful couture for the ordinary girl, at prices she can afford. For brides.

"Oh my God, Chaz," I say. "Did you hear that?"

"Hear what?" He still has his arm around me. "The part about the full body massage I'm going to give you?"

"Them." I open my purse and start digging around in it for my cell phone. "Did you hear what they said?"

"About going to Kleinfeld's? Yeah. Hey, maybe that's where you should get a job. That's where everybody goes to get their wedding dresses. That's where my sister went. Not that it helped. She still looked like me. In a wedding dress. Poor kid. She tried waxing and everything."

"No," I say, stabbing at the numbers on the keypad of my phone. "Not that part."

Be there, I pray. *Pick up. Pick up.*

A second later, a voice chirps, "Hello?"

"It's me," I say. "Please don't hang up. I know you hate me. But I've got a business proposition I've got to talk to you about. It's important. And you won't regret it. I promise. Where are you?"

"Me?" She sounds slightly confused. "I'm at the dog run. Why?"

"Stay there," I say. "*Do not move.* I'll be right over."

A HISTORY
of
WEDDINGS

Carrying the bride over the threshold is a tradition that harkens back to the ancient practice of capturing brides from rival tribes or villages. It was also thought to—say it all together now—trick any evil spirits that might be lurking in the new home.

Today's modern bride may find the practice sexist or—often more alarming, considering the state of many HMOs—may fear her groom will throw his back out in attempting to lift her.

It is, for these reasons, a tradition that is losing popularity and may safely be skipped in lieu of a kitchen witch.

Tip to Avoid a Wedding Day Disaster

There is a rumor flying around that the cost of the gift you give at a wedding as a guest should roughly equal the amount of the cost of the food and wine you are served at the reception. This is ridiculous. Your gift should be tasteful—and does not even have to come from the bridal registry—but does not in any way have to be proportionate to the cost of what you are being served. Any bride who suggests otherwise deserves the wooden spoon you give her applied to her backside.

LIZZIE NICHOLS DESIGNS™

Chapter 21

Love is composed of a single soul inhabiting two bodies.

Aristotle (384 B.C.–322 B.C.), Greek philosopher

Wedding gowns?" Ava echoes, her carefully plucked eyebrows raised. "At Geck's?"

"Why not at Geck's?" I'm perched beside her on a park bench next to the small dog run at Carl Schurz Park. The small dog run is actually a raised, fenced-in stage along the boardwalk by the East River, where pedestrians can stop and watch the tiny dogs as they skitter after tennis balls thrown by their owners. This seems a source of particular delight to toddlers, whose parents lift them to stand along the edge of the stage, and who shriek in delight every time a Pomeranian or miniature pinscher comes dancing in their general direction.

Ava, however, is holding an exhausted Snow White in her lap. The Chihuahua has apparently run after so many tennis balls that she is virtually unconscious on her mistress's smooth, tanned thighs, a fact of which the reality television crew, filming Ava for the pilot she hopes gets picked up, *Slaves of Ava,* is taking pointed note. I can't help staring at the cameras looming over me, even though Ava has told me not to pay any attention to them.

"You don't even see them after a while," she says, with a yawn that, I can't help noticing, is made all the more elfin and charming by the fact that her bee-stung lips are perfectly glossed.

"Ava." It's even harder than usual to get her full attention due to the fact that DJ Tippycat is still inside the dog run with his French bulldog puppy, and Ava's gaze keeps straying toward him every five seconds. "Listen to me. You said you wanted to do something with your life. Remember? After you broke things off with Prince Aleksandros. You have to have meant something more than just another tired old reality show. Well, this is your chance. Not only to prove to the world that you're more than just a bubbleheaded heiress, but to help out millions of brides who want to have a beautiful gown but can't afford it."

Ava doesn't look remotely interested. She's gazing through the enormous black lenses of her sunglasses at a tugboat chugging down the river in front of us. I glance over my shoulder at Chaz, who is waiting for me out of camera range. He refused to sign the waivers the film crew demanded in order for me to speak to Ava while she was on camera, so he has to wait out of the shot until I'm done. He doesn't look too unhappy. He's found a hot dog vendor and is munching away, enjoying one with everything, along with a cold soda, in the shade.

"I don't know," Ava says. "What do I know about clothing design?"

"You don't have to design the gowns," I say through gritted teeth. "*I'll* take care of that part. You just have to market the clothes. And Geck Industries have to provide the labor and materials. I'm not talking sweatshop labor or cheap materials, either. I'm talking quality craftsmanship, sewn here, in America. The gowns have to look gorgeous and feel nice against the skin. But nothing can retail for more than four hundred dollars. It all just has to be designed by me and marketed by you . . . the Lizzie Nichols–Ava Geck bridal line."

She perks up at this. "Hey. I kind of like the sound of that."

"I thought you might," I say, eyeing the camera uncomfortably as they swoop around us.

"Lizzie and Ava," she says. "Or Ava and Lizzie?"

"Whichever," I say. I can't quite believe she's actually going for it. I'd been shocked she'd even taken my call, let alone agreed to meet with me. I hadn't planned much beyond my initial pitch, not thinking I'd get further than that. "Either works, I think."

"That's *so cute,*" Ava gushes with so much enthusiasm that Snow White nearly tumbles from her lap. "Can we, like, do brides-maid dresses too?"

"I don't see why not," I say. One of the cameras comes in for a close-up. I am acutely conscious of the fact I haven't powdered my nose all day, and that I am sweating copiously. I pray to God this show won't ever get picked up by a major network. Or Bravo.

On the other hand, if Ava accepts this deal, who even cares?

"And flower girls?" she asks.

"Sure," I say.

"What about clothes for dogs," Ava says. "When DJ Tippycat's divorce from that ho wife of his comes through, we want Snow White and Delilah to be in our wedding."

I look down at Snow White, struggling to find purchase on Ava's vinyl mini. One of the cameras zooms in on Ava's crotch. I switch my prayer to a different one . . . that she's wearing panties.

"Um," I say. "Sure. We can do a line of wedding wear for dogs."

"Okay," Ava says. "That sounds like fun." She eyes me a little uneasily. "But if we're going to work together, Lizzie, I need to know we're not gonna have that same . . . *problem* we had before . . . are we?"

I shake my head. "Ava, I swear on my grandmother's grave, I will never blab something I'm not supposed to ever again." And I know, as I say it, that this time I really mean it.

Really.

"Okay," Ava says cheerfully. "Lemme call Daddy." And she gets out her cell phone.

"Wait." I stare at her. "You're going to do it *now*?"

"Yeah," she says, dialing. "Why not?"

"Um." I glance over at Chaz. He beams at me and gives me a thumbs-up. "Nothing. Go ahead."

A second later, Ava's removed the gum from her mouth with a murmured *Sorry* in my direction, and is saying, "Daddy? It's me. Yeah, hi. So, I want to start my own line of bridal wear at the store. What? The reality show? Oh, whatever, that's so two thousand and seven. Anyway, I'm working with Lizzie, the girl who did my dress for my wedding to Alek? Uh-huh. Yeah, the one who outed me to the paps. But that, like, wasn't her fault, really. Her sister did it, and she's, like, a fat-armed cow. I know. Anyway, she wants to—well, here, I'll let her tell you." To my horror, Ava holds her pink Swarovski-encrusted phone out to me. "Tell him the thing about the beautiful gowns for girls at prices they can afford."

I fumble for the phone, my mouth going instantly dry. "Um, h-hello? Mr. Geck?"

"Yes?" A voice, gravelly from too many years of cigar smoke, demands impatiently.

I repeat Luke's line about beautiful gowns that brides can actually afford, and somehow the same spiel I'd given Ava just seconds ago about how Geck's would be in charge of labor and materials—but they couldn't be cheap!—and I'd be in charge of design while Ava would be in charge of marketing comes spilling from between my lips.

And in that moment, sitting in the sunshine by the river, with the *Slaves of Ava* camera crew on me, and Henry Geck on the phone, and Chaz a few dozen yards away, watching over me like a shaggy sheepdog, I'm pretty sure I have an actual out-of-body experience. It's as if all the times I have ever blabbed a secret involuntarily or said something I didn't mean to or revealed an intimacy probably best left unsaid, and was called upon to exercise my powers of charm in order to make amends come back to me with laserlike intensity and focus on a single point—the man on the other end of the phone. I am no longer Lizzie Nichols, almost-certified professional vintage wedding gown refurbisher, fiancé of Luke de Villiers, on whom (by the way) she is cheating with his best friend, currently probably a two on the Bad Girl Scale, about to lose her home, her business, and her life.

I am Elizabeth Nichols, cool and collected designer of wedding attire, with a single desire: to make beautiful bridal gowns—and bridesmaid and flower girl and dog clothes—available to the masses, at a reasonable price.

Suddenly I am on fire. I am invincible. The cameras swing entirely from Ava and onto me. Even though, as she gazes at me, her thighs swing apart, and it becomes apparent she's going commando today. And she's gone and gotten herself a Brazilian.

"Well," Mr. Geck says when I'm through and have paused to take a breath. "Miss Nichols, I must say. That sounds like an interesting idea. I'd certainly like to hear more. Why don't you and Ava come over for dinner tonight and we'll talk about it some more? Put her back on the horn."

I hand the phone back to Ava, feeling dazed.

"He wants to talk to you," I say.

"Oh, goody," Ava says. "Hi, Daddy. You like Lizzie's idea? Yeah, I know, me too. Okay. Eight? Yeah, we'll be there. Okay, buh-bye." She hangs up and looks at me. "He wants you to bring some sketches. Do you have any?"

I look at her, feeling slightly nauseous.

But it's a good nauseous. It's a *great* nauseous, actually.

"By eight tonight," I say a little hazily, "I will have."

•　•　•

"You're going to design a line of bridal gowns for Geck's?" Chaz asks as we hurry down Seventy-eighth Street, back toward Chez Henri. "And Ava Geck is going to do . . . what, exactly?"

"Be my spokesmodel slash corporate representative," I say.

"Does Geck's even sell nice clothes?" Chaz wants to know.

"They will after they start selling mine," I say. "Ava will make sure of that. They're going to have her name on them too."

"And you trust her?" Chaz sounds dubious. "Ava, I mean. No offense, Lizzie, but—"

"If the next words that come out of your mouth are 'skanky crack whore,' you're never setting foot in my apartment again. For however little time left I have it."

"I'm just saying, like another person whose name I won't mention, Ava doesn't exactly have a reputation for stick-to-it-tiveness. Except where pudding wrestling is concerned."

"Maybe because no one has really given her a chance to prove herself," I say defensively. "I mean, she's an heiress. When has she ever *had* to stick to anything? But she seems really serious about this. The dog clothes were her idea."

"Oh yeah," Chaz says, with a chuckle, putting his arm around my shoulders. "She's serious about this all right."

"Chaz," I say, leaning into him. I don't care that I'm hot and sweaty (and so is he). Even when I'm annoyed with him, like now, I can't stop myself from touching him. It just feels . . . *right*. "People love their pets. They really want them to be a part of their special day."

"But doesn't the idea of your enabling them to do so by designing mini doggie tuxedos for them make you the slightest bit queasy?"

"No," I say firmly. "Not if it's going to save the jobs of everyone at the shop."

"And how is your designing doggie tuxedos for Geck's going to do that?" Chaz wants to know.

"I haven't figured that part out yet," I say as we hurry along. "I'm just taking this one step at a time. First I've got to get these sketches done. Then get the deal in place. Then I'll get to that part."

"You're incredible," Chaz says. And there's no hint of sarcasm in his tone now.

Still, I pull him to a stop and narrow my eyes as I peer up at him. "Are you mocking me?" I demand suspiciously.

"Absolutely not," Chaz says, looking down at me with a perfectly serious expression on his face. He's dropped his arm from my shoulders, but now he puts both his hands there instead. "I told you before—you're a star, Lizzie Nichols. And I am humbled to be allowed to hitch my wagon to your star. Just tell me what you need me to do to help, and I'll do it."

I blink up at him and my eyes fill with sudden tears. It's still astonishing to me how blindly stupid I'd been, refusing to see what was right there in front of my face for so long. That I could have been this happy six months ago, if I'd just been willing to admit to myself what I'd clearly known all along . . . that it wasn't Luke I was in love with anymore after all.

But I don't say any of this to Chaz. There's no reason to. Not now. Because I've said it already.

Instead, I say, "Diet Coke."

He tightens his grip on my shoulders. "You need Diet Coke? To get the drawings done?"

I nod.

"Done," he says. "I'll get you every six-pack in the city. I—"

Then his voice trails off, and I notice his gaze has as well. We've reached Chez Henri, where I'm startled to find, when I turn to look in the direction he's gazing, Shari sitting on the front stoop.

She climbs to her feet when she sees me looking at her, her hemp tote bag dangling from limp fingers as she stares.

"Well," Chaz says, dropping his hands from my shoulders. "*This* is awkward."

"Hi, Shari," I say unsmilingly, aware that Shari is close enough to have overheard every word we've just said to each other.

"Hi, Lizzie," she says. Shading her eyes from the sun with one hand, she squints down at us from the stoop and says, "Hi, Chaz. I need to talk to Lizzie for a minute."

"This is a really bad time," I say. "I'm in kind of a time crunch. Can we talk later?"

"No," Shari says and comes down from the stoop. "Look. I'm really sorry about what I said earlier. I was out of line."

"You were really trying to fix us up the whole time?" Chaz wants to know.

"Please stay out of this," Shari says to him. To me, she says, "Lizzie, you're my best friend in the whole world. I would never do anything to hurt you. I should never have said that about the Carvel cake. That was in poor taste, and I owe you an apology."

"What Carvel cake?" Chaz wants to know.

"I know you didn't mean it," I say to Shari, feeling suddenly remorseful over how I've treated her. "And I shouldn't have run out of the café like that. I'm a dork. I'm sorry too. Do you forgive me?"

"Of course I do," Shari says, and pulls me in for a hug. I inhale her Shari-like scent—grapefruit body lotion and Labrador retriever—and then let go of her.

"And now I'm sorry, but I really do have to go," I say. "I have to design a line of bridal wear for Geck's."

"Geck's?" Shari looks confused. "They sell bridal wear?"

"They do now," Chaz explains. "Or they will after they see Lizzie's drawings. Lizzie and Ava Geck are going into business together."

"Is that really such a good idea?" Shari asks, looking dubious.

"Why does everyone keep asking me that?" I demand. "*Yes*, it's a good idea. Now, bye—I have to go get to work."

I give them both kisses—Shari on the cheek, Chaz on the mouth—and hurry into the shop to find Monique reading the latest copy of *Vogue*.

"Lizzie," she says, looking up when I come in. "*There* you are. God. Finally. Everyone and their brother has been looking for you, it seems."

"Keep taking messages," I say. "I've got some work to do upstairs. I'll be gone for the rest of the day."

"But, Lizzie," Monique says, looking dismayed. "You *do* know that—"

"Yes, of course I know all about it," I say. "I'm doing the best I can to save our skins. So hold all my calls, will you?"

"All right," Monique says. "But—"

"Thanks!"

I pop out the side door and hurry upstairs to my apartment, crank up the A/C, peel off my sticky, sweaty sundress, grab the last Diet Coke in my fridge—Chaz better hurry with his delivery—and get to work.

A HISTORY
of
WEDDINGS

Ever wonder why it's called a "shower"? In the late nineteenth century, a bride would invite her closest friends and relatives over for a little stress relief right before the wedding. Everyone would bring small token gifts that would be placed in an upside-down, umbrella or parasol. This would then be raised and turned over the bride, and the gifts would "shower" down on her for luck.

How this charming little tradition transformed into the monstrosities we know as showers today is a mystery for the ages.

Tip to Avoid a
Wedding Day
Disaster

*Bathrooms. No one wants to think or talk about them . . .
until there aren't enough of them, or they're overflowing . . .
during your reception.*

We know you've got a lot on your mind, but when choosing a place for your reception, make sure you take into account the little things . . . like where your guests are gonna go. Because they're gonna hafta.

Are you going to be the one to tell them to hold it?

LIZZIE NICHOLS DESIGNS™

Chapter 22

Marriage is the mother of the world and preserves king-doms, and fills cities, and churches, and heaven itself.
Jeremy Taylor (1613–1667), English clergyman

I am in a state of such advanced shock when I emerge from the Geck's limo shortly before midnight that I don't notice at first that the hall lights are on in the Henris' building when I stumble through the door. I didn't leave them on when I left, because I was in so much panic about my drawings—some of which were still only half-finished—I completely forgot.

But they're on now. Who could have switched them on? Not a burglar, surely. Why would he want to announce his presence to the world?

Could it be Chaz? He has a key, of course.

But Chaz would *never* let himself in knowing I'm not there. Especially when I'd made it very clear I'd call him when I was ready to see him. He just isn't the let-himself-in-unannounced type.

And while Sylvia and Marisol have been known to work late,

they've never worked *this* late—and they don't answer when I call out toward the workroom.

Great. This is the one disadvantage of living alone. The part where I could at any time be murdered, and no one in the building can hear my screams. Because I'm the only one in my building.

Gripping my keys so that each one protrudes from between a knuckle, my hand now resembling Wolverine's from *X-Men*, I start up the stairs, my body tense as I strain to hear any heavy breathing or scraping of Freddy Krueger–like claws that will give away whoever is waiting to strangle me on the top floor.

But I hear nothing. The hallway is silent. Maybe I'm imagining things. Maybe, in the excitement of the evening, I *did* flick on the lights before I left.

I've almost convinced myself of this as I unlock the front door to my apartment, throw it open, and find a strange man standing beside my living room couch.

I let out a scream loud enough to wake the dead.

"Jesus," Luke cries, laughing. "Lizzie! It's me!"

It is. It's Luke. Luke—my fiancé. Who is supposed to be in Paris, France.

Only he's not in Paris, France. He is standing in my living room.

"Surprise!" he cries.

Oh, I'm surprised, all right. I'm very, very surprised.

Just not as surprised as Luke might have been, had I not come home alone. And it's mere luck that I didn't.

"What are you doing here?" I can't help bursting out.

"I felt so awful about everything you were going through," Luke says, coming toward me. "I heard Uncle Gerald had booked a private charter to the city for a meeting, so I grabbed a seat on it."

He looks so handsome in his cream-colored linen suit, with his pale blue tie, and his dark tan and flashing white teeth. It's almost as if he were another species from Chaz.

But not a species I care to know. Anymore.

I can't help taking a quick step backward as Luke approaches me.

"Wow," I say. "A private charter! How . . . luxurious!"

"Yeah," Luke says, taking another step toward me. "I got here in six hours. Total travel time. From France! Can you believe it?"

"That's amazing." I take another step backward. If this keeps up, soon I'll be in the hallway again.

"I know," Luke says with another of his dazzling smiles. "Isn't it?"

Luke takes another step forward, and I'm trapped with my back against the door. He twines an arm around my waist and leans down to kiss me. I have to use every ounce of self-restraint in my power to keep from jerking my face away from his.

And then his lips are on mine—those lips I used to love so much—and he's kissing me hello.

And I feel . . . nothing.

Nothing! How can I feel nothing? I used to adore this man! I made love on a wine cask to this man! I wanted nothing on earth but to marry this man and have his babies and be with him for the rest of my life.

But I guess there's more to a relationship than making love on wine casks. Like making the other person laugh until milk comes out of her nose.

And being there for her when she really, really needs you.

I guess that's how, after not having seen him for nearly a month, when Luke kisses me, I'm capable of feeling nothing.

Luke lifts his head and looks down at me through half-lidded eyes—those eyes I've always found so dreamy, with those impossibly long, dark lashes.

"Is everything all right?" he wants to know.

"Sure!" I cry. "Everything's fine. Why wouldn't it be?"

"I don't know," Luke says. "You just seem . . . nervous about something."

"Oh," I say, laughing like a hyena. I'm aware that his hands are on my hips. My hips that are unadorned by Spanx. I think this is the first time ever. Since last summer, anyway. I mean, that he's touched my un-Spanxed hips and I haven't been naked in bed. Lying down in a prone position. "I am. I just came from a meeting with the Gecks."

"The who?" Luke looks confused.

"The Gecks. You know, *Get it at Geck's*?"

"Oh," Luke says. But I can tell he has no idea what I'm talking about. "And how did that go?"

"It went *great*," I say. I can still hardly believe it. Suddenly my nervousness is forgotten in my excitement over recounting my incredible evening. "Luke, you don't even know . . . your idea—offering brides beautiful dresses at prices they can afford—it was brilliant. A brilliant idea. Ava Geck and I—her whole family and I, as a matter of fact—we're going into business together. My designs, their business savvy. We're going to give brides across America beautiful, *nice* dresses that they can afford. Not just brides, either. Bridesmaids, mothers of the bride, flower girls, dogs—it's going to be *huge*."

Luke laughs—mostly at my enthusiasm, I think. It's pretty clear he has no idea what I'm talking about. I don't think he's ever even heard of Geck's. Well, his family probably never shopped there in their lives. Maybe his mom sent their housekeeper there to buy cleaning supplies.

But, ever the loyal fiancé, he *acts* like he knows what I'm talking about.

"Lizzie," he says. "That's *great*! I'm so proud of you!"

"Thanks," I say. "This all just happened. Just now. I . . . I'm still a little shell-shocked, I guess. It's exactly what I've always wanted,

Luke. It's going to solve everything. Mr. Geck made me an offer—you can't even believe how much."

"Well, that's even better," Luke says, grinning more broadly. "We can both fly back to Paris in style, then!"

I stare at him. And realize I need to sit down. Fast.

Oh God. How can I do this? I can't—I can't do this. I'm *not* a Bad Girl. I'm not!

And yet, for the past week, that's exactly what I've been acting like. Maybe—deep down—I *am* a Bad Girl.

Either way, it's time to pay the price for my actions.

"Yeah," I say, heading for the couch, where I sink down before my knees can buckle beneath me. "Listen. About that."

"Uh-oh," Luke says. The grin has vanished. "I don't think I like the tone of your voice right now, Lizzie. Should I be scared? Because suddenly I'm scared."

I look up at him—his gorgeous, perfect face. I can't help shaking my head.

"Luke," I say, in a *Who are we kidding with this?* voice. "Come *on*."

He spreads out both his hands in a *What, me?* gesture. "What?"

"Seriously," I say. "Get real with me. For once. I know you're Mr. Nice Guy and everything. But was that not the worst kiss ever?"

He drops his hands.

And suddenly he drops the pretense as well.

And I realize I may not have to pay anything at all.

"Okay," he says in an entirely different tone, coming over to the couch and collapsing onto it beside me. It's as if all the bones have gone from his body. I can see the jet lag has finally kicked in. "Yeah. I'm glad you said something. God . . . Lizzie . . . I thought it was me."

The relief that surges through me is like an electric pulse. It leaves me slumped beside him like a rag doll. I think I must feel almost as exhausted as he is—and I haven't just traveled thousands of miles to get here.

"It's not you," I say. It's horrible to be falling back on a tired cliché like this. But in this particular case, it really is true. "It's me."

"No, Lizzie," Luke says. "It's not you."

"No," I assure him. "It really is."

But I'm not going to tell him about Chaz. If I have my way, he's *never* going to know about Chaz. At least, not until a suitable mourning period for our failed relationship has passed, during which Luke's had time to find a fabulous new girlfriend—maybe someone like Valencia, a size 2 who'll fit into that Vera Wang wedding gown I saw in that display window today—and who will cause him to forget all about me.

"I think I just . . . I pushed you too hard for a commitment you weren't ready to make," I say.

"No," he says valiantly. "That's not true. It's just . . . we're just at such different places in our lives right now. Jesus, Lizzie, we even ended up on different *continents*. How could we ever have hoped to make this work?"

I can actually think of a lot of ways we could have made it work. But considering it's clear neither of us *wants* to make it work anymore, it seems better to leave them unsaid.

So instead I say, "Well, we can still be friends, right?"

"Always," Luke says, trying to look sad. But I can see such relief in his sleepy brown eyes, it's almost comical. It's the same relief I'd felt out on my stoop that night before he'd left for France, when I'd told him we were taking a break.

I know exactly how he feels. How is this even possible? How could we have disentangled ourselves from this without so much as an angry word or even a tear? Is it possible that we're just . . . well, *adults*?

"Here," I say. "I want to make sure you get this back."

And I pull off the diamond that's been weighing down my left ring finger for so many months. It slips off so easily, it's almost scary.

"No," Luke says, looking slightly panicky, putting out a hand to stop me. "Lizzie—no. I want you to keep it."

"Luke, I can't keep it," I say.

"Really," Luke says, looking completely panic-stricken. I'm not imagining it. "I don't want it. What am *I* going to do with it?"

"I don't know," I say. I don't understand this. Why won't he take it? "Sell it. Luke, I'm breaking off our engagement. I can't keep it."

"No, *I'm* the one breaking off our engagement," Luke insists. "*I* can't keep it. *You* sell it."

The relief is gone from his eyes. Now I see genuine terror growing there. He *really* doesn't want the ring.

Something, I can tell, is wrong. Very wrong.

And our breakup had been going so nicely up until now.

"Okay," I say gently, slipping the ring under some magazines on the coffee table, since the sight of it seems to upset him so much. "I'll keep it."

The relief creeps back into his face.

"Good," he says, visibly relaxing again. "Good. I want you to have it. I do."

Um . . . okay. What kind of guy wants his ex to keep the ring? Especially a ring that cost as much as mine had to have. (Okay. Twenty-two thousand. Tiffany looked it up one day on the Cartier Web site. She was bored.)

I'll tell you what kind of guy: a guy with a guilty conscience. That's what kind.

But surely not. Not Luke. Not my sweet, handsome, loving Luke, whom I so cruelly wronged by boinking his best friend in a Knight's Inn when I went home for my grandmother's funeral.

(Which, by the way, Luke did not fly home for. But he did fly home when I lost my job and apartment. Except that I was more upset about losing Gran. Let's face it, you can always get another job and find another place to live. You can never replace your grandmother.)

Luke would never do anything for him to have a guilty conscience about. He's exactly what Shari accused him of being—too perfect. Sure, I *thought* he might be cheating on me all those nights he spent studying at his place and those afternoons he was at the library, when he said he didn't want to see me.

But that was just my overactive imagination. *I'm* the only one with a guilty conscience in this relationship.

Luke yawns—then *does* look guilty. But only about his rudeness.

"Oh my God," he says. "I'm so sorry . . ."

"You must be exhausted," I say. "You should go. I'd offer to let you crash here, but—"

But we just broke up.

I don't have to elaborate. Luke gets the message.

"No," Luke says, getting up. "Sorry. I'll go to my mom's. God, this feels so weird. It's weird, isn't it? Is it weird?"

"It's weird," I assure him, standing as well. It's just not as weird as he knows. "But I think it's good. It's a good thing."

"I hope so," Luke says.

And, as we hug good-bye at my doorway, and he gazes down at me, I see that there are actual tears gathered in those deep brown eyes of his. No, really. They're hovering, like the tiny Swarovski crystals that dot Ava Geck's phone (only not pink) on the edges of his tremendously long eyelashes.

As if I didn't feel guilty enough. Now I've made him cry.

"You know I'll always love you, right, Lizzie?" Luke asks.

"Of course," I say. Though I'm thinking, Oh my God. This is so

. . . Are those really tears? *Actual* tears? Why aren't I crying? Should I cry? I guess so, I'm the girl. Oh God, I should be crying. But I don't feel like crying. Is that because I'm not in love with him anymore, because I'm in love with Chaz? Shouldn't I cry for what might have been, for the children Luke and I will never have now? Is this because of the hives? It's hard to cry for a guy who gave me so many hives, I guess. And because he gave up medical school to be an investment banker. If he'd gone through with the doctor thing, I'd be crying, for sure.

I think.

Then Luke gives me one last affectionate hug, kisses the top of my head, and leaves.

As soon as I hear the front door close, and I see him walking slowly down my street through my front window, I'm on my cell phone.

"Get over here right now," I say into it.

"Is this a booty call?" Chaz replies, sounding delighted.

"You are never going to guess who was just here," I say.

"Seeing as how you were at the Gecks this evening," he says, "I am going to take a wild guess and say . . . Neil Diamond?"

"Luke," I say, clutching my phone so tightly my fingers hurt. "He shared a private charter over from Paris with his uncle. We just broke up."

"I'm on my way," Chaz says, not even a hint of humor in his voice.

A HISTORY
of
WEDDINGS

The first known bachelor party took place in Sparta in the fifth century B.C. Military comrades about to conduct a raiding party to fetch themselves some new brides toasted and feted one another. Since then, men have gathered on the eve before one of them is about to tie the knot to become inebriated, mourn the passing of their friend's singlehood, and ogle dancing girls.

Brides are encouraged to ignore this long-standing rite of manhood. It's been around way longer than you have, honey. Let him have his fun. You'll get your revenge . . . on your wedding night.

Mother of the bride (or groom), don't think we've forgotten you. You'll want to look your best on the big day as well. How? It's easy. Start shopping for your dress early, so you'll have plenty of time to find the perfect look for you. Neutrals are always elegant (leave red to your husband's trashy new wife and white is, of course, for the bride only), as is black if it's not a morning ceremony. Nothing too glitzy unless it's an evening reception.

And remember, you can never go wrong with a good support undergarment, such as Spanx.

LIZZIE NICHOLS DESIGNS™

Chapter 23

Let us celebrate the occasion with wine and sweet words.

Titus Maccius Plautus (254–184 B.C.), Roman playwright

He is at my apartment in fifteen minutes. It's amazing how fast a taxi can travel seventy blocks uptown along First Avenue after midnight.

"I want to know everything," he says, slinging his backpack— we have not progressed to the point where either of us has a drawer at the other's apartment yet—onto my couch. "But first . . . how did it go at Ava's parents' place?"

"Oh, Chaz . . ."

And the next thing I know, I'm in his arms, and it's— I don't know how to describe it. It's completely different from being in my former fiancé's arms. Instead of feeling self-conscious and strange and awkward, the way I had when Luke and I hugged a little while ago, I feel safe and comforted and, most important of all, loved—completely and wholeheartedly loved—when Chaz's arms are around me. I close my eyes, letting his warmth envelop me, and suddenly the tears that hadn't been there with Luke show up.

"Whoa," Chaz says with a gentle laugh, kissing my cheeks. "It was that bad? They didn't like your drawings? How could they not have liked them? I've always loved your little stick women. Did you put top hats on them? I love it when you put top hats on them."

"N-no," I stammer, shaking my head as he grips my waist. "Th-they l-loved the top hats! Well, I mean, I didn't put top hats on any of them. But they loved the drawings."

"They did? Then what's the problem?"

"I—I'm just so happy!"

It's true. I feel so happy, standing there in my living room slash dining room slash kitchen, with Chaz's arms around me, and—now that I'm no longer engaged—my status on the Bad Girl Scale back to negative, I think my heart might burst.

"So the Gecks are buying your designs," Chaz says.

I nod. "I'm in charge of design and quality control. Ava's doing marketing. Her dad's taking care of everything else. Chaz . . . I think this could be really great. It's not going to be crappy. It's really not. Because Ava's super-invested in it. Because her name's going to be on it. She's actually taking it seriously. I've never seen her take anything this seriously. It helps that she's so into this DJ Tippycat guy, and he turns out to have a business degree from Syracuse. His real name is Joshua Rubenstein. He was there tonight too."

Chaz looks impressed. "And what about the shop? Tiffany and Monique, and Sylvia and Marisol?"

I chew my lip. "I have a plan for them too," I say. "But . . . it's going to involve some driving."

"Driving?" he echoes. "Driving where?"

"To New Jersey," I say, taking his hand and pulling him down onto the couch. "But first . . . Chaz, seriously . . . and no joking around. Just tell me. I *need* to know. What did you mean when you said that stuff about Luke not being a Boy Scout while we were dating? Because when we broke up just now . . . he insisted on my keeping this." I lean over and pick up the ring from where I've hidden it beneath a copy of *People*. "Chaz, this is an expensive ring. Why would he insist on my keeping it unless he felt *super*-guilty about something? Huh? It doesn't make any sense."

Chaz looks down at the ring and shakes his head.

"God," he says. "I can't believe he didn't take it back. Did he cry?"

"When we broke up?" I look at him in surprise. "Yeah, he did, a little. How did you know?"

Chaz takes a deep breath. Then he lets it out in a whoosh.

"Luke wasn't exactly Mr. Innocence himself the whole time you two were going out, all right?" Chaz lifts his gaze from the ring and locks it onto mine. "Did you really think he was studying all those nights he said he was at the library? Because that's not what he was doing."

I blink. "I *knew* it," I say. "Shari was right! He really *was* too perfect. There *was* something creepy about it." Then I add, "Wait. You'd better not be making this up to make me feel better about what *we've* been doing . . ."

"Better?" Chaz echoes. "Hell, all this time, I've been afraid to tell you. I thought you'd have a nervous breakdown if you found out."

"If this is a joke," I threaten, still not sure whether or not I believe him, "to make me feel less like a two on the Bad Girl Scale, it really isn't very funny . . ."

"I'm not joking," Chaz says gravely. "And I don't know what a Bad Girl Scale is. It was that girl Sophie, from his class, all right? The one who knew the guy who got us a table at the Spotted Pig that night. He was doing her behind your back all last semester. You should have seen her. You'd have flipped out. She wore that

Juicy Couture stuff you hate. And those giant sunglasses with Dolce & Gabbana written on the side?"

I shake my head.

"No," I say. "Nice try. But you'd never have kept something like that a secret this long. You'd have told me."

"Actually," Chaz says, sounding dead serious for a change, "I couldn't tell you, Liz. How could I have told you about Luke sleeping with another woman behind your back when you were still so in love with him—or at least when I thought you were still so in love with him? How would that have looked? Consider my position, being in love with you, and wanting you for myself. Had I come to you before I'd actually, ahem, managed to win you over, as I apparently have now, and suggested to you that your fiancé was sleeping around behind your back, what, exactly, would I have accomplished? Yeah, you might have broken up with Luke, and yeah, you might have slept with me. But how would I know that I wouldn't have been just some revenge screw—some way for you to get back at Luke for what he'd done to you?"

I blink at him.

The thing is, I believe him. Mostly because of the details—he couldn't make up that Dolce & Gabbana thing. Chaz doesn't know anything about designers—look at his shorts. But also because of the incredibly coarse way he was putting it.

What he was actually saying is incredible.

But, given his bluntness, it might just be true.

"That's not what I wanted," Chaz goes on. There isn't a hint of sarcasm or laughter in his tone now. His blue eyes look almost pained. "That's the *last* thing I wanted. For the longest time—since way before New Year's, since the day I helped you move into this place—I wanted you any way I could get you. And that's the truth. But I wanted you for keeps, Lizzie. And you weren't going to stick around if that's all I was to you, a revenge screw, a way to hurt Luke. So . . . yeah, I didn't tell you. Until now. So sue me."

Then, his shoulders still hunched, he whips out his cell phone. "Besides. I can prove it to you."

The next thing I know, he's pressed a button on his keypad. A second later, he's saying, "Luke?"

"Chaz," I cry. "No—"

But it's too late.

"Oh, hey, man," Chaz says conversationally, into the phone. "Oh, sorry, did I wake you? Oh no? You're in town? What are you doing in town?"

I cannot believe this is happening. I flop back against the couch, slapping my hands over my eyes. I can't watch.

"Oh, you did? Really? Oh yeah? Oh, she did? Oh, really. Oh, that's too bad." Chaz leans over and pokes me, but I don't take my hands from my eyes. Finally, after a few more "really"s, I hear Chaz say, "Yeah, so, if you and Lizzie are splitting up, I guess that means things are really going to heat up with Sophie."

Chaz must have put the phone close to my ear, because I hear Luke's voice saying, "Well, you know, I'm going to be moving to France, so I guess I won't be seeing as much of Sophie. But you know there's this fantastic woman I've been seeing in my new office, that one I was telling you about, Marie . . ."

I take my hands away from my eyes and just look at him. Chaz's expression is a beguiling mixture of anxiety—that my feelings are hurt—and laughter. It is kind of hard not to see the humor in the situation. It's not as if I *care* who Luke's been doing behind my back.

I just hope he, like me, has been using a condom.

When he sees that I'm smiling too, Chaz puts the phone back to his ear and says, "Uh, Luke? So, listen, since you and Lizzie aren't seeing each other anymore, I was wondering . . . how would you feel if I asked her out? Because, you know, I think she's a great girl, and I've always sort of—"

Even from where I'm sitting, three feet away, I can hear Luke's voice curtly cutting Chaz off.

Chaz's grin grows more broad.

"Oh," he says, his blue eyes twinkling at me. "You don't think that would be a very good idea? Why? You think you're such a sex god you should just have *all* the great girls for yourself, even after you're done with them, is that it?"

Laughing, I gasp, "Chaz, don't!" and reach out to wrestle the phone away from him.

"No?" Chaz is saying into the phone, even as he wraps an arm around my waist and wrestles me noisily to the floor. "Oh, because she's in a very fragile state right now? I don't think she's in quite as fragile a state as you might think. What was that noise? Oh, I think that was just . . . my upstairs neighbor. Yeah, he just brought home another trannie from that bar down the street. Hey, Johnny"— Chaz takes the phone away from his face and yells at the walls as he tickles me mercilessly, while I try not to blow our cover by laughing—"it's called abstinence! You should give it try! Oops, Luke, I gotta go, he's puking in the hallway. Yeah, he's sliding around in his puke. I'll call you later."

Chaz hangs up, throws his cell phone over his shoulder, then dives on top of me, burying his face in my neck. I can barely breathe I'm laughing so hard.

And I realize something: I've never had such a good time in my entire life.

Which is a lot to say, considering the day I've had.

A HISTORY
of
WEDDINGS

Anyone familiar with her historical romances knows that any young bride worth her salt went to Scotland to elope in nineteenth-century Europe (even back then girls under eighteen weren't allowed to wed without their parents' permission). Even Elizabeth Bennet in Jane Austen's *Pride and Prejudice* despairs when she learns her flighty sister Lydia has not gone to Gretna Green with her lover, Wickham, for it meant he had no intention of marrying her.

Scotland is still a popular wedding destination for Americans, and many travel packages for that purpose can be purchased. Although care should be taken to fill out the necessary paperwork stateside before going, or the unwary bride could find herself in the same situation as poor, unhappy Lydia.

Eloping doesn't necessarily mean a couple has to miss out on the fun of wedding gifts! The couple's parents or other relatives or friends can still choose to host a reception for them upon their return. They can even still register for gifts and be within the confines of good taste and etiquette. With weddings growing to be so costly these days, some parents are finding it less expensive to pay their daughters to elope.

We should all be so lucky.

LIZZIE NICHOLS DESIGNS™

Chapter 24

There is nothing nobler or more admirable than when two people who see eye to eye keep House as man and wife, confounding their enemies and delighting their friends.

Homer (eighth century B.C.), Greek poet

I find Monsieur Henri in his back garden the next morning, precisely where his wife said he'd be: practicing on his homemade *pétanque* lane.

He seems surprised to see me.

Well, I don't suppose it's often he receives visitors from Manhattan to his suburban Cranbury, New Jersey, home.

Especially while he's still in his terrycloth bathrobe.

"Elizabeth!" he cries, dropping the *pétanque* ball in the dust and hurrying to close his robe. He casts an indignant look at his wife, coming up behind us with a tray of iced tea.

"I'm sorry, Jean," she says. But if you ask me, she doesn't look the least bit sorry. "Elizabeth phoned earlier this morning to say she was coming with something important to discuss with us. I did call out to you. But I suppose you didn't hear me."

Monsieur Henri watches, dumbfounded, as his wife sets the

tray down on the small metal table beneath the rose-covered arbor at the end of his *pétanque* lane, then takes a seat on the bench beside it. Always a large man, her husband has lost a lot of weight since his surgery. But he is still sweating in the summer heat, even in the shade of the arbor. He looks down at the three glasses of iced tea before him.

"Well," he says. "I suppose I can take a break. For a moment."

"That would be nice," I say. I flick a glance toward the house. Chaz is driving around the neighborhood, having assured me he'd be back in half an hour to pick me up in the car we rented from Avis that morning. "I'll just cruise the strip malls," he'd said. "Pick you up a thong from Victoria's Secret. I've never seen you in a thong. Or anything from Victoria's Secret, for that matter."

There's a reason for that, I'd assured him.

I take a seat on the bench beside Madame Henri, after carefully tucking my vintage Lilly Pulitzer wraparound skirt beneath me, waiting until Monsieur Henri has lowered himself carefully into the teak Adirondack chair opposite us before I speak.

"I'm so sorry to bother you here at your home, Monsieur Henri," I say. "But it's about the building—"

"Now, Elizabeth," Monsieur Henri says with hearty kindness as he reaches for one of the glasses of iced tea and swirls around the twig of mint his wife has plopped into it. "I really don't think there's anything more we can say about that. We're listing it with Goldmark, and that's that. I'm very sorry about your having to find another job and an apartment, but like we said, we'll put in a good word for you with Maurice—you'll have the best references there are . . . you'll have no trouble at all finding a job—and you will just have to be satisfied with that. Really, this begging . . . it's not attractive. I'm rather surprised at you, I must say."

"Actually," I say, reaching for my own glass of iced tea, pleased to see that my hand isn't shaking at all as I hold it. Way to go,

Lizzie! "I'm not here to beg for my job, Monsieur Henri. I've found another job. I'm here to make an offer on your building."

Monsieur Henri nearly drops the glass he's holding. Madame Henri chokes a little on the mouthful of iced tea she's just taken.

"I . . . I beg your pardon, Elizabeth?" She coughs.

"I know I ought to have gone through your Realtor," I say quickly. "But the thing is, I don't have *all* the money. Yet. But I will. Soon. And the rest I can pay as we go along, but it will have to be over a period of a few years. Which I know isn't exactly what you were hoping for, but"—I lean forward, speaking to both of them in a low, urgent voice, while somewhere off in the distance, a lawn mower roars to life and a bird begins a plaintive but still melodious song—"the advantage of selling to me, as opposed to some stranger, is that you won't be paying any Realtor fees. We can cut out the middleman completely, and you'll be saving yourself hundreds of thousands of dollars. I'm willing to make you an offer right now, here, today, no inspection, no nothing, of four point five million dollars. And before you say you think the building is worth more," I say, cutting off both of them, since I hear them inhale, "allow me to point out that I live and work there. I don't need an inspection because I know how much work the place needs. I've seen the cracks, plugged up the leaks, called the exterminator myself for the rats down in the basement more times than I can count. And I'm making my offer to you now, today, with my guarantee that you will have the whole amount five years from today. I'll sign anything you want guaranteeing it. All I ask is that you remember where the two of you were when I first walked through your door a year ago. And where you both are now."

I lean back against the bench and take a long swig from my iced tea. Even for a talker, I am spent after having given such a long speech. I eye the two of them as they stare uneasily back at me.

Then Madame Henri looks at her husband.

"The Realtor fees *are* a lot," she says in French. Even though they both know perfectly well by now that I speak their native language more or less fluently, they still slip back into it when they don't want me to overhear what they're saying, out of force of habit. "We could save a lot of money."

"But we'd have to wait for the money," her husband says petulantly. "You heard her."

"So?" his wife demands. "What are you planning on buying? A yacht?"

"Maybe," Monsieur Henri says with a snort.

"You heard what the inspector said," Madame Henri says. "About the asbestos in the basement."

"He also said if we left it alone, it wouldn't be a problem. *All* pipes in Manhattan are lined with asbestos."

I listen to this without blinking. I already know about the asbestos. The plumber told me months ago. I'd planned on using it as leverage if they balked at my offer.

"It's going to cost thousands to get it removed," Madame Henri goes on. "Maybe tens of thousands. Do you want that hassle?"

"No," Monsieur Henri pouts.

"This way," his wife says, "we can be done with it in an afternoon. We don't even have to pay to have our things moved out! She'll keep them!"

Monsieur Henri brightens at this. "Eh! I didn't think of this! But where's she getting all this money? She's not even thirty."

"Who knows?" his wife asks with a Gallic shrug. "The dead grandmother, perhaps?"

"Ask her," Monsieur Henri says.

Then they both turn to me. And Madame Henri asks in English, "Did you hear all that?"

"Of course," I say testily. "I'm not deaf. And I speak French. Remember?"

"I know." Madame Henri shakes her head. "The money is from your grandmother?"

"No," I say. "It's from a deal I made last night with Geck Industries. I'm going to be designing a line of wedding wear for their discount department stores."

Monsieur Henri looks confused. "But if you are going to work for Geck, then why do you still want the shop?"

"Because I'm still going to be doing gowns for my own customers," I said. "Independent of Geck. Besides, your shop . . . *my* shop, if you'll agree to sell it to me . . . it's *home*."

I feel ridiculous, but as I say the word, tears fill my eyes. And yet . . . it's true. That pokey little apartment—which I fully intend to renovate if it ever becomes mine—is the place where I've known some of the highest highs, and lowest lows, of my life. I can't let it slip away from me. I won't. Not without a fight.

Madame Henri blinks a few times. Then she looks at her husband. He arches his eyebrows.

"Well," Monsieur Henri says. "In that case . . . I think we have to sell the building to Elizabeth. Do you not agree, *chérie*?"

Madame Henri's face breaks into an enormous smile.

"I agree," she says.

Which is how, a half hour later, I end up drinking champagne in the noonday sun with Madame Henri in her back garden, while the birds chirp all around us, and her husband shows Chaz, who's returned from his odyssey at the mall, how to play *pétanque*—a sport at which, it soon becomes apparent, he excels . . .

Almost as much as he excels in coaching me in how to get my former bosses to sell me their place of business.

A HISTORY
of
WEDDINGS

It's important to remember that many of the most sumptuous and expensive weddings in history didn't always lead to romantic bliss. Look at Henry VIII and his many wives; Prince Charles and Princess Diana; and of course the always optimistic but unlucky in love Miss Elizabeth Taylor.

No matter how large or small your wedding, what's crucial is that you're marrying the right person, someone who loves you for who you are, not whether or not you can provide him with a male heir, how much money you have, or whether or not you look good in a bathing suit. Love is a many-splendored thing, it's true. But there is nothing more important than making sure your life partner is someone who can make you laugh when you are feeling down, will bring you cinnamon toast when you're feeling sick, and is willing to share the remote.

When the guests are gone, the gifts all unwrapped and put away, and the last thank-you note finally written, you might feel the tiniest bit depressed. This is normal! After all, you've just been through the most joyous time of your life—your (hopefully) only wedding! It's natural that you feel a little sad it's all over. But keep in mind you're about to embark upon the most wonderful and joyous journey ever . . . married life!

Still, it's okay to put your wedding gown on every now and then . . . even just to watch TV. Everybody does it.

Really.

LIZZIE NICHOLS DESIGNS™

Chapter 25

He is the half part of a blessed man,
Left to be finished by such a she;
And she a fair divided excellence,
Whose fulness of perfection lies in him.

William Shakespeare (1564–1616), English poet and playwright

Six months later

O h, you make the most beautiful bride ever!"

"No, I don't," Tiffany assures me. "I look fat."

"Tiffany," I say severely. "You're four months' pregnant. You're *supposed* to look fat."

"Is it odd that that still frightens me?" Monique asks no one in particular. "The fact that Tiffany is going to be a mum, I mean? Does it frighten anyone else?"

Shari raises her hand, along with Sylvia and Marisol.

Tiffany glares at them. "I hate all of you," she says.

"What's nice about the fact that Tiffany is going to be a mum," Monique goes on, "is that it's turned her into such a sweet, caring person."

"This gown is what's making me look fat," Tiffany says to her reflection in the gilt-framed full-length mirror in front of her.

"No, it isn't," I say indignantly, offended. "You're pregnant. That's what's making you fat."

"This is a fat dress," Tiffany says, pouting. "You designed a fucking fat dress for my fucking wedding."

"You know what's awesome," Shari says, slipping a Milk Dud into her mouth from the box she's brought into the shop for the show she's been anticipating for days. "When brides swear. Especially pregnant brides."

Sylvia and Marisol make tsk-tsking noises and fuss over Tiffany, foofing out the train of the exquisite—and completely nonfat—original gown I've designed for her.

"I did not design a fat dress for you, Tiffany," I say, restraining myself with an effort from strangling her. "And that's not a very nice thing to say to the person who is responsible for paying you enough so you can work part-time for me and finally quit that job you hated at Pendergast, Loughlin, and Flynn."

Tiffany just glares at my reflection. "So? I'm just going to quit working for you in five months so I can stay home with Raoul Junior."

"It's a boy?" Marisol asks excitedly.

"Who knows?" Tiffany glares at her reflection. "Whatever."

"Seriously," Shari says, dropping another Milk Dud into her mouth. "This is better than *American Gladiator*."

"You can afford a nanny, Tiffany," I say to her, giving her sash a tug that is perhaps a little harder than necessary. "You aren't going to have to quit. And I picked out a health care plan that gives all you ladies a full four months' paid maternity leave, remember? Now, I designed this gown for you *personally,* with a gorgeous empire waist and a sweetheart neckline and a chapel train—which, by the way, is entirely inappropriate for the quickie wedding you and Raoul are about to have in the office of the city clerk . . . even if we *are* partying afterward at Tavern on the Green—so that your bump is completely disguised. No one can see it. How dare you call it a fat dress?"

Tiffany eyes Shari's box of Milk Duds. "Are you going to give me one of those?" she asks. "Or what?"

"No, she's not," I snap. "You are not getting chocolate on this dress I've slaved over for weeks."

"*We've* slaved over," Marisol corrects me. "I stayed up until two last night doing that crystal beading on the train."

"Right," I say. "That *we've* slaved over."

"Whatever," Tiffany says again, rolling her gorgeously made-up eyes. "Like there's not going to be a knockoff available off the rack at Geck's next week for two hundred bucks."

"There's not!" I cry. "I told you! It's a Lizzie Nichols Designs original! There'll never be anything like it at Geck's. I mean . . . there'll be something similar. But it will retail for three ninety-nine."

Tiffany tosses her head until her newly coiled ringlets bounce. "I knew it," she says with another eye roll.

"The cars are here," Monique says in a bored voice.

"All right, let's go," I say quickly. "Or we're going to be late."

And we all troop out into the crisp winter air, past the new hot-pink awning with the words "Lizzie Nichols Designs™" emblazoned on it in white curlicue writing, and splitting up into the two waiting black Town Cars that Raoul ordered for us, me carefully folding Tiffany's train in after her, then climbing into the car behind hers with Shari.

"Thanks for coming," I say to her gratefully.

"Are you kidding me?" Shari says, pouring more Milk Duds into her mouth. "I wouldn't miss this for the world. So what happened? The guy finally got his green card?"

"And just in time. Five more months, and he'd be a dad before he was a legal."

"That has to be the quickest divorce in the history of mankind."

"Well, the former Mrs. Raoul got a pretty hefty settlement for being so accommodating with INS," I explain. "You know, not mentioning the part about how they hadn't lived together as man and wife in years."

"That's so *romantic*," Shari says with a sigh, snuggling down into the leather seats.

When we reach One Centre Street, I jump from the car and hurry to make sure Tiffany emerges from her own without damaging the gown we've all worked so hard on. She manages to do so, though she isn't exactly gracious about it. Thanks to a united effort, we get her up to the hallway where the men—and Pat, who's rushed over on her lunch break—are waiting.

All of my anxiety turns out to have been worth it, though, when I see the look on Raoul's face as he gazes upon his bride for the first time in her wedding finery. Tears fill his eyes, and I'm so touched when he takes Tiffany's hand and whispers, "Baby, you look beautiful," that I have to look away.

"I know," Tiffany whispers smugly back. I guess she doesn't think she looks so fat after all.

An arm slides around my waist, and a second later, a man in a charcoal gray suit is kissing my neck.

"Hey," Chaz says. "You did good."

"Thanks." I giggle. Yes, really. I giggle. That is what Chaz does to me. "Do you like the ribbon work around the neckline? I thought that was a nice touch. I'm going to do that to the new line of flower girl dresses we're introducing for next year's resort line."

"It'll sell like hotcakes," he says.

He's wearing the yellow tie I love, in honor of the occasion. My knees are melting. The sight of Chaz in a suit and particularly that yellow tie still has the power to turn me into butter on a hot stove. I wonder if that will ever change.

I have a feeling it won't.

A bored clerk has just called Tiffany's and Raoul's names, and we're getting ready to crowd into a tiny chapel with them when there's a commotion in the hallway as a familiar voice shrieks, "Wait! Wait for me!"

"Oh God," Shari groans. "Who invited *her*?"

I bite my lower lip. "Um . . . I might have mentioned that Tiffany was getting married downtown today . . . right about now."

"Oh my God, Lizzie," Tiffany snaps. "Aren't you *ever* going to learn to keep your mouth shut?"

Before I have a chance to answer, however, Ava bursts in, wearing a demure business suit (complete with pillbox hat) and clutching the arm of her husband, Joshua Rubenstein, aka DJ Tippycat, followed, as always, by Little Joey.

"I'm so sorry I'm late," Ava says, with all the regality her recently acquired position as president in charge of marketing of Geck Industries has given her. "We got stuck in traffic on the way from the helicopter landing pad."

Tiffany glares at her, but Raoul says amiably, "So glad you could make it."

Then the clerk calls their names again, and we all file forward for the mercifully brief—but meaningful—ceremony.

It isn't until Latrell has uncorked the champagne, and congratulations have been exchanged all around, and we've been told to file out again to make room for the next couple, and Raoul's instructed us to get back into the Town Cars he's provided to take us back uptown to Tavern on the Green that Chaz snags me by the elbow and pulls me into a corner by a water fountain and a bulletin board listing clerk's office personnel. There he shows me something he has hidden in an inside pocket of his suit.

"Do you know what this is?" he asks, a suspiciously bright twinkle in his sapphire eyes.

I look at the plain white envelope.

"It's the deed to my building?" I ask eagerly. "You paid it off with your secret inheritance, and I don't owe any money on it anymore?"

Chaz looks disappointed. "No. Is that what you want me to do? I thought you wanted to do it all by yourself, stand on your own two feet, and all of that stuff you said last summer?"

"Um, yeah," I say, trying to hide my disappointment. "I do. Totally. So what is it?"

Chaz opens the envelope and pulls out the folded paper inside. It's a pamphlet with *Office of the City Clerk of the City of New York* written on the top. Under it, it says, *What You Need to Know to Apply for a Marriage License.*

"Yeah," Chaz says when I turn my stunned gaze toward him. "I took one. And before you throw up, you can say no. I won't be mad or offended or anything. I don't care if we ever get married. It's not important to me at all. I love you and only you, and I always will. No piece of paper is going to change that. I just know it used to be important to you, and if it still is, well . . . we can do it. And this might be a way we can do it that won't cause you to break out in hives, or me to york. We could just fill out the application now, come back tomorrow—there's a twenty-four-hour waiting period—and do it. We don't have to tell anyone. I just figured, you know, since we're here anyway, we could go in there real fast—I wrote my name down on the list when I got here, the application office is downstairs. It's okay, we've got time, we're like number ninety on the list or something—while everyone else is getting into the Town Cars, and then join them up at Tavern on the Green. And no one will be the wiser. We'll be exactly the same. Only we'll be getting married. Tomorrow. Or whenever. They're good for sixty days. The licenses, I mean."

I am still staring at the pamphlet he's holding.

"You're asking me to marry you?" is all I can manage to choke out.

"If you want to," Chaz says. "You don't have to. And I'm not talking about one of those big monstrosity things your clients have, with a chocolate fondue fountain and the chicken dance. I don't want that. I will never want that, do you understand? My sister had that, and it was—" He shudders. It is clear he is beginning to lose it. I lay a steadying hand on his arm as he goes on, "Your parents will probably want to have that for you, and I am telling you right now . . . I will run. I will run as far and as fast as I can away from that. I will come back to you at night, when it's safe. But I'll hide during the day, where they can't find me. Even if I have to take to the swamps. I know there aren't any swamps in Michigan, but . . ."

I give him a gentle shake.

"Chaz," I say. "It's all right. I don't want that either, okay? I like your idea. Doing it this way, just you and me here tomorrow. No one else. Because that's what getting married is really about, right? Just us. No one else."

"No one else," Chaz says. "Because we're the only ones who matter. I mean, I guess we can tell people . . . someday."

"Someday," I agree. "When we feel like it. We can just mention it. Like, by the way . . . we got married. Although they'll probably be mad we didn't invite them."

"I don't care," Chaz says. "Do you care?"

"I don't care," I say. "We don't even have to tell them if we don't want to."

"I should probably mention to Luke that we're going out first," Chaz says. "To sort of cushion the blow. I can tell him we're married in a few years. Although he's juggling approximately four steady girlfriends in Paris right now. I don't know why he still thinks my seeing you is such a bad idea."

"Aw," I say. I still can't seem to summon up any animosity toward Luke. I'm still holding on to his engagement ring to give to my own daughter, if I ever have one. Or to my niece Maggie, from whom I'm expecting great things. "That's so cute."

"Cute, my ass," Chaz says. "Let me see your arm."

Obediently I roll up the sleeve to the vintage Lilli Ann pink wool suit that I'm wearing. We both stare at the inside of my elbow.

"No hives," Chaz says.

"That's a good sign. Do you feel like throwing up?"

Chaz shakes his head. "No."

I'm feeling optimistic about this, and about the number we are on the list. Ninety. That was Gran's age when she died. They both seem like gifts from above. Like maybe . . . maybe someone is watching out for us . . . someone who wants to make sure we aren't on the highway to hell after all.

Or that maybe we are, actually. Because maybe that's a good place to be.

Chaz and I both look down at the pamphlet in his hand. It is divided into frequently asked questions, which include, *Is a premarital physical exam or blood test prior to the ceremony required?* (Answer: No) and *Can two first cousins legally marry in the state of New York?* (Answer: Yes) and *Can I use the marriage license in another state?* (Answer: No).

It all seems so . . . *legal.*

"You really want to do this?" Chaz asks.

"I think so," I say. "But . . . you once said I'd make a terrible wife."

"I've sort of amended my opinion on that," Chaz says. "I think you'd make sort of a spiffy one now."

"Spiffy?" I grin up at him. "Did you really just say that?"

He grins back. "I think I did."

I grin even harder. "Do you promise to cherish and obey me?"

"I already do," Chaz points out. "Especially the obey part. In bed, when you get saucy with the whips and chains."

"Then," I say gravely, "Charles Pendergast the Third, I will gladly marry you."

"You guys," Tiffany shrieks from the doorway through which everyone is filing. "Are you coming or *what*?"

"We're coming," Chaz calls after them. He nudges me. "Hey, I don't think they heard me. You've got the big mouth. Tell them not to wait for us."

"Not me," I say happily. "I think I've finally learned how to keep this big mouth shut."

MEG CABOT was born in Bloomington, Indiana. In addition to her adult contemporary fiction she is the author of the bestselling young adult fiction series The Princess Diaries. She lives in Key West, Florida, with her husband and one-eyed cat, Henrietta.